LUSTFULLY
EVER AFTER

LUSTFULLY
EVER AFTER

FAIRY TALE EROTIC ROMANCE

Edited by
Kristina Wright

Foreword by
Sylvia Day

CLEiS
PRESS

Published in the United States by Cleis Press, Inc., 2246 Sixth Street, Berkeley, California 94710.

Printed in the United States.
Cover design: Scott Idleman/Blink
Cover photograph: Carlos Emilio/ANYONE
Text design: Frank Wiedemann
First Edition.
10 9 8 7 6 5 4 3 2 1

Trade paper ISBN: 978-1-57344-787-4
E-book ISBN: 978-1-57344-800-0

Contents

FOREWORD

Sylvia Day

The Disney Company made sure we all grew up with fairy tales. Most girls grow up with a favorite Disney princess or two and a stack of video cassettes or DVDs (depending on the era) of their favorite princesses' stories. It's become a part of girlhood to dream of Prince Charming and the miracle he's supposed to bring to his true love's life, staging grand rescues from evil stepmothers and their curses and spiriting his mate away to his castle to never again have a care in the world.

I was twelve when my notion of Prince Charming changed. That was when my mother handed me a romance novel featuring a virile, ultra-alpha sheik and the woman he desires to the point of obsession. Looking back now, with our modern feminist sensibilities, we both admit the book is a "bodice ripper," but at the time it was powerful, sexy stuff. Prince Charming wasn't rescuing the heroine; he was her antagonist, her kidnapper, her beast to tame while he exposed her to her own potent sensual nature (and fell helpless to it himself).

Many years later I discovered erotic romance via the futuristic novellas of Liz Maverick and Angela Knight. *Now this,* I thought, *is my kind of reading.* Stories in which sex was as integral to the characters as breathing, the means through which they most deeply communicated with each other. Kick-ass men and women who had well-rounded lives all by themselves, they needed rescuing in only the most personal and profound ways; the rest they had covered on their own. For me, that's romance.

Where are the fairy tales for readers like me?

Once upon a time, fairy tales were darker, grittier, and sexier. Rapunzel let down her hair and lifted her skirts. Sleeping Beauty wasn't awakened by a mere kiss. Little Red Riding Hood is an allegory for the wolfish, predatory qualities of men. Fairy tales were written for adults, then later adapted to be suitable for children. They were softened and sweetened, removing most of the spice.

Somewhere along the way we've come to believe that the magical and fantastical are for kids. To prove maturity, one is expected to cast off belief in the imaginary, but adults need fairy tales, too. We brave the dangerous forest of commuting every weekday, fighting off the trolls and goblins in our lives, outwitting the witches and villainous overlords we work alongside, and trying not to strangle the stockbrokers who manage our golden nest eggs.

I've outgrown the softened and sweetened fantasies of childhood. The stories I crave are raw, laced with dark magic and unfettered passions. Adult fairy tales should be gritty yet illusionary, edgy yet sinuous, violent yet dreamy. They should take what is recognizable in us to the farthest degree, making it marvelous and terrifying, fascinating and titillating.

I still have a soft spot for Prince Charming, but I prefer him as a reward for the prince or princess who slays his or her own dragons. He should carry a bit of the beast inside him and more than a little wickedness. He should bring his adventurous spirit into the bedroom, and he should be respectful of the value and independence of his true love. But that's *my* fairy tale. For others, tales may include princes or princesses who master them, one (or a few) who save them from themselves or exposes a hidden beauty, like the swan from the ugly duckling.

The beauty of *Lustfully Ever After* is its celebration of the individual fairy tales in us all. I relished taking the ride, seeing how fluid the journey can be and how unique each creator's vision was of something known and familiar. As a writer, it's natural to say I'll write what I wish was out there for me to read, but then I would be trapped by the limits of my own imagination. Within the pages of this collection, I was invited to join in the fantasies of others, which took me in directions I would never have thought to go, wrapped within the enchantment of fairy tales and folklore, and deliciously flavored with sex and love.

Here are the fairy tales for grown-ups. Enjoy!

INTRODUCTION: THEY LIVED HAPPILY EVER AFTER

When I edited my first collection of erotic fairy tales, *Fairy Tale Lust,* and received an overwhelming number of submissions from authors—and an enthusiastic response from readers and reviewers—I knew I would be editing another fairy tale collection soon. There were just too many fairy tales in need of retelling—tales that were ripe for reinterpretation. And so, the idea for *Lustfully Ever After* was born, sitting on a back burner in my imagination while I wrote other stories and edited other books. But the excitement about another fairy tale collection wouldn't wait long and before I knew it I found myself pitching the idea to my publisher. Happily (ever after), they were as enthusiastic about it as I was—as were the authors when I put out my call for submissions. Fairy tales, it seems, are such a part of our culture and imagination that we long for more.

While there are similarities between *Fairy Tale Lust* and *Lustfully Ever After*, there are also notable differences. *Fairy Tale Lust* was a collection of original and classic fairy tales written as erotica and erotic romance; the stories ranged from light and playful to eerie and intense. For *Lustfully Ever After*, I knew I wanted only reinterpretations of the classics and that I wanted them to lean more toward the dark tones of the originals. The stories themselves, while steeped in the history and tone of the classics, are as different in *Lustfully Ever After* as they were in *Fairy Tale Lust*.

Some of the stories in *Lustfully Ever After* are the tales that you know by heart but likely never dreamed of quite this way. Others, while still based on classic stories, will be less familiar but I hope just as entertaining. Among the stories you will recognize immediately are Anya Richards's "Rosa Redford," a delicious reinterpretation of "Snow White and Rose Red," and Lisabet Sarai's reimagined Rapunzel in "Shorn." Emerald gives us a corporate "Beauty and the Beast" in "The Beast Within," while Shanna Germain shows sympathy for—and the passionate, Sapphic side of—Snow White's evil stepmother in "Mirror, Mirror."

Some less easily recognized tales include Charlotte Stein's "You," an imaginative retelling of "The Three Billy Goats Gruff," and Michael M. Jones's retelling of the somewhat obscure "The Boots of Buffalo Leather" in his adventurous and sexy "The Long Night of Tanya McCray." Andrea Dale delivers a contemporary version of "The Steadfast Tin Soldier" in her poignantly erotic "Steadfast," Anna Meadows has written "Matches," a passionate (and happier) blend of "The Little Match Girl" and Mexican folklore, and Sacchi Green dreams of a different kind of pussycat in "Kit in Boots."

Michelle Augello-Page has penned a romantically charged BDSM version of "Little Red Riding Hood" in her tale "Wolf Moon," while Jeanette Grey tackles "Hansel and Gretel" (or at least Gretel's story) in "Gretel's Lament." Contrary to the title,

Lynn Townsend's "Garden Variety" is no typical "Jack and the Beanstalk" tale, nor is Evan Mora's "Real Boy" anything you've ever imagined about "Pinocchio." Other classic fairy tales make appearances, including "Twelve Dancing Princesses" in Kristina Lloyd's erotic threesome fairy tale "The Last Dance" and "The Princess and the Pea" in Donna George Storey's creative "Sensitive Artist." My own story, "A Sea Change," is "The Little Mermaid" revisited in reverse, and A.D.R. Forte's "Name" is an ambitious and passionate retelling of one of my favorite fairy tales, "Rumpelstiltskin."

The stories here were chosen for being original, erotic interpretations while maintaining the fairy-tale elements and literary integrity of the original tales. I was seeking as much variety as possible in these stories—not wanting to duplicate the table of contents of *Fairy Tale Lust*. The few classic tales that appear in both collections are as different from each other as they are from the original stories. I think that says as much about the talented authors' imaginations as it does about the diverse appeal of fairy tales.

Unlike *Fairy Tale Lust*, every story in *Lustfully Ever After* has a romantic relationship and a "happily ever after" or "happy for now" ending. So relax, dear reader, and curl up with this delightful collection of fairy tales that will lead you down a magical path into forbidden romance and erotic love. I promise you won't need those bread crumbs to find your way home—for home is where the heart is, and the authors of *Lustfully Ever After* know your heart's most wicked and secret desires.

Kristina Wright
The dark woods of Virginia

ROSA REDFORD

Anya Richards

'm not hungry." He held out his hands, as though showing her those strong, hairy fingers would be proof enough. "I've already...supped. All I want is companionship. The world is such a cold place."

Behind him the snow fell in thick flakes, drifting down like feathers to settle on his fur-covered head and shoulders, clinging to the long eyelashes. Dark, all-too-human eyes glowed with silent entreaty from the beastly face. But despite his horrifying appearance, Rosa removed the chain and let him in.

As he slowly entered, his dark gaze swept over the second-hand furniture and old stage props, the detritus of their theatre jobs and myriad potted plants. What he thought about any of it, the marks of their occupations and personalities, she couldn't tell. He expressed no opinion, simply prowled around the edge of the living room, looking and sniffing at everything before plunking down on the couch.

"What's going on?"

Blanche came down the passage rubbing her eyes, the hem of her short nightie swinging around her thighs. His gaze sharpened. Blanche gasped, seeing the hairy man-thing.

"I just wanted some company."

Once more loneliness echoed in his voice, and, when Rosa glanced at Blanche, her friend's mouth pursed into a winsome pout. A spark of annoyance fired in her belly. Why did Blanche always have to be so cute, even with her pale, straight hair all over the place and sleep lines on her face?

"No problem." Blanche dropped onto the couch too, folding her long, slim legs up under her ass. "Company is always a good thing, right Rosa?"

Well, there was company and then there was company, and Rosa wasn't sure what to make of the present kind.

"Would you care for a drink?" She shifted from one foot to the other, asking more out of the need to say something rather than politeness.

"What do you have?" He was still casing the joint, so to speak, but his eyes now went from her to Blanche and back again.

She glanced at the cabinet, trying to remember what was left. "Vodka, gin, maybe scotch. We killed the tequila last night though."

He laughed, and the deep, rich chuckle, the strong, sharp teeth made every hair on her body stand on end. "Just as well. Tequila makes me want to live *la vida loca*. You don't want to see that."

Strangely though, she kinda did. Would he climb on the table—*climb on her*—and howl to the moon?

"So, nothing then?"

Now his gaze settled fully on her, eyes seeming to penetrate into her soul, and warmth flashed over her skin. Beneath her white T-shirt her nipples came to attention and a buzz of arousal took residence in her pussy. She wasn't aware of licking her lips until his attention dropped and a low growl issued from his throat. Even when she forced herself to stop, his eyes didn't move, stayed on her mouth.

Her legs wobbled.

"I'll have whatever you're having."

"Screwdrivers," Blanche said, uncharacteristically decisive, already heading for the kitchen. "I'll get the ice."

With trembling hands Rosa poured the vodka, awareness tightening her skin, blood flowing thick and hot, like lava, in her veins. Blanche came back and dropped cubes into the glasses, added a splash of juice to each, but she may as well have been a ghost. All Rosa could focus on was the creature across the room—the hint of his scent filling the apartment.

Blanche took her drink, leaving two glasses behind. Rosa stared down at them for a moment, trying to pull herself together, but his allure was too strong. Picking up the drinks, she walked over and gave him his, shivering slightly at the brush of his fingers, her heart rate picking up speed. Her mouth was dry so she took a sip, hardly noticing the cool bite of the alcohol going down. Like a mirror image he did the same, and she watched the powerful throat move, yearned to put her lips there, feel the muscles shift.

Who are you, she wanted to ask, *what are you?* But although the questions lingered, they didn't seem important. The only one that mattered was whether it was her or Blanche he chose. With her long legs and willowy figure, quiet Blanche attracted lots of guys, although Rosa couldn't complain. Her more rounded figure, Latin looks, and outgoing personality garnered attention enough, and they never fought over men. But, this time, Rosa wanted the beast for herself.

He growled, a low, sustained sound, and leaned forward slightly. His eyes burned, matching the heat already inundating her body, melting whatever hesitancy remained. Letting her gaze drop, she saw his cock rising, long, dark and thick, from the hair of his groin. Stepping toward him, she nudged his legs apart, knelt between them.

"Damn," Blanche sighed.

"She's the one," he replied. "But you can watch, if you like."

Rosa ignored them, intent on his growing cock. It curved up toward his belly, the head so smooth she salivated to taste it. He plucked the glass from her hand and she smiled, reaching for him. When she circled his cock with her cold fingers, he growled again, and a giggle escaped her.

Then there was no more time for laughter.

His glans filled her mouth—texture, taste, and arousing scent exploding in her head all at once. It was like she'd been starved but now had a feast, and she wanted to devour him. Licking and sucking, learning the shape of him with her tongue, his fingers tunneling into her hair to hold her in place, she couldn't get enough. The base of his cock pulsed, and she laved a thick bead of pre-come from the tip, knowing he was close, wanting to hear and feel him let go in her mouth.

When he pushed her away, she fell, gasping, on her ass, the sense of loss indescribable.

"Oh, no you don't," he growled, and she saw his muscles bunch, poised to spring. "No, no, no..."

He was on her, ripping her T-shirt away, tearing at her panties with his teeth, and everything became a slow-motion blur, a cacophony of growls and gasps and moans, a tsunami of sensations. He licked and nibbled his way over her body, pushing her breasts together with his powerful hands, sucking and growling around her nipples. Working his way down, parting her legs, swirling his tongue between the lips of her pussy, surrounding her clit, the knowledge of those strong teeth close to her flesh bringing her to a screaming climax.

And could he fuck! He made her glad for the stamina and flexibility brought on by years of dancing, because *missionary* clearly wasn't in his vocabulary. Twisting her, this way and that, clutching with his claws, cock unerringly finding its way home, he gave her orgasm after orgasm. At the end Rosa found herself practically doing a split on the back of the couch, his cock driving into her from behind as she held herself aloft with a death grip on the cushion in front of her hips. Blanche stared up at them, blue eyes wide, her usually pale cheeks bright pink, lips open as she panted. She was thrusting a neon-green vibrator into her cunt, fingers of her other hand pinching and tugging at her nipples.

His cock went deep and he leaned into Rosa, teeth grazing her shoulder, scraping up to her neck. No reason why that should make her lose control, but it did. Entire body shuddering, she was the one who howled, pumping her hips with short, hard, movements, his cock moving with delicious friction in her pussy.

"So tight," he growled into her ear. "So wet and sweet."

She couldn't answer, could do nothing but let the waves of orgasm break over her, revel in him filling her, hearing his words dissolve into the primal sounds of his release.

The last things she remembered was asking, "What would happen if I gave you tequila?" and his answering chuckle.

Waking up, blinking against the sunlight coming in through the window, she realized the warm, soft body snuggled with hers on the couch was Blanche's.

"Wow," Blanche stirred, yawned. "I had the wildest dream."

"Did it involve a hairy man-beast thing?"

Blanche went still. "Yeah," she replied slowly.

"And do you own a neon-green vibrator?"

"Damn...so it wasn't a dream?"

Rosa didn't bother to answer. What was there to say?

The winter fell into an otherworldly pattern—working during the day and Bear, as they took to calling him since he wouldn't tell them his name, at night.

For the first time in years Rosa and Blanche were working on the same project, an off-Broadway production by the world-renowned team of Short and Dean. Still in rehearsals, Rosa had one of the leads while Blanche worked on the set designs, so they spent even more time together than usual. Normally Rosa would have been stressed to the max with opening night only six weeks away, but somehow she floated through. Not even the tantrums and scathing remarks of producer David Short, who often came to monitor the cast's progress, fazed her.

This easygoing attitude must be linked to Bear's nightly visits. They didn't have sex every night, but for the first time she was getting both quality and quantity, along with a friendship she came to treasure. Although Rosa was the focus of his attention, Blanche didn't seem to mind.

"I never thought myself a voyeur," she said one day when they were standing near the stage door at the end of the lunch interval. A touch of color brightened her pale cheeks, and her eyes sparkled. "But watching you two together is amazing."

"Well, we all knew I was an exhibitionist, although not in that way," Rosa replied. "Bear brings out the beast in me."

They were both laughing when David Short came by, the heavy woolen cloak he affected swirling around his ankles.

"Well, what have we here? Two of my favorite girls. You really must come by my place one evening." He winked, his lascivious gaze causing a shiver of distaste to trickle up Rosa's spine. "We'd have fun, I guarantee."

He left without waiting for a reply, letting a blast of cold air and a swirl of snow into the corridor. As he went out, the wind slammed the heavy door shut behind him, catching the hem of his cloak between it and the jamb. Rosa and Blanche stared at the fabric for a moment then exchanged a look. There was no way for Short to open the door from the outside.

"Asshole," Blanche said. "His partner seemed nice when he came that one time, but this guy gives me the creeps. Ignore it— the porter will be back in a while and set him free."

Rosa shrugged, already moving toward the exit. "He's a jackass but also the producer, and it's cold out there."

But the fabric had jammed the door shut and it took both of them shoving before the door sprang open. Short had obviously been tugging hard on the other side, and the sudden opening of the door sent him flying, face first, into a snow bank. Rosa bit her cheek in an effort to stop the laughter welling inside.

"You stupid bitches," Short snarled, once he'd spat out the snow. "Look what you did. I'll have you fired for this."

Without a word Blanche nudged Rosa back inside and closed the door. "Wow," she said. "Just, wow."

"Asshole," Rosa bunched her fists. "The union will make him eat his balls for breakfast if he tries it."

But at night, when she let Bear in, everything outside the apartment fell away, and he was all Rosa cared about. She'd never had a lover like him—one who concentrated solely on her, even ignoring Blanche who often stayed to watch while they made love. Whether she was there or not, it was always the same. Bear made sure Rosa was exhausted with pleasure by the time he slipped back out into the cold dawn, and she'd drift to sleep, carrying the memory of his eyes into her dreams.

Sometimes he was fierce, fucking her hard and long, slamming his cock into her pussy until the entire world shrunk to just that one amazing point of contact and she exploded into orgasm. Other times he was tender, loving her slowly, touching, kissing, licking, sliding into her with infinite care or rolling so she was on top and could take him at her own pace, in her own way. Then there were the nights when he took one look at her and suggested a game of poker if Blanche was around or a movie if they were alone.

It was always right. Somehow whatever she needed on any given night, he willingly, ably, supplied.

On the mornings after a night of sweaty, limb-tangling, balls-to-the-wall sex, Rosa would be energized, raring to hit the street running. After one of the slower, dreamier nights, she woke up mellow, able to take everything in her stride. How much better life seemed with Bear in it—more balanced, easier to handle.

He made her feel indomitable.

Spring approached, along with opening night. The theater was chaotic but Rosa moved through final rehearsals with confidence, despite a number of run-ins with David Short. They were all silly incidents, like him getting angry when she told him his phone, which he'd left on a seat while he spoke to one of the grips, was ringing. Or the day he pushed past her on the stairs and tripped. She'd instinctively grabbed and stopped him from falling, but he'd still bawled her out for inadvertently tearing his shirt while she did.

The director called Rosa aside one day.

"I don't know what you've done to Short," he whispered, obviously not wanting anyone else to hear, "but you better watch yourself. He's talking up your understudy, nitpicking about your performance."

A chill of fear careened through her veins. The part was her big break, her first lead in a production of this size. "Are you thinking of replacing me?"

"*I'm* happy with you—think you're doing an excellent job—but I don't hold the purse strings." Raking his fingers through his hair only made the strands stand up even more, and the nervous energy emanating from him was palpable. "I wish the other partner, Dean, was handling this project. Word is he's far easier to deal with."

He didn't say any more but the inference was clear. Short could force Rosa out if he really wanted, and the director couldn't—or wouldn't—protect her.

When she told Blanche, her friend was horrified and recounted her own problems with Short.

"He's been constantly questioning everything I do. Worse, today I accidentally caught him and Daria in the prop room, fucking."

"He's screwing my understudy?" Rosa had the urge to punch something.

Blanche nodded, "Yep, and apparently doesn't care who knows. They weren't even discreet."

Rosa dropped her head into her hands. "Between that and the incident with the snowbank, we're screwed. If we both lose our jobs, we'll be in shit for sure."

That night Bear was later than usual, and anxiety sparking under her skin wouldn't let Rosa sit still.

"Calm down." Blanche checked her watch and picked up her clutch purse. "I've never seen you so keyed up. I almost hate to leave you in this state."

Rosa forced herself to sit, realized she was convulsively tapping her foot and held it still too. It was the first date Blanche was going on in ages, and she didn't want to spoil it. "I'll be fine."

Once Bear gets here.

Finally there was a knock, and she ran to answer. Bear came in, but there was no lessening of her nervous tension. Instead it ratcheted higher.

As the door closed behind him, Bear picked her up and carried her down the hall toward her bedroom. Rosa clasped her legs around him, pressing close, burying her face in the soft pelt on his neck, digging her fingernails into his back. His chest vibrated with a barely audible sound, his cock rising, nudging her satin-clad pussy, and she rocked against it, already yearning to feel it inside, stretching her, bringing her to orgasm.

Dropping her in the middle of the bed, he straddled her legs.

"Why do you insist on wearing so much clothing?" he growled, breaking the straps of her bodice with strong twists of his hands. "I don't want you hiding from me."

She was caught in the dark need of his gaze, hunger for him churning inside her, making her nipples tingle and ache, her hips rise in silent invitation. In reply he shredded the central lace panel of her teddy, peeled aside the satin covering her breasts, chuckled as a shudder of anticipation wracked her frame.

Swirling his tongue from one side to the other, he didn't miss an inch, teasing the undersides, the outer curves and valley between, scraping his teeth against her skin. Holding on to his shoulders, she tried to open her legs but he effortlessly held them closed between powerful thighs. His cock rubbed against her mound, the sensation entwining with those from his mouth, and Rosa arched upward, eyes closing in ecstasy.

Straightening, shifting forward, he pressed her breasts together.

"Yes," she groaned, lifting her head to watch his cock slide into the valley created by her soft flesh. Opening her mouth to receive his glans as he thrust forward was rewarded by a groan of approval.

Tasting his excitement and feeling the evidence of it on her skin only increased her arousal. Longing overwhelmed her and she curled upward, wanting him fully in her mouth.

As though knowing her desires, he lifted away and turned so he was lying beside her, facing her feet. With a moan of satisfaction Rosa rolled onto her side and, just as he tore at her G-string, she engulfed his cock, taking him as deeply as she could. For a moment he went rigid, his muscular body stiffening, hips thrusting instinctively. The feel of him on her tongue, his balls contracting in her hand, took her excitement to new heights.

Bear's mouth covered her pussy, lips sucking, tongue flaying, teeth scraping, and she was forced to let him go, her body going into overload, convulsing with shock after orgasmic shock. And he held her there, keeping her on the knife edge of passion until, with a strangled shriek, she once more succumbed, writhing under the strength of her release.

While she was still trying to catch her breath, her body shuddering with aftershocks, he moved with lithe speed to roll and cover her body with his, bringing them face to face. His gaze was fierce, the tip of his cock poised to thrust into her still-quivering pussy. Instinctively she wrapped her legs around his hips, her arms coming up to hold on to his neck, and he trembled in turn.

"Remember this," he growled in a passion-thickened voice. "Remember *me*."

And she knew even as he penetrated her, causing her body to spasm anew, he wouldn't return. So she held him tighter, tighter yet, lifting her hips to accept and encourage each desperate thrust, wanting to brand this final coming together in his memory—to in turn never be forgotten.

Buried as deep as possible inside her, holding still, he lifted his head.

"Look at me, Rosa," he demanded.

Blinking against tears she obeyed, meeting his gaze, seeing fear, sadness, and an indefinable something that caused her breaking heart to suddenly soar. When he began to move again it was with slow intent, each motion imbued with the magic he'd brought to her life, filling her soul as well as her body. She would never be completely free of him, she knew, never be the woman she was before Bear entered her life. But she was better for knowing him, and she couldn't regret anything. Including these exquisite, beautiful, excruciating moments when, staring into his eyes, she felt the end approaching.

There were no words, only emotion and the language of their bodies straining together, climax only one more thrust, one swivel of the hips away. She felt her orgasm start—ripples turning to waves and then a surge of pleasure—heard herself cry out in ecstasy. He responded, driving into her again and again, his voice joining hers in a cacophony of mutual bliss, prolonging her pleasure as he took his, not stopping until the final shudder had receded and she grew quiet once more.

Silently they held each other and Rosa fought sleep, not wanting to miss a single second of being in his arms. Eventually the aftermath of the emotional storm claimed her, but as she drifted off she thought she heard him whisper:

"I'll be back—if I can."

Dress rehearsal passed in a blur, but Rosa knew her performance was the best she'd ever given. Losing Bear, missing him, was a constant ache that gave her strange new strength, and she put all the emotion tearing at her into the part.

"Fantastic!" The director grabbed her, kissed both her cheeks, grinning like crazy, his hair only moderately askew, which she took to be a good sign. "You were brilliant, love. Do that on opening night and I'll drink champagne from your shoe."

He whirled off to speak to someone else and Rosa heard a voice murmur behind her, "He might be happy, but he's not the one you have to please."

She turned slowly toward David Short, fighting to keep the smile on her face.

"Did you find my performance lacking in some way, Mr. Short?"

A mocking smile twisted the producer's lips as he replied. "I thought it a bit wooden. Maybe you need to loosen up a bit. I can help you with that—especially if you bring your blonde friend along."

There was no mistaking his meaning, and a rush of mingled fear and fury burned through Rosa's blood.

So this was what it all came down to—a choice between her job and her self-respect? Despite all her hard work she still had to screw the producer or throw away the past six months of effort?

Leaning close, she smiled even wider and softly said, "Fuck you, Mr. Short. I'd rather go back to waiting tables."

"You'll have to," he said as she turned to walk away. "That, or stripping, is the only job you'll be able to get."

Fuming, she pushed through the still-milling crowd, refusing to look back. Going backstage, she pulled off her costume and, without stopping to remove her makeup, threw on her street clothes. She hesitated about packing up her bits and pieces, finally left them scattered on the table. If they really were going to fire her, it was going to have to be in front of the entire cast. There was no way she'd go quietly.

The rest of the company was still celebrating, and it took a while to find Blanche. Pulling her aside, she said, "I have to get out of here. You coming?"

Blanche shook her head, although concern showed in her expression. "I have to stick around. Some of the crew members are moving on to other jobs after tonight and I promised to hang with them for a while. Are you okay?"

Rosa grimaced. "Short just threatened me again."

"Shit." Blanche glanced over her shoulder at the crew. "I can cry off."

"No," Rosa squeezed her arm. "I'm fine. We'll talk about it when you get home."

She slipped out the stage door into the foggy night, pulling up her collar against the drizzle. As she started down the shadowy alley the door opened behind her, and she heard Short's voice.

"What do you mean it's delayed? I booked the car for eleven. Tell the chauffer to get his head out his ass and get here, now."

There was a click as he snapped his phone shut and, hoping he hadn't noticed her, Rosa glanced back just in time to see a figure stalk out of the shadows and approach him. She froze, wanting to call out, warn him, but something held her frozen in place.

"David," it was a low, dangerous growl, and Rosa's heart leapt. "I've been waiting."

Short spun toward Bear, backed up a step. "A...Alex. What are you doing here?"

Bear paced closer, light from the bulb above the door glinting in his eyes, off his teeth and claws. "Did you think I wouldn't realize you were the thief? I'm here to get the talisman, and my life, back."

Short gave a little scream, turned to run, but Bear was on him. In a flash it was over, and Short lay curled on the damp ground. Bear took something from the other man's neck, placed it around his own.

"Rosa," he came toward her, stopped an arm's length away, holding out his hand. "Come."

Without thought she placed her hand in his, heard his little growl of pleasure as he lead her to the mouth of the alley, where a limousine waited. When they were settled inside, he put his fingers around the amulet hanging around his neck from a heavy gold chain. A blinding flash of light and a sharp tingle, like electricity, filled the car.

Rosa opened her eyes, blinking to dispel the spots dancing across her vision, and gasped. The handsome man, with smooth chocolate skin and an attractively shaved head, was startlingly familiar.

"You're Alex Dean."

Bear—Alex—nodded. "David knew I'd be trapped in my other form without my amulet and decided to steal it, and our company, from me." He shrugged lightly, his fingers tightening on hers. "There were others who could have done it, so it took a while to figure out, especially since it was so hard to move around looking the way I did."

"Why...?" She hesitated, not knowing how to ask, but she didn't need to say any more.

"I saw you the day I came to rehearsals and knew you were mine. I couldn't stay away, even risking your revulsion."

Rosa shook her head, still marveling how, even almost hairless, it was still unmistakably *him*. "I didn't truly notice you when you came to the theater—too caught up in my own world—but when you came to my door I knew you were mine too."

He growled—an endearingly familiar sound—and leaned close. She raised her face, anticipating his kiss, heat uncurling in her belly, uncontainable happiness storming through her heart.

Their lips were only a breath apart when he paused to murmur, "I have to warn you. We mate for life."

"So do I," she whispered in reply, cupping his cheek and urging him closer yet. She wouldn't be content until they were skin to skin, but this would do for now. "So do I."

GRETEL'S LAMENT

Jeanette Grey

He slid his mouth along my throat, over the thrumming flutter of my pulse and to my jaw. At my ear, he paused, his breath full of sweetness and promises of candy as he asked me to follow him upstairs.

It was an offer I'd heard before.

Still, he wore me down with the way he touched my lips with his, broad hands on my hips and a posture that told me he knew how to do this. How to touch and how to kiss. I wondered what else his lips could do.

Another breath against my ear was all it took, and I felt myself nodding, my fingertips seeking out buttons, eager for the drag of a zipper. I longed to grip the width of firm male flesh. And it was easy to be swayed by promises.

On the way upstairs, I scattered my clothes like bread crumbs. I knew full well the dangers of wandering out into the forest of love alone.

Laying me down across his bed, he put his mouth to the

center of my collarbones before surrounding the tip of my breast. And then he went lower still. Succumbing to the soft pleasure of that warmth against my flesh, I held my own legs open with my hands. It gave him the freedom to explore.

I'd heard a man could eat a girl alive, and that's exactly what he did. Licking and sucking, stroking lips and teeth and tongue across my apex, he devoured. From the sounds of things, the low moans and quiet words against my flesh, he relished it. In the heat, I burned, and when he pressed his fingers deep inside, I felt myself consumed.

And yet I survived. I lived to kiss my liquid from his lips and to feel his body's sweetness. Intermingled with salt and bitterness, he fed himself into my mouth, and I took everything he chose to give, sucking greedily until he grunted low and deep and flooded me.

I licked it all up. Just like candy.

In the morning, I slipped out from underneath his arm and followed the trail of my own scattered clothing back to safety. Only my apartment felt cold, the shelves all barren. There was nothing there to eat. There was nothing to sustain me.

When he called again a few days later, I was sitting on my counter, nibbling at my fingertips and staring at cobwebs. Over the phone, he asked me, "Will you come?"

"Repeatedly."

On my way to his apartment, I bought a loaf of bread to feed the hunger in my stomach and my heart. It was a good, rich bread. Poppy seed.

Although I had traversed it many times before, the route I took to love that day felt unfamiliar. Squishing bread between my finger and my thumb, I let a lump fall to the ground, and then another. Behind me, the white puffs looked far too small against the sidewalk.

So insubstantial—so impermanent—my tether to the place I'd called my home.

With the last of it deposited, I stuffed the final piece into my mouth and chewed. I knew that I could be alone and that I didn't have to starve.

But I wanted what he offered me.

I knocked, then held my breath as the door swung open, uncertain what precisely I would find. Staring at the tender lines of his face, I searched for warts. I sniffed his breath for a hint at what he'd been eating, and I kept on the lookout for the charred bones of children.

A single girl had to be careful, after all.

He laughed and pulled me forward, tilting my head back to kiss me. I let him. I let him slide his lips along my skin and to my ears and throat. And his promises were still so sweet.

We didn't make it to the bed this time. This time, he stripped me down beside the door, slipping hot fingers through the lips of my pussy before holding them up for me to taste.

"It's so good," he whispered. He kissed my cheek and let me suck on his fingers. "You taste good enough to eat."

Some memory haunted me. Some plea for caution. But in the face of pleasure, I let my safeguards slide away, my breath catching as I asked him, "Then why don't you?"

He sank to his knees, still half-dressed, bare chest against my thighs and warm hands parting me. With one leg over his shoulder, I threw my head back, and my hands moved to his hair to keep him where he was. To pull him closer.

And as I tightened, my whole body soaring, I wondered if this was what I'd been missing. I wondered if what I'd really needed was someone to feed.

He drank down everything.

Still trembling from the brilliance of climax, I melted against the door and pooled across his shoulders, stroking his hair as I laughed and smiled and breathed.

"God, you're beautiful," he told me.

Maybe he was the one feeding me.

Rolling us until I lay beneath him, he asked me if he could, his body hard and naked then and pressing to my thigh. His tip was wet, the whole length of him hot, and I was wanting still. So I told him, yes, please, to take me.

As he sank into my body, I gripped him just as tightly as I dared, all arms and legs around his frame and lips around his breath. He felt so good, hard and male and filling me up, up, up, pushing and making all these sounds inside his chest. I made them, too. I made them when he pulled almost all the way out and pressed back in. When he ground himself against my hips. When a hand snaked in between us and he begged me, *Please*.

When I shattered around the hot bloom of his release.

And after that, nothing was the same.

First it was one night a week and then two. And then it was more. There were dates and dinners, and I while I never stopped looking for warts or for danger in his choice of what to eat, I let myself enjoy his company. I particularly enjoyed his bed.

Sitting in the middle of it one night, naked and slick, sated from our lovemaking, I waited for him. He came to me with a tray full of cheese and wine and bread. Breaking the loaf, he pressed a piece against my swollen lips. I took it in, but as I did, I remembered how I always used to feed myself. I wondered how the cobwebs in my apartment were doing.

"Come on, love," he said, a wicked smile upon his face. "Eat up, now. You know you'll need your strength."

As I chewed and swallowed, I thought of all the times that he had told me I was beautiful, a low hint of caution tingling in my spine. The feeling only grew as we ate. His hands were at my face so many times, touching and stroking and placing morsels on my tongue. I accepted it all. The food. The affection that was so warm it hurt my heart.

The praise.

We made love with the lights out, tumbling roughly. Swift strokes in and out, and his fingers in my mouth, my teeth restrained as I came and came and came.

Afterward, he curled himself around my body with a hand against my abdomen. Through the hum of his sleeping breath, I imagined he wanted it to grow.

My earlier uncertainty resurged. With my hand over his, I pulled his arm away from me, slipping out from underneath him to stand beside his bed. I saw my own reflection in the mirror and tried to see if I was fuller in my figure, or if it was just inside my mind.

I *felt* fuller. Like I was more than I had been.

I remembered that he could just be fattening me up. The way he fed my belly and my heart, I would be ripe for the slaughter. And he had so much power now. In just his words, he had all he needed to make me bleed.

He was still sleeping as I pulled my clothes back on. I didn't say good-bye, and I didn't leave a note.

But when I stepped outside, I found that all the crumbs I'd left were gone. Somehow, in the intervening months, they had gone to seed, and the sidewalks bloomed with the flowers of my previous hesitancy, a brilliant rainbow of poppies. I could have followed them. I knew where they would lead me.

Instead, I picked a small bouquet of blooms and went inside. Most of them I left in a little plastic cup, filled with water to keep them alive. But one I took to bed with me.

For half the night, I trailed its scarlet head across my lover's skin, relearning the shape of him and opening my mind to hoping for more from him.

The next day, I followed the path of poppies to my old apartment, and I packed a box. One by one, I moved my things into his space. I never told him. Still, he knew.

For a week, the poppies sat there on our kitchen table, beautiful and colorful and new. When they started to wilt, I kept them fresh, heading out into the field that now covered the walk and gathering another bundle of blooms. They reminded me that I could always find my way back to my own lonely bed.

And that, in retrospect, the path that I had taken to the one I slept in now was beautiful.

A few days later, I came home from work to find our apartment hot and sweltering, the drywall dripping. As the heat overtook me, I leaned against the wall beside the door.

When I pulled my hand away, it was covered in sticky-sweet.

Stepping forward, I called his name, and he called back. I found him in the kitchen, hovering over the oven. Through the window, I could see the orange lines of flames.

In the corner, the poppies were wilting.

With a smile, he turned toward me. "You're just in time."

All my old uncertainties told me I should flee. His face was still clean, no hints of warts or green, but surely this was enough of a sign.

I wanted to trust him, though. God, but I wanted to.

"Just in time for what?"

"For this."

And then he threw the oven wide.

I jumped back, my skin raw, like it was blistering. He was bent over, his arms reaching, and in the flames behind his body, I saw my opportunity.

My thoughts screamed, *Save yourself!*

But I couldn't harm him without harming myself.

A second later, it was all rendered moot as he turned back around. His smile was just as devilish as I had always feared. And it was even more beautiful than that.

But he didn't push me in. He didn't burn me.

Instead, he swung the oven closed, and when I looked again, his arms were full of bread. What I'd mistaken for a leer was just a grin.

"Come on," he said, reaching over to kiss me. "It's cooler in the bedroom." As we walked, he told me how the oven had been malfunctioning, but how he'd persevered.

"Wait," I begged. "You did all this....You almost roasted yourself because you wanted to feed me?"

"What can I say?" With his eyes soft, his hand on my cheek, he explained, "I love you."

So many times, I'd thought of love as a forest one walked in alone. It was dangerous and frighteningly dark.

How could I have known that it was also warm and bright? That it could smell of bread and poppies.

"Take off your clothes and lie down."

I followed his instructions with brimming eyes, my own assurances of love hanging silent on my lips. He didn't let them spill out. Instead he pressed a bit of crust into my mouth.

I ate it happily.

Spread out on the bed the way he'd asked of me, I lay there and waited for him to join me. Instead, he stood there at the edge, tearing off pieces of bread. "What are you—"

"Shh."

One by one, he laid the pieces on my body. A lump on my shoulder and another on my breast, all of them leading to the very center of me. So tenderly, he tore a final chunk and placed it on my mound. Sitting back, he licked his lips.

Taking care to keep still, I look down at the trail he'd left across my skin, and then I asked, again, "What are you doing?"

His mouth and eyes were shining as he stared down at me, slowly bending down to kiss me. With one fingertip, he traced the bread crumb line from my throat to my heart and to my sex. He followed it with his lips.

At the juncture of my legs, he paused to look up at me.

"I'm making sure I can find my way home."

MATCHES

Anna Meadows

On the night of my eighteenth birthday, my mother's boyfriend handed me a box of candles and locked me out of the house. He said if I sold them all I could come back the next morning.

They had belonged to his mother, who'd taught me to make dolls from yarn and cornhusks and let me call her my *abuela* even though we were not related. The deep red wax let off the perfume of rose oil as I walked to *la plaza*. It was empty this time of night, the men home or drunk at the *tavernas*, the women asleep or waiting. The church was dark, the water in the fountain still, and the cobblestones shone from the last rain.

A few men stood at the opposite side of the *plaza*. I wasn't afraid. The men in this town were too lazy to do anything but call out, "Wanna take me to church, *santa guapa?*" But one of them kicked at something on the ground. Another bent down and hit it with the side of his fist. When I got closer, I heard them saying the same thing over and over. *Chucho.* Mutt. I wondered if they were beating a young coyote or a runt mule.

I knocked my heel against the stone of the fountain. "Leave it alone."

They shuffled enough that I could see between their legs. Not an injured coyote, but a young man lay curled on his side. He couldn't have been much older than I was. His hair was as dark as mine, but his skin was lighter, like the inner peels of birch bark. Just the rings of his irises showed around the blacks of his eyes. They were green as an agave frond. That was what they had meant by calling him *chucho*. He was half-dark, like me, like the men who were beating him, but the rest of him was pale. I wondered which of his parents had been which.

He lifted his head a little when he saw me. Blood shone on his lip and temple. He still had a watch on. I doubted they had taken his wallet. For them, it was about the fun of it, not what he had on him. If it was, they would've picked a man with a better watch.

"*Princesa* likes *los chuchos?*" asked one of the standing men.

I struck a match, lit one of the candles, and held it out, a sheet of light between them and me. The two men holding the young man down did not let him go. I remembered the prayer my *abuela* had taught me, *De las doce verdades del mundo*. The twelve truths of the world. I said the first truth, *la Casa Santa*—the Lord's house.

The two men holding the young man took their hands from him and stood up. They each took a slow step back, as though I clutched a handful of cursed rock salt over their mothers' graves and was slowly opening my fingers.

I held the candle just in front of me so they could see my face. I said the second truth, *dos Tablas de Moisés*—two tablets of Moses—and the third, *tres Trinidades*—three trinities. The man on the ground began to move his lips, first silently, and then his mouth slowly gave the words sound. He knew the prayer, and said it with me. *Cuatro Evangelios*—four gospels.

The men startled to hear him speak. *Cinco llagas*—five wounds. The men backed away like tadpoles scattering from a firefly's light. *Seis candeleros*—six candles. The men left *la plaza* and vanished into the dark.

The man on the ground mouthed the rest of the prayer, eyes closed. I thought he might have been too hurt to move, but then he crossed himself.

"Can you get up?" I asked.

He did, wincing a little. He had on jeans, and a leather jacket that was cracked and worn enough that it must have been at least a generation old. He was too clean to be homeless. His jeans had the soft look of being worked in all day, but there were no stains except new ones from his blood and the wet ground.

"Are you a *bruja?*" he asked.

"No," I said. "Are you?"

"My *bisabuela* was," he said. "A *curandera*, I mean."

He must have had a young *bisabuela*; my great-grandmothers had all died years before I was born. I didn't know why he used the word *bruja* at all if his great-grandmother had been a *curandera*. *Bruja*—witch—was a word used by those who feared the women who healed with herbs from midnight gardens.

He tossed his head to clear his hair from his forehead. He had a browbone and a mouth like other brown men, but the *gringo* in him showed up in the shape of his nose and in those eyes. Even in the dark, with the shadow of his hair as it fell back over his forehead, his eyes were green as a tree's first sprouts. He was that strange kind of handsome that only *chuchos* were, freckles on brown skin, green eyes, and hair dark as a river at night.

"My name's Roman," he said, and he stood there looking at me.

"Are you stupid?"

He shook his head.

"You gonna wait around here for them to come back?" I asked.

He shook his head again, slower this time, and put his hands in his pockets to leave. He looked over his shoulder and said, "Thank you," no trace of an accent. It made me wonder if he was all *gringo,* and the men had made a mistake.

He tried locking eyes with me. I blew the candle out so he couldn't see my face.

When I couldn't see his shape anymore, I huddled into a corner of the church steps with the box of candles. There was no one to buy them at this time of night, not unless I walked down to the bars, and those weren't the kind of men who cared for *las rosas de la virgen.*

I wished I had my heavier coat. My fingers were red with the cold, and the tips of my breasts grew hard enough to spread pain through my upper body. The smell of winter, of ice crystals and frozen earth, spun through the air. I relit the candle. It was already ruined for selling; no one would buy a black wick. Seeing the light turn gold and amber on the cobblestones warmed me more than that small flame.

A tear slipped from the inner corner of my eye. I gasped to fight it, but it slid easily down my cheek. I pulled my knees into me, shielding the candles. Wind brushed the back of my neck, and as I fell asleep I imagined it was my *abuela* stroking my hair. In those last few moments before I slept, I thought I saw her in the light on the still fountain water, laughing and kneading dough with the heels of her hands.

I woke up to snowflakes spinning in the dark, each catching the moon through the clouds. A light layer of snow stuck to the cobblestones in the *plaza.* I would have found it beautiful if I hadn't been so cold. I shivered off the dusting on my shoulders and lap. My body was stiff. I felt as brittle as new ice. The candle had gone out; the wick was damp and dotted with snowflakes. It would not light again, no matter how many matches I spent on it.

The feeling went out of the tips of my fingers. Lighting another candle, one with a dry, new wick, would at least give me that little light to hold my hands near. The glow in my corner of *la plaza* would turn the snow to gold.

The candle flickered to life, and I saw my *abuela* again, the shape of her in threads of light. But snowflakes stuck to the wick and put the candle out. I lit the next one, and my *abuela* appeared from the light, this time sewing a dress I had torn playing in the rose bushes. The snow dampened the wick again, and it dimmed. I lit the next, not caring that I wouldn't be able to sell it, and I saw her cutting roses from the same bushes. I lit the one after that, and the one after that. Each time the snow, falling harder now, put out the flame and ruined the wick.

The last candle went out. I tried to light it again, but the flame wouldn't take. I tried each of the others, but they had soaked through. I tried until the book of matches was nothing but stubs. A tear froze just below my eye, and the ice stung my cheek. The cold prickled, then deepened, the sting of rose thorns turning to the pierce of a scorpion's barb. Snowflakes gathered on my eyelashes so that the whole world shimmered with ice.

A falling star broke through the clouds and streaked to earth, and the light slowly went out of the world. I remembered my *abuela* telling me about *los meteoros*. If I saw one, she said, it meant one of only two things: a soul was being welcomed into heaven, or two souls had fallen in love and were becoming one. "They're close, no, *m'ija?*" she had always asked.

I thought I was dead by the time I saw him. I thought the

green of Roman's eyes was the last thing I would think of before I met my *abuela* again. Strange, how much I must have wanted him, even from those few moments in the rose candle's light, that I would think of him then.

Roman put his hands on the sides of my face, and the warmth of his palms felt so good it tore a scream from me. The sleeves of his jacket smelled like ash tree bark in summer. The hollow of his neck shared the same color and scent as agave nectar. I was all ice now, and the warmth of him was breaking me. He put his jacket around me, and the lining held so much of his heat that I thought it would splinter me into snowflakes.

He shook me to get me to look at him. "Stay with me, okay?"

His breath was hot against my mouth, and my lips stung with thawing. He put my arm around his shoulder and picked me up off the steps. My body was too numb to fight him or hold onto him. I was still dying, and though I felt the warmth of Roman's chest against my cheek, I could still see the falling star.

He shook me gently. "Don't fall asleep," he said. "Look at me."

I didn't listen.

The last thing I felt out in the cold was the snowflakes melting from my eyelashes and slipping down my cheeks. After that it was the soft pain of my skin warming again, of his hands stripping away my clothes. I fought him then. I tried slapping him, but he only grabbed my hand and looked at it, front and back, like he thought I might be bleeding.

"I'm not gonna hurt you," he said.

I fought harder when I realized I was in his bed. The wood scent of his skin and the smell of that old leather were on the sheets.

"Your clothes are wet," he said. "They're gonna get you sick." He pulled my blouse off hard enough that I sat up from the force, falling when my arms were free of the sleeves. He held the small of my back to slow my fall. The tips of my breasts brushed against the quilt. He put a hand on my forehead and whispered something I couldn't make out. His fingers shone with oil, and his hand smelled like wild blue sage.

He held my hand. I tried to pull it away.

He pinched the middle of my palm between his thumb and forefinger. "Do you want to lose half your hand or do you want me to help you?" he asked.

I stopped fighting. He cut a blade from a potted *áloe* and spread the wet inside over my fingers. The pain dulled at his touch. I must have talked in my sleep as he took me away from *la plaza*, because he knew to show me one of the rose candles. He pinched the blackened wick with his thumb and third finger. He drew his fingers up quickly, and the candle lit. I looked for a match hidden in his palm. There was nothing. He'd ignited it with his bare hand, but he looked neither surprised nor impressed with himself.

"How did you?" I asked.

Now he bowed his head to let his hair fall in his eyes. "It happened the first time when I was five," he said. "I lit a candle but I didn't mean to." He winced in a way that told me someone had beaten him for it, thinking he'd been playing with matches. "It was always things that were supposed to be lit," he said. "Candles. Lanterns. But my *bisabuela* taught me to control it."

The light, orange-gold as a harvest moon, brought out the olive in his face as he set the rose candle on the table next to the bed.

"*Tiene un corazón solitario, pero usted no es el único,*" he said—*you have a lonely heart, but you're not the only one.* It must have been something he had learned from his *bisabuela*, who had been kind to him, who had never beaten him for making fire between his fingers.

What a strange man, who lit candles without matches, who called the woman he had cared for most *bruja*.

He turned just enough for me to see a streak of dirt in the wound on his temple. Flecks of dried blood still clung to his lip. He had not taken the same care with his own body as he had taken with mine. I wondered how long the men in *la plaza* had kicked him and hit him before he and I drove them off with the twelve truths.

I brushed away a few flecks of blood, my thumb grazing his lower lip. "You're hurt."

"I'm all right," he said.

I pulled his shirt off anyway. He let me. Bruises darkened his body, some already violet as blackberries. They shaded the contours of his chest and back. My *abuela* would have said that was good, that him bruising quickly meant he would heal quickly.

My hands were ice on his bruises. Each time I moved them, he winced at the cold, but then relaxed to feel it spread.

"*Las malvarrosas*," he said, because he must have known I was wondering why he had been out in *la plaza* so late. "They grow wild in the hills on the other side of town, but I gotta get them at night, or they don't keep."

I'd seen them, the fluffy flowers that turned the hillsides red and gold and blush pink in springtime. I didn't ask why he wanted them. Maybe their scent helped him sleep, or they were his *bisabuela*'s favorite.

His back was darker than his chest, the brown of a clay jar. His skin was so warm I thought a little of the sun must still be in it, that I could see it letting off light if I looked close enough. I kissed the darkest bruise on his back, just below his left shoulder blade. I'd meant it as kindness, more out of gratitude for him pulling me from the cold than out of desire for the heat of his body, but I felt the flinch of his muscle under my mouth. He knew.

I did the same with his chest, kissing a patch of blue over his heart as though it would veil the longing. But I realized my hands were on his jeans, and wondered if the tensing in his thigh muscles was from that same desire or only because he could feel the chill of my palms through the fabric.

The inside of me spun hot as a new star, but my skin was still so cold I felt like I was cracking whenever I moved. I shuddered with the ache of coming back to life. It began below my collar-bone and ended with a rush of warmth and wetness between my legs. With every new scent I picked up on him—the ash bark, the green herbs, the jacket he must have inherited from his father or uncle—I wanted him in that new way.

The feeling came back to my fingers like light across water. I kissed him hard enough that the breath at the back of his throat deepened to a low, quick groan. His mouth tasted like copper rock salt.

He pulled the quilt around my shoulders. "No," he said. "*No ahora. No porque usted tiene frío.*" *Not now. Not because you're cold.*

"*No es porque tengo frío,*" I said. "*Es porque soy vivo.*" *Not because I'm cold. Because I'm alive.*

It must have been enough of an answer, because he kissed me, one forearm under the small of my back. He pulled my panties off with the same urgency of tearing my wet clothes away. He unhooked my bra as if it were made of ice and it would kill me if it stayed on my skin.

The *áloe* had brought most of the sensation back to my fingers, but they were just numb enough that I struggled to unbutton his jeans. He was patient, even as he grew hard against my hands. I got his pants down around his knees and kicked them the rest of the way off his legs. My hands found the warmth of his bare thighs and then strayed to his erection.

He didn't thrust against my palm, but he moved a little toward me, letting me know he didn't mind the cold. I couldn't understand it, how any man would let a woman with so much cold in her fingers touch him where it could hurt him most. But maybe there was enough heat in his body that he liked it, his nerves responding to the sudden change. He got harder against my hand. When I offered my mouth to his, he took it.

The gash on his lip reopened from kissing. Without thinking, I tongued the trickle of blood. He startled. I stopped and gasped, afraid I'd stung him, but he breathed in with a soft noise that told me he liked it.

The heat of his body spread over me. I was a shimmer of cold sand, and he was the salt of a warm ocean, turning my million rough grains back into flesh. I cried out at the pleasure of it. He did not startle again, not until I opened my legs and guided him into me. He set his teeth like the feeling surprised him, like he'd never felt it before. I didn't ask; it would've been cruel. I could see the desire in the tensing of his muscles, but there was something chaste in the agave green of his eyes. It made me think I should handle him gently. I couldn't. I was still too cold. My fingers could not touch him delicately. They were too hungry for his warmth.

"It's inside me," I said.

"What is?" he asked.

"*El frío,*" I said. *The cold.*

He pushed deeper into me, reaching that last part that was iced over and armored in snowflakes. The same finger that had lit the candle touched me until I felt like a close star. He was all warmth and salt. I bit his shoulder, and even there he tasted like rock salt. I opened to take him in. The black of his eyes flinched as the inside of me pulsed around him. The green darkened, and the last ice inside me shattered. He still looked kind, but not chaste. I still had the glisten of snowflakes on my skin, but there was no winter inside me.

When he came, it spread through me like hot amber, melting the part of me that still fought what his hands were doing to me. "Roman," I said, calling for him like we were in darkness. I finished, and he held onto me tighter, like he was catching me. Coming down from the feeling of his touch made me dizzy, like falling into grass after spinning under the night sky, and I slept.

His arm was around my waist when I woke up. It wasn't yet dawn, and snowflakes still spun outside the window. The glow of my *abuela*'s candle let me see the spice jars and potted plants along the wall of his bedroom. Agave and moonflower. Cayenne and blue lavender. The same plants that skilled women used to heal children with nightmares or fevers and men and women with *susto*. Roman went to the hillsides in the dark for *las malvarrosas* because he wanted them for his *remedios*.

"You are a *brujo*," I said.

He slowly ran his fingers through my hair. "Sort of," he said. "Apprentice *brujo*. For now I pay the bills with carpentry work."

"Who do you apprentice to?" I asked. I didn't know a *curandero* in town, man or woman.

"Nobody," he said. "It was my *bisabuela*, but she died last year, so I'm figuring it out as I go."

"That's why you knew the twelve truths."

"Since I was six," he said. "I fought it for a while. Then I gave up. The *gringos* were calling me warlock, and the rest were saying *brujo*. I figured I'd better take it."

I stroked my fingers along the side of his face. The constellations of freckles on his temple and the bridge of his nose seemed as unlikely as the life flickering in my blood. "Last night," I said. "How'd you know?"

"Something didn't seem right," he said. "So I came back."

"You live here alone?" I asked.

"My *bisabuela* lived here."

"You're young," I said. "To be a *curandero*."

"She said I was ready, before she died. Sometimes I don't know though."

I kissed the bruising on his temple and on the side of his mouth.

"What were you doing out there?" he asked. It wasn't a question I was meant to answer with my lips. He put his hand to my forehead, not so much reading my thoughts as feeling the shape of what I was willing to let him know. I'd heard of *curanderos* doing the same, but never one so young.

"Oh," he said.

I didn't meet his eyes.

"You could stay here," he said.

"You don't know me," I said.

"You got those guys off me. That's as much as I need to know. *Los corazónes solitarios* gotta stick together." He got up from the bed and, one by one, lit my *abuela*'s candles by sliding each wick between his fingers. The whole room glowed rose-gold.

He lit the last of my *abuela*'s candles. I caught his hand and pulled him toward me, the heat of a falling star between us. He covered my body with his, so close I could watch the muscles in his back as I stroked that bluish bruise on his shoulder blade. I shivered when he took the most sensitive part of me between his thumb and his forefinger, nervous that it might turn to fire at his touch. He stroked it like a candle's wick, and the pleasure spread so quickly it felt like embers on his fingertips.

I could have gone back to *la plaza* and waited for the cold to take me to my *abuela*. I could have gone to my mother's and waited on her front porch. But I didn't want any of it. I wanted nothing more than this man with the fire on his fingertips.

THE BEAST WITHIN

Emerald

In the headquarters of Castle Jewelers, the young CEO sat, as usual, locked away from everyone in his high tower office. He glared at the email from the board of directors open on his computer and the corresponding appointment notice on his calendar and snarled out loud to himself as he turned his chair away and stood up. The CEO was a notorious figure among the employees who sat in the offices on the lower floors—his internal ugliness had become legendary, making his chosen reclusion in his office welcome among all who worked for him. The impeccability of his blue suit and expensive gold jewelry did nothing to hide the beastly disposition his workers had always seen in him.

Across town, Julie Bellevue had been called from her small cottage by the lake by her father, who had fallen from his ladder and hurt his ankle as he was fixing the siding on his house. Julie hovered now by her father's hospital bed as the doctor informed them that the ankle was indeed broken.

Mr. Bellevue moaned. "Oh, what am I going to do? I have my first appointment with Castle Jewelers in an hour. I must be there!" Julie, who was his youngest daughter, reached for his hand, her beautiful face drawn with sympathy. He turned to her. "Julie. Sweetheart, I'm going to need you to go and take over the job in my place."

Julie felt some apprehension at this request. The young woman was already an employee of her father's consulting business that specialized in conflict resolution for businesses and organizations. Though her father had been grooming her in his line of work for years, and the recent acquisition of her master's degree in transpersonal psychology was already supporting the next step of her getting to take on her own clients, she had not yet served in a capacity beyond providing her father assistance with his cases.

"Please, Julie. This is a very important client—I can't afford to lose it right now."

Julie recognized the desperation in his face, and she knew this job was a significant one, both financially and for his reputation. If it were lost, the hard work he had put into forming and running his consulting business for the past several years could be in jeopardy.

So, to save her father's business, Julie agreed to go to Castle Jewelers headquarters in his place. As she was about to take her leave of the room, her father called to her again.

"Julie," he said, concern evident on his face. "Your meeting is with the CEO—Heath Castle. The board has hired us to work with him individually in addressing the conflict between him and, well, the rest of the company. I was to coach him in sensitivity training and interpersonal communication.

"I want you to be warned—Heath is not said to be a nice individual. He has, in fact, an ugly reputation. He is reputed to be a rather beastly manager, very difficult to work with. His workers mostly vacillate between fear and loathing of him, and he's not even usually seen around the workplace. Generally he locks himself in his office in the highest tower of the building."

"What makes him so not nice?" Julie asked her father.

Her father shook his head. "I don't know." His face crinkled into a smile. "That's what they pay us to find out."

Julie smiled and leaned down to kiss her father's cheek, then turned and hurried out the door and across town to make her father's appointment at Castle Jewelers on time.

At the highest office in the top of the headquarters building, Julie met the eyes of the company's thirty-eight-year-old CEO. As she'd read her father's file, she had been struck by the young age of the head of such a large and lucrative company. Upon reading further she had found that the circumstances surrounding his position were a bit mysterious—it was a family company, and Heath's mother had taken over after his father had died several years before. She had run the company for a short time before Heath had abruptly assumed the leadership role. There was no further information about his mother's current status with the company or why this turnover had taken place.

The man in front of her had a tall, sturdy, and potentially intimidating build as he stood behind his desk with his arms crossed. His hair was dark and longish, his suit tailored to fit his bulky frame flawlessly. The truth was that Heath was a handsome man, but no one who worked for him even noticed his physical attractiveness anymore, so accustomed were they to the hideousness of his demeanor.

It was when Julie looked into the man's eyes that she saw what her father had warned her about. They appeared flat, dark with hostility and emanating an energy about as welcoming as a prison. In fact, Heath had eyes of a lovely bright blue, but they had reflected darkness for so long that they appeared black to most who looked at him now.

Julie's father had been retained to conduct a one-hour session with Heath each morning for two weeks. Julie understood immediately the complaints of those who worked for him and the reason the board had procured her father's services. The voice of the man in front of her was low and menacing, and not once while she was in his office did he smile. At times his demeanor seemed downright ferocious, almost animal-like in the refined environment of posh furniture and spectacular views from the broad windows behind his desk. That day's meeting was the initial consultation, and Julie's heart sank a bit as she realized she would be trapped in this office tower with him every weekday morning for the next two weeks.

The beautiful young woman also found herself forgetting the attractiveness of Heath's physical appearance as she interacted with the internal ugliness that had so obviously alienated his colleagues and employees. Even so, when she stood up at the conclusion of their first session, she found herself admiring his solid build and chiseled features, formed into a frown as frequently as they were. She approached him to shake his hand and bid him well for the day, and his eyebrows came together in an even deeper frown as he hesitated before offering her what may have been the coldest handshake she had ever experienced.

As the week progressed, Julie discovered the predictable resistance to warmth or consideration that Heath displayed. Each day when she came and went, she passed by Vivian, the receptionist, who had made no secret of the fact that she found Julie's job far from enviable.

"Good luck doing that kind of work with such a beast of a

man," she'd said not unpleasantly when Julie had introduced herself her first day there. "He'd just as soon growl a nasty comment at you as say hello."

Julie just smiled and went on her way. To be sure, she found working with Heath distasteful sometimes, and at times she even grew frustrated. But Julie had been raised very consciously, and she knew that the only way to overpower hate was with love. Love could take many forms—kindness, protectiveness, fierceness—but it was essential in all dealings in order for them to be true. So she took a deep breath and found that awareness in her heart, and she responded to Heath from that place.

Though Julie was a clever girl and had discerned an understanding of many things about Heath thus far, she was unaware that an unwanted attraction he felt toward her was making him even edgier than usual. He felt no desire to give in to any kind of connection with anyone, and the carnal pull inside him whenever the image of the beautiful young woman floated across his mind was something he simply clenched his jaw against and pushed from his awareness, as he had so many other things.

When she was physically present in his office, the challenge became considerably more intense. One such time he even found himself idly remembering the single unopened condom he had tossed carelessly in the bottom drawer the morning he had discovered it mysteriously lying beneath his desk. (This was only mysterious to Heath, because he was unaware of the pastime the cleaning crew had begun to enjoy of having irreverent sex atop his desk after hours.) When he realized where his mind had drifted, he had slammed a fist onto his desk and said some vicious thing to the beautiful woman sitting on the other side of it. She had met his gaze, never losing her cool. Heath, on the other hand, found himself shaking and clamped down with even greater resolve on the unwelcome libidinous urges that had crept their way into his consciousness.

Monday morning of the second week, Julie entered the office in a bright yellow power suit with a lavish bouquet of red roses in her hands. Vivian looked up from her desk as Julie passed by with the large vase.

"Ooh!" the receptionist said, her eyes lighting up. "Who gave you flowers?"

Julie gave a tinkling laugh as she paused. "No one, Viv darling. I bought them myself."

Vivian's brow crinkled. "You bought a dozen red roses for yourself?"

Julie laughed again. "They're for my father. Red is his favorite color. I'm taking them to him later to cheer him as he heals."

With a little wave she turned and continued down the row of cubicles to the elevators, and a smiling Vivian went back to the work at her desk. Though Julie had been headed to Heath's office carrying a bouquet of flowers, it never occurred to Vivian or any of the workers at any of the cubicles that the roses might be for him, as no one liked him enough to even consider that anyone would take such interest in him.

Heath didn't look up as Julie sailed into his office, and she accepted this slight with her usual grace. At the soft sound of the glass vase as she lowered it onto a shelf, his head lifted. He did a double take as his gaze landed on the flowers.

"What the hell are those?" he demanded, his gaze darkening even more than usual.

"Roses," Julie said, stating the obvious. "I'm taking them to my father's house on my way home."

Heath's glare had grown more pronounced as she spoke,

even as it didn't leave the blooms now set atop the shelf. "I don't want them in here. Get rid of them!"

Julie looked at him evenly. "Heath, a little brightness in this room while I'm here is not going to hurt you."

Heath looked enraged, and he stood up, slamming his palms on the desk in front of him. "If you don't get them out of here, I'll do it myself!"

He made a move from behind the desk, and Julie stepped calmly in front of him. Neither spoke for a moment as they stood toe to toe, Heath breathing heavily, Julie meeting his gaze with the silent strength she had always shown in the face of Heath's hostility. It was this time that she saw, as she looked into his stormy gaze, the flicker of sadness she suspected he didn't even consciously register. His aggression, his maleness, stood inches from her, and while she felt the stirring of arousal in her gut at the challenge, she took a deep breath and tempered it in the face of her immediate duty.

"What do you have against roses?" she ventured in a quiet voice.

The flicker grew then, but it was quickly replaced by an even stronger fury. "I hate them!" he snarled, moving to push past her, but Julie stayed rooted, and her steadfastness made Heath back up.

The progress Julie had made working with Heath over the past week began to show when Heath chose to offer more information. In a low, furious voice, he muttered through clenched teeth, "They remind me of my mother."

"What?" Julie was surprised by the disclosure, and she stepped closer to him.

"Nothing!" Just as quickly Heath retracted, and Julie felt his energy draw back in as his nostrils flared with anger.

"Would you like to tell me about your mother?" Julie's voice was quiet, the invitation like a feather floating through the air between them.

"My mother was an evil witch! It's because of her that I'm the way I am!" With this furious outburst Heath stood and stalked to the window, sending his rolling chair flying back to bang against the wall.

Julie looked at him, sensing the importance of his words. "What way is that?"

Heath whirled on her and glared. "Do you think I don't know what people think about me? What they say? That no one wants me around? Why the fuck do you think I stay locked in my office all damned day? Because I like it so much?" He gave a dry laugh that scraped like metal against concrete. "Not quite, sweetheart. It's because I know people don't want me around. Which is fine, because I don't want to be around them either."

Julie didn't answer, sensing, despite his anger, that she should let him continue. The young woman was surprised to find that his use of the word *sweetheart* had given the undeniable arousal in her a jolt. She took a deep breath, however, and released the distraction, focusing again on her present responsibility. She stood still and remained quiet, holding a place of safety for him to speak if he wanted to.

After a few minutes, she heard his voice start up again. "I had a younger sister. We grew up rich, of course. Materially, we had all we could ever want." His jaw clenched. "But my father worked all the time, and my mother—my mother hurled nothing but cruelty at my sister and me. We threatened to run away, but my mother told us we were ugly children, and that no one else would ever want us." He turned away from Julie, and she could see him trembling as he stared out the window.

"Michelle killed herself." The words were like the wretched creak of an abandoned, centuries-old castle door. He stayed facing away from her. "After that, my mother ran off. I never saw her again." He turned slowly from the window. Fury seemed to spark from his eyes as he trained his seething gaze on the bouquet of roses on the shelf. "She sent a spray of red roses to Michelle's funeral, even though she knew Michelle hated red."

Julie remained silent, allowing Heath's words to land and be heard.

After several minutes, she spoke, barely above a whisper. "I'm so sorry about your sister." She paused, then went on. "And I can understand your feeling very hurt by your mother's actions."

Heath didn't move, though she saw his jaw clenching and unclenching.

"And it's because of that hurt that you've treated people so cruelly yourself." Julie said it as a statement rather than a question. In Heath's eyes she saw the understanding of the declaration as truth.

It encouraged her, and she spoke again. "What might that tell you about why your mother treated you so cruelly?"

"What?" he snapped.

She repeated herself, pausing to allow the question to register before adding, "I don't know what happened in her life or why she herself felt so much pain, but the bottom line is, it was likely the pain in her that hadn't been released that made her treat her children that way."

A look of sadness came over him like the sun from behind a cloud. "I know what happened to her." His expression became so distressed it looked as though he might cry. "She *was* hurting." Then his expression hardened. "But it wasn't fair for her to take that out on us."

Julie acknowledged his comment with an emphatic nod. "You're right, Heath. It isn't fair to take our pain out on others."

Her gaze stayed on him as he looked at her, the internal struggle smoldering in his expression. His eyes were dark again, and Julie could see he had not understood. The defensiveness was rising up in him again, threatening to take over and burst through at an even stronger degree than before. Julie knew it was not unusual for defenses to arise in the face of revelation, for the mental processing of words alone to not be enough. She saw the opportunity, and she knew she would need to take a different tack.

The pain, like a spell, needed to be broken.

Anger continued to rise visibly in Heath, and Julie took a deep breath, allowing fierce love, love in its warrior form, to rise inside her as it was called forth. When she felt it fill her being, she stepped forward and met the stony gaze of her client head-on, her own reflecting the hardness of twin diamonds.

"Sit down." Her voice had changed. She heard it, and she could tell by the look on Heath's face that he did too. Wariness among the fury and bitterness now, he hesitated only a second before lowering himself back into his chair.

Julie reached forward and started to untie his tie. Her closeness made Heath's breath hitch even as he began to demand to know what she thought she was doing.

The sharp connection of her hand with his face resounded in the office before his sentence was even finished. Heath's jaw dropped, though the countenance of Julie, who happened to know how to deliver such a slap without damaging anything, didn't change.

"I'm doing whatever I want, and you will do so as well until I release you from that order." She pulled his tie the rest of the way off and stepped back. "Stand up."

Julie minced no words as the orders came through her, the alignment of fierce love displaying its unique beauty.

Still stunned, Heath did so without a word. Julie turned him around and secured his wrists behind his back with his tie. She felt his muscles tense beneath her hands, and she left one hand on his arm after she was finished, sending warmth from her body into his via the physical contact. She kept it there until she felt a degree of relaxation beneath her fingers. Then she put a hand on his shoulder, bending him at the waist and pushing his cheek down to the surface of his desk.

Though Heath would never have wanted to admit it, Julie's sudden treatment of him seemed to make the arousal he had clamped down so tightly rocket into his consciousness like an erupting volcano, his cock providing immediate and granite-like evidence as such. He stayed still in the position in which she had put him, desperately hoping she wouldn't notice this incriminating evidence. He made a move to speak, but the pressure of her grip on his body relegated the sound to only a whimper.

Then Julie was behind him, her body pressing against his as she leaned forward and grabbed his hair. Reaching below the desk, she grabbed his crotch without preamble. Heath jerked with humiliation, his face burning from being caught in such a state of arousal. Julie, on the other hand, almost breathed a sigh of relief. Though she had fully expected it, she was more than a little relieved to feel the hardness between his legs. Her instincts had been correct.

The revelation also made the wetness grow between her legs. The arousal she had felt earlier was in full force now, but she still relegated it to a secondary position, inviting her slick pussy to be patient while she attended to the struggle taking place within Heath.

Julie held his hair unflinchingly and squeezed the base of his erection just hard enough to keep his attention.

"Do you like that?" she hissed in his ear, tightening the grip of both her hands. She let go of his cock and undid his belt as he whimpered incoherently. She yanked his trousers open unceremoniously, and his pants and underwear fell to the floor.

The smack resounded in the cavernous office as Julie brought her hand down against his behind. Heath jumped and cried out as Julie's hand, already poised for the second blow, found its target again before she paused and ran her hand over the red blossoming over his skin. She kept her grip on his hair, the warmth of her hand exuding a strength she knew was founded on compassion and alignment, whether or not Heath felt it consciously yet. Over and over she hit him, then caressed him, checking the surging of his cock periodically and barking orders as he squirmed beneath her hands. The energy swelled and retreated like an orchestra, the harmony and dissonance of hers and his and that which was unique to their connection administering just enough pain to touch that which was repressed within him.

Julie watched as the immediate and past hurt melded together, rising into Heath's consciousness as his body shuddered. She held on tighter, holding steady and guiding him with her hands and her heart to release, the place where what had been trapped for so long was experienced, processed in a moment of agony that for an instant seemed everlasting before it exploded and vanished, just another form of light in the infinite array of all that is. Finally Heath's cock erupted at the same time he did, his body collapsing in a roaring sob as come spurted to cover her fingers.

Julie yanked the tie off his wrists and moved immediately to cover his body with hers, holding him tightly as he released beneath her. The energy affected her deeply, and she found herself feeling awash in the beauty that broke forth from beneath the beastliness that had covered it for who knew how long. The transformation took her breath away, transferring effortlessly through her body to the arousal spilling between her legs.

Seamlessly Julie slid her mouth to his ear. Careful to only complement and not interrupt the long-overdue expressing as it came from him, the words were barely a whisper, almost simply a movement against his skin:

"You're beautiful."

Heath's body convulsed, his sobs continuing long after his orgasm had culminated. Eventually he fell silent. His eyes closed, Julie watched him take a deep breath as he rose to his feet. She stood as well. He turned to her and opened his eyes.

Julie blinked at the transformation. She was startled to discover how blue Heath's eyes were, as though the tears had literally cleaned them out, polished the tarnish away to restore them to their original luster.

They were also, she noted, filled with desire, a potency of a purity she had not yet seen from him. Before she could respond, Heath stepped toward her and lifted her from the floor, almost crushing her in his embrace as he backed her up against the wall, his mouth on hers with a sizzling urgency that made all professional considerations drop from her consciousness. Nothing but her sex commanded attention now, the wetness between her legs covering Heath's fingers as he slipped his hand beneath her skirt.

Gently Heath lowered Julie to the wooden floor, unbuttoning her suit jacket and sliding her bra out of the way as he took one nipple then the other into his mouth, eliciting in Julie a burning desire over which she felt she had no influence. Rising to his knees, Heath yanked open the bottom drawer of his desk and scrabbled through it frantically until he found the tiny foil packet he had remembered only days before.

Then he sank into Julie, who was waiting beneath him with flushed face and rapid breath. The two of them cried out in unison as he entered her, and her arms came around his strong shoulders as he pumped into her, somehow knowing exactly how to move his hips so that her breath grew even faster as Heath felt her start to tremble beneath him.

When her release came, she wailed with abandon, releasing all the earnestness Julie had collected while caring for Heath and succumbing to her own state of sublime luminescence.

They lay on the floor together, neither speaking nor moving, for some time. When Julie rose eventually and began to straighten her outfit, Heath stood up as well.

"I'll walk you downstairs," he said. For the first time, Julie saw him smile.

Moments later the two stood just inside the glass door in the entryway of Castle Jewelers headquarters as their lips came together in a kiss softer than the rose petals adorning the stems in Julie's hand. Behind them, Vivian's eyes practically popped out of her head as she stared from her desk.

As they eased apart, Julie extracted, with exquisite delicacy, one of the scarlet blooms from the vase. With reverence, she extended it gently to the man in front of her.

Heath swallowed and looked down at the flower before lifting his big hand to accept it.

"Please don't tell me I must wait until tomorrow to see you again," he whispered back as he looked up at her.

Julie smiled. "I'll text you my address right now." Palming her phone from her purse, she gave Heath a last kiss on the cheek and strode through the glass door into the sunlight beyond.

And so it was that the beast within was released in the face of unconditional love. Because Julie had loved and accepted even what was ugly in Heath, it had transformed and returned to the beauty inherent in all things. And from that day forth Heath became beautiful again to all who knew him, and especially to Julie, who continued to visit his tower office long after their two-week contract was up, whenever he wasn't already taking the day off to spend at her small cottage by the lake.

WOLF MOON

Michelle Augello-Page

Master says, "Strip."

I remove my red hooded cloak; finger the straps of my brassiere and pull, slide my hands down along the sides of my body, ease my underpants away with my thumbs, and allow the lingerie to fall in a tangle to the ground. I meet his eyes and smile, sharp-toothed careless girl. I stain my lips blood-red; Little Red I am, bloodthirsty, half-woman, half-wolf.

The hunter grabs my hair and crushes my mouth with his mouth, lips, tongue, teeth; he is as hungry as I am. He ran to me, through the woods, past evening primrose, trembling ash and pine. He ran through the garden of thorny wild roses, barely touching the path of crumbling stone leading to the cottage door leading to me, open, waiting.

His eyes burn into mine; I feel the depth of the full moon in his desire, this time he will own me. He exposes his cock and forces me to kneel before him. I take his balls into my mouth greedily, graze and nip hungrily between his legs. A low growl escapes me; he pulls me up and slaps my cheek. I am sorry.

He slaps me again.

He knows I could tear him apart; I am flesh and blood, hunger.

Once upon a time, and again, the hunter held my life in his hands. I had grown reckless, believing the woods free of men, and his cottage was camouflaged deep in the forest. His shotgun was loaded with silver bullets, cocked and aimed at the red-flecked creature in the shadows. Though he could hardly believe his eyes, he saw at once who I was. He overcame me, strapped my mouth and tied my arms and feet; he carried me home to Grandmother's cottage, across his back, dead weight.

He knew I was wild; I had never known a master. He knew I was afflicted, cursed by the moon, by the wolf-beast who left me part changeling as a child, leaving only a scream and strewn flowers on the forest floor.

The hunter had heard my frightened echo as he was cutting wood, preparing for winter. He raced through the woods, still holding the axe, following the sound and the path of my foot-steps to the cottage. From the window, he saw the wolf-beast sleeping, bloated and sick with satiation, and he broke through the door. The hunter slashed the wolf-beast's stomach to release Grandmother and me. With a strong stroke of his axe, the hunter then liberated the beast's head from his body, killing the wolf-beast instantly.

Blood, and more blood. Grandmother and I covered in gore substantial as afterbirth. In shock, numb, we could neither move nor speak. The hunter wrapped the head and body of the wolf-beast in a bed sheet and placed it outside the cottage. When he returned, he cleaned us off with a damp towel, soothed us with gentle words. I held onto Grandmother as the hunter wrapped me tight in my red hooded cloak and placed a shawl around her shoulders. He set about cleaning up the cottage and put the door back on its hinges. He told us that he would take the body of the wolf-beast deep inside the forest to burn; he would never bury something so evil in the nourishing earth.

Not long afterward, Grandmother died; she had been sick, and her old frail body was unable to sustain the internal changes caused by being inside the wolf-beast. But I was still young and lived, returned to Mother and Father with the promise to never stray from the path in the woods again. I never strayed, but I remained lost.

Time passed, and when it became clear that I had changed, I changed again. The cycles of the moon brought blood and breasts, fur and teeth. Mother wept and Father held his head. They could not keep me. I was no longer Little Red, they said.

"But I am Little Red," I cried. "Still Little Red," I pleaded.

They turned their faces away, disgusted at the sight of me. They didn't know what I was; the girl they loved as Little Red had become a beast, half-woman, half-wolf. Each month, I was stained with blood; each month, they found the carcasses of creatures I hated to kill. I needed to feed. I was hungry. I was sorry. I was no longer their daughter. I wanted to die.

I made my home in Grandmother's dilapidated cottage, my bed from thickets of leaves, dirt, and thorns. I could no longer live as the others lived. I saw no one. I wanted no one. Eventually, I forgot the ways of the village. I lost language; I lived in the shadows of night and crawled on all fours. Thus, Master found me. Still, he recognized me. He wanted me; and when he took me, there was nothing to leave behind.

I am his pet, his companion, his beautiful and wild treasure. The hunter brings me flowers and skinned rabbits, red cloth and needles and thread. He smells like man; he leaves in the day and comes back at night; he has known many women, but none like me.

He does not mind my silences, my guttural sounds; he reads

to me from leather-bound books, stories about animals and princesses and faraway places. He wants me to learn the words again; he is teaching me the sounds, he is teaching me the ways of woman, to walk upright, to wear clothing underneath my tattered red cloak, to kiss instead of bite.

The first time he tried to take me during my full transformation, he retreated outside the cottage door, a bruised ribcage, bloody gashes on his cheek and neck. He was angry; he punished me severely. He caged me, then.

He reminds me that he rescued me twice. He says he is destined to save me, to care for me, ever after, and in return, he only asks that I accept him as my master. I serve him well, and he cares for me well, but under the swollen moon each month, I am slave to no one.

"Wolf moon," he says, "is the first full moon of the New Year."

It feels like want, deep want within me, ruthless, ice-bright and cold. He kisses me and pets the soft fur on my body, warming me. He leads me to the leather table he built for me, lifting me so I could sit upon it. I nuzzle against his rough cheek, and turn upward, looking into his face.

"What big eyes you have."

He takes his time touching me, teasing me, pink-gold dusk slowly turning to royal evening blue. He says he loves me. Do I understand? He kisses me deeply, his cock rising hard and thick and wanting. He wants to train me; he wants to tame me. He wants to fuck me, to punish me, to take me as the moon breaks me; neither woman nor wolf, perhaps both, choking at the bit, shivering in my eclipse. His.

I am his obsession, his addiction. I am dangerous to want, to own. I change.

"Lie down," he says and I submit, my hair gliding across the table, my body finding the leather dry and firm, cold against my skin.

I watch him as he begins to work, rope in hand. He binds my wrists together and spreads my legs apart, licking and kissing each foot after tying each ankle to the table. I am stretched tight, knot, bound and secure. The hunter's eyes burn like coal, deep and black, red hot at the center, lit by flames of desire and focus; absolute concentration crosses his face as he attends to me with such care; I see him. And all at once, I know love, and I know I love him.

He tried to save me, once upon a time; he cut red ribbons through flesh to release me. For so long, I wished that I would have died. Instead I lived, Little Red, still Little Red, cursed by the fairy tale moon, the happily ever after sky.

He saw me through the eye of a shotgun; he found me when I was so lost I would not recognize myself, matted with dirt and ragged red cloth, more wolf than woman.

And still, he knew me.

He pulls a thick leather belt across my waist and belts me to the table. He pulls a strap across my mouth. My long hair spills black against pale skin against black leather; my lips open, red and wanting. Silver clasps hold my nipples; each clasp attached by chain, pulled tight, pleasure waves of pain.

Then there is this slow arousal, the feathery touch of a fan brush dancing across the surface of my body, tickling my feet, the tips of my toes, in between my legs; wisps of intense longing heighten my desire, my infinite ache, and I shiver, gasping, laughing like a little girl.

"What big teeth you have."

My jaws snap against the leather strap, wanting to taste, to tear the moon from the sky. His voice in my ear, deep and steady, is an anchor. "I own this body, whatever form it takes. I own you, do you hear me? You are mine. You are my slave. Say, 'Yes Master.'"

"Yes Master." I am fully present, my delirium swirls, light expands and contracts, I ache.

My legs stretch as I grow, stronger. I pull at my tight restraints and remember the cage; my heart races, quickening to fear. Pain. Tears blind my eyes; I cannot move. He smoothes his cool hand across my forehead, relaxing me. He says I am a good girl, he would never hurt me. I believe him. I trust him. I breathe the way he taught me to when I get scared, in and out, steady, calm.

Master adjusts my bindings, resecuring each ankle with leather cuffs and chains. He tightens the belt around my waist and keeps the clasp chain of my nipple clamps suspended and held tight. Chains linked to chains, heavy ropes of silver hanging from the eaves, my legs spread in a wide V.

Master draws back, drawing a sharp intake of breath at the sight of me; he inhales the scent of me, beast he is. I am forest flowers freshly dug, dirt still clinging to the roots.

"Little Red, I am the wolf."

He feasts between my feral thighs, licking and sucking my pussy, devouring me. I cannot think; I claw at the rope, howl as his tongue flicks inside my lips bringing me to wild orgasm, again and again, as I growl and thrash, my body pulsating, bucking. He grabs my hips and fucks me with his mouth; over and over, I am moaning with pleasure, each movement pulling and pressing ropes and chains and belts of leather. I beg him to stop, not wanting him to stop, never wanting him to stop, my master, my god.

Moonlight moves through the curtained window; hours have passed. His eyes flicker across my body, sleek and strong, half-woman, half-wolf; I am panting. He kisses me, my sex on his mouth, and releases me slowly from my bondage. He holds me standing as I sway in subspace, shifting form, emptiness, being, nonbeing, not knowing who I am, what I am. He rubs a collar of cold link chain against my cunt; cooling the red-hot heat between my legs, making me whimper and cry out, slave.

Around my neck, a pure silver choke-chain; Master owns me.

He kisses my lips then pulls the chain attached to the nipple clamps. I wince as he pushes the chain between my sharp teeth. "Take them off," he says, testing me.

I bite down, brace myself, and pull up the chain hard; they snap, slaps of delicious pain.

"Kneel on the bed."

I am eager to please him; I want to show him how I love him, how I want to suffer his power and lay in submission at the command of his desire. A hunter, he saved me; a beast, he entered me; a master, he conquered me. I kneel as he disciplines me. Lashes of exquisite touch sting, slap, and tickle. He spanks me red with the palm of his hand.

He grabs my hair and pulls me up, letting the heavy chain leash fall down my back. Holding the reins of my hair, he ravages me, riding me mercilessly, hitting my flanks with the crop. I whimper and arch my body, wanting more, more. We are savage; we could fuck each other numb. I am fur and claw; he is more animal than man.

Master enters me from behind, tearing within me, caressing me with his thick hard cock. He tortures my pussy, teasing me in and out, sliding and thrusting, fucking me with a whisper, with slow hot breath. Rising, he rages within me, he takes his pleasure from me; I am bound helpless, sobs and moans, songs of praise and worship, I am his. He comes, his hot cock swelling inside me, bursting inside me. Little Red I am, yes Master. The wolf moon howls, ever after, happily ever after, breaking the night into stars.

MIRROR MIRROR

Shanna Germain

She has a raven the color of coal. No, not coal. Blacker. The darkest night on the darkest day in the darkest minute of the year. An absence of light that is so full of nothing it makes everything around it shine like a jewel. Even if it isn't.

Which is why she keeps the raven perched always on her shoulder. She's no jewel anymore, and the creature offsets her graying pallor, her growing wrinkles, the way the half-moons beneath her eyes are the color of maid-bucket water. She's growing thin, too.

What she can't hide, she passes off to the king, and the kingdom, as mourning. "Your daughter," she says to her husband, choking, as if that's all she can bear to say. As if she cares so much for her stepdaughter that she is eating herself from the inside out.

And maybe she is. She's called for the huntsman's head on a platter, after all. Proclaimed him murderer. Sent search parties to the woods for the body that no one has found. She is taking it harder than the kingdom might have expected, and they love her for it. Her unexpected generosity, her grief that mirrors their own.

The queen, she despairs, but not for what they think.

As for me? I despair for the missing Snow, for the king without a daughter. Of course I do. I even despair for the huntsman, who had small, delicate fingers, a lovely growl, and a bit of a masochist in him to boot. Well, perhaps more than a bit of a masochist, if even Snow found him satisfying enough.

But mostly I am happy. I have the queen to myself, for now, and there is nothing to despair of in that.

Today, like every day lately, the queen is having trouble getting out of bed. There's a celebration of some sort, a baby shower that she must attend, and the sun is already halfway through the sky. Yet she lies beneath the covers, the ends of her black hair tipped silver.

I stand at her bedside, as I've stood for hours, waiting. There is no pushing the queen. Not yet. Even her raven sits still upon her headboard, quiet except for the occasional click of his jaw.

"Girl," she says, finally. Her voice is ragged with age and exhaustion. The hand that tugs the covers is thinned to the bone, the long nails broken to claws. "Bring me my breakfast. The purple one."

I do her bidding, quick and quiet, because I am a good girl, the best girl. Because even though I know my queen for all that she is and all that she is not, I love her. Because I am hers and she is mine in the way that all queens and their girls have ever been, will ever be.

I open her secret closet—I overheard the magic word from Snow before she was gone, and the queen is not well enough to notice that I have hold of something I shouldn't. Inside, there are dozens of bottles, of all sizes and colors. Some are clear as water and as still. Others bubble and sparkle inside the glass. Still others, the ones I find hard to look at, hold golden rings and skeleton keys, preserved toads and coils of snakes, finger bones and stag hearts.

The purple one is so deep and inky it's nearly black. It is small, and I carry it to her in the palm of my hand. She takes it without opening her eyes. The color stains her lips and teeth and tongue so that when she grimaces, her mouth becomes a black, endless maw.

She lets the bottle fall to the floor, not enough left to worry about staining the rug. The transformation is not as instant as it once was. She is farther gone, and luster takes longer to paint, even with magic.

Old becomes young, grey blooms to pink, flesh shifts and plumps. Her eyes are the one thing that don't change—black as her raven, deep as the end of the world.

"Girl, my red dress," she says. Red for blood, red for mourning, red for death.

"Perhaps a bath first, your Highness?" I venture. She doesn't need one, not with the potion, but we are in no hurry. She is the queen; the world will wait.

"Ready the bath, then," she says as though it were her idea.

"I've done so," I say. I've learned a few things from her too. How to be still like a spider in a web. How to keep a bath warm at all hours of the day. How to be someone I am not.

She pushes back the covers and reaches an arm out so that I may help her from bed. She's naked, her body still shifting, breasts filling, hips growing rounder. Even as I let her lean on me, inhale the scent of stream water and crushed petals, I have to look away from her so that I don't drop her. Only the raven notices, his beady black eye watching.

I lead her to the tub, its steam rising to cloak us both. Her skin is soft and warm, tingling with magic. She leans back, and I soap her curves, the hollows of her shoulders, the gorge of her breasts. Her nipples pucker in the steam. Faint pink lines crisscross the upper half of her back, a few graying bruises show on the inside of her arms, between her thighs.

Poor work, really. An amateur is what she had in Snow, although I doubt she knows it. Still, I scrub those pained places harder, just to hear her soft moans of protest, the quiet whimpers. When I run the cloth over her tight nipples, into the closed space between her thighs, she shudders a little, splashes on my white cotton dress, and I let the warmth sink into my skin, imagine it's something other than water.

The magic is doing its work, and soon she is stronger, doing the work herself, relegating me to hand her soap, a new cloth, a dry towel.

As she dries, I pull the red dress from the not-secret closet. It's one of her proper dresses, fully covering her in its scarlet sheen, the headdress imposing and regal. It's a bitch dress, a top dress. A queen's dress. Not like the dresses farther back, the purple one that is corset top and black embroidered sheer along the arms and legs. Not like the emerald one with the cut-out cups, the waist straps for tying her wrists together. Not like the one in the very back, the one I've only seen her in once, its tiny bits of fabric the same alabaster as Snow's skin, the splashes of red the colors of rubies, of lips, of blood.

Naked, she stands and faces the mirror. Its surface has been covered since Snow disappeared. Every day, she lifts the cover and watches her own reflection, just as she's doing now.

"Mirror, mirror...," she begins. She can't finish. She never finishes anymore. She is afraid to ask, afraid the mirror will tell her the thing her heart knows to be true. That Snow is not dead, not, after all, murdered by the handsome and wicked huntsman for her trophy heart, but that she's run off with him. That Snow is still out there, beautiful and living, without her queen.

"Let me prepare you, Your Highness," I say.

She acquiesces, lowers the drape back over the mirror and sits at her dressing table. There's a mirror here, too, but it's not magic. It isn't forced to tell her the truth, and so she can eye herself in it, slyly, from the side with half-closed lips while I powder her pale skin and lipstick her mouth in red. She doesn't need the makeup—the potion has done its work fully, and it will keep her until tonight, at least—but this is part of the ritual, and it means she does not yet have to leave her room. I wrap her hair the way she likes, two tall black cones that will fit into the circle of her crown. It's how I first came to be her girl, my deftness with her hair and later, with Snow's, and I relish the pull and tug of the strands between my fingers.

While I work, the raven flies over and perches on her bare shoulder, fluffing his feathers, watching me. She shoos him away for once. His claws have left pale pink indents in her skin. I ache to touch them, to run my tongue over their clefts.

When she stands, I pull the dress around her, delighting in the brush of the crimson fabric over her curves, the sound of it sliding, each small hook and eye to be closed, the touch of skin to skin.

"Exhale," I say, my fingers tight on the stays.

She sighs, the sigh of a million small things lost in the woods and never found, and I pull the stays.

"Again," I say.

A second time and the stays pull her tight, wrap her in their silk so that her breath is forced from her in a low grunt.

"Again," I say.

This exhale is from the belly and the heart, the wind of the south when winter leaves, the bear waking from hibernation, the whoosh of bluebird wings through air.

My fingers wrap the stays, pull until she is gasping for breath. She can barely look at herself, even now.

"Do you want to stay, my queen? Skip the party?" I ask. It's bold. It might be too early to make this move, and yet I've waited a hundred years, it seems, through the king and the couriers and finally through Snow. It is now or never.

"No," she whispers.

"No?" The stays are cutting into the crooks of my fingers, turning them pale at the knuckles. I can't imagine what it must feel like inside that dress; the stays are made for a queen. They will not stretch nor break.

"Yes," she said. "Please." It's the first time she's ever said please anything to me.

"Please what?"

Her eyes close against the reflection of her. Her crown of hair shines black as wings.

"Please let me stay."

I laugh—oh, it is the laugh of pleasure and power—and loosen the stays until her breath rushes in a gasping inhale.

"You have to go, my queen," I say. All proper servant girl now. "It's what's expected."

It is hard to be queen. All that power all the time. All those expectations. All that topping.

Her cry is the anguish of a rabbit being released from a trap into a coyote's mouth. She lets her head fall to the dressing table. From her bedside, the raven caws, a chatter of black song.

I undress the queen each night. I had done so for many years, loosening her stays, sliding the fabric from her skin. For the past week, since the party, she's eyed me warily, a startled deer unsure whether to run or go still, knowing only that she wants to be caught. I stay the good girl, her good girl. Doing only what is asked of me. It's a small dance, a bit of sport, and occasionally when she looks at me, it brings a bit of life back to her cheeks.

Every day that she must be in public is hard for her. Tonight, her potion is worn to a bare glimmer. Her eyes sink into grey pools, her skin is returning to its rash-marked rudd. Not fit for a queen. Not fit at all. I will make her beautiful again. Not with her silly potions, their temporary glamour.

When she's naked and in front of her dressing table, I take her silver comb in my hand. The tangles are thick and spidered, coarse as horse hair. I go slowly and carefully, letting her rest, letting her regain her strength.

"They won't find Snow," she says.

She's right but I don't say so. I weave her hair into small braids, make them into reins, as if she were a horse, bridled and ridden.

I fist my hand in her hair, pull her back so that she must look up at me. Her face, her throat, pale and pink.

"Enough mourning," I say. "Do you understand?"

She glares at me, sparks of life. From her bedside, the raven caws, flaps his wings.

"Do…" I say, a tug of her hair for every word, my fingers tracing the long line of her neck. My nails turn in to lightly score her skin. "…you understand?"

"She…" My queen closes her eyes as she says this. "…made me feel beautiful. She made me beautiful."

I want to slap her silly face, I want to rake my nails over her skin until she bleeds, I want to uncover the mirror and make it speak the only truth it knows. But the queen's not ready for that.

Instead, I keep my hand tight in her hair, lean over her upturned face, kiss the red lips of her mouth. She tastes of potions and despair, her tongue a sleeping thing that must be coaxed into waking.

I will make her beautiful too.

I pinch her nipples, one after the other, pull them into points and then release them, loving every time she moans into my throat, every time she shudders. Still holding her hair, keeping her still, I push my hand between her thighs, play in the wetness that already fills her, a stream of want. I tease her until she's bucking against my light touch.

"Please," she says.

I pull her back, take the comb from its spot on her dressing table. The silver makes a pretty smack against the curves of her breasts, the insides of her thighs. It brings her skin to flush, petaled and pink.

"Beautiful," I say in her ear as the comb does its work against the point of her clit, as it hits home again and again. "Beautiful," I say.

But I know she doesn't believe me.

From her bed, the raven caws and caws.

Snow has been gone seven months. The huntsman hasn't been found. Even the raven has been spending more and more time elsewhere. It's time.

While my queen bathes—she's almost fully herself now, no potions needed—I open the closet and pull the white dress from the very back of it. My queen gasps when she sees it.

"No," she says. "Not that one."

"Do you trust me?" I ask. I'm already bringing the dress to her.

"Yes," she whispers.

"Do you love me?"

I can't hear her answer over the rustle of fabric, as I settle the alabaster strips around her skin. It barely covers any of her, only the curve of her hips, a line up her belly, swatches below the hang of her breasts. I can't hear the answer, but I know what it is.

"On all fours."

She does so without protest, the dress moving like white feathers around her. Swan Queen. Down on her hands and knees in front of me. So beautiful. So mine. "Open your mouth," I say.

She does. Obedient. Wanting. Willing.

Into her mouth goes the apple-red gag, tied in place with leather stays. She looks up at me, her eyes wide.

"It's a good color for you. Red," I say.

She shudders lightly. She knows what I mean.

I kiss her around the gag, laughing as she tries to kiss me back. My fingers find her nipples, tighten over them until they're as red as the gag. Until she's moaning, her breath quick and heaving.

I lean her forward, tease the places that the fabric doesn't hide. I spread her open until my fingers, all of my fingers, my small fist reaches deep inside her.

My other hand wields the leather riding crop that leaves long thin lines on her skin.

She's screaming inside the gag, writhing into every lash, opening herself up more and more around the push of my fist. The alabaster fabric shows every bit of sweat, every drop of blood. They glitter like pearls, like rubies.

Her clit is an easy thing to find, even with the crop still in my hand. Tall and pointed as a glass mountain, the very tip a delight to the curve of my fingers. It doesn't take long; I flick her clit two, three times and she's bucking me nearly out of her, sucking breath around the gag.

She comes quiet and hard, like a queen should, all shudder and arch and breathstop.

Barely waiting for her to finish, I take the gag from my

queen's mouth. Her breathing is so fast it's barely there. Her eyes are glazed over, unfocused.

"Do you love me?" I ask.

"Yes," she breathes. Like the mirror, in this moment she cannot lie.

"Then ask," I say, and I turn her face toward the uncovered mirror.

She shakes her head, a tiny movement.

"Ask," I say again.

"Mirror, mirror..." She closes her eyes, swallows hard. "I... can't."

Oh, my queen. The things we do for love. The crop makes such beautiful lines, crisscrossing the already red bleeds of her ass, her hips. She whimpers, bows her head.

"Ask," I say. Third time, and she knows that she must.

She looks at her reflection, really looks. The mirror is magic, yes, but it is not her magic, and it owes allegiance to nothing but the truth. It shows her herself, on all fours and naked before it. Her chest is crisscrossed with raised welts, their surface pink and purple. Bruises flower on the inside of her arms, across the ridges of her collar bone. Her makeup is smeared, the black of her eyes, the ruby of her lips. Her ass is snow white and blood red. Her skin is stained with a thousand drops of blood that bloom like the smallest of roses.

There is nothing more beautiful in this world or any other.

She begins again. This time she makes it through. "...who's the fairest of them all?"

"You, my queen," says the mirror. "Are the fairest of all."

It's true. Snow is dead. The huntsman is dead. Even the raven is dead. Don't ask me how I know. What I do know is that there is nothing more truly alive in this whole country than my queen.

From her place on the floor, my queen lifts her gaze to mine.

Her smile is a radiant thing. It alone could force roses to bloom, cause ravens to talk, turn servant girls into rulers, get princesses lost in the darkest of woods.

And it is only for me.

Love is a thorny thing, fraught with peril. I have held a lot of beating hearts in my hands, but hers is the one I love best.

THE LAST DANCE

Kristina Lloyd

D on't get me wrong, I love my sisters, but being the youngest of twelve totally sucks, especially when my siblings are such famewhores. They drag me here, there and everywhere, and when I try to refuse they accuse me of being selfish and spoiling it for everyone. "Eleven? What will people think if part of us is missing?" Emotional manipulation and its best mate, guilt, are so entrenched in our family dynamic I'm tempted to lay places for them at mealtimes.

We were conceived on the IVF program and are the world's only surviving dodecaplets. My mother needed two hospital beds, one for her body, one for her belly, before she pupped her litter of twelve. Hardly surprising, but she didn't survive. We were brought up by our father—or publicity agent, as I prefer to call him.

Our lives have been sponsored by a range of companies taking care of everything from baby booties to buzzing sex toys. I swear, the house practically levitated the weekend we received our first box of freebies from LoveStuff, a dozen Double Fun Pocket Rockets. But you don't get anything for free in this life. "Who do you dream of?" the marketing people wanted to know. For me, with my new toy taking me to heavens I'd never explored, the question wasn't "who" but "what." Oh, and I'd dreamed all manner of terrible things; of being abducted, tied up, and spanked; of sucking cock till I couldn't take any more; of muscular men getting soapy in the shower; of being fucked by strangers who called me "slut" and "whore."

"David Beckham," I told them.

"He's married," said my father. "Say Prince Harry."

Ultimately, I could forgive my father for being overbearing, controlling, and insensitive. After all, bringing up twelve identical daughters isn't easy or cheap. However, he lost my sympathy by contracting us to appear in a fly-on-the-wall reality TV series when we were too young to appreciate the consequences. Our lives have been lived in the spotlight, and the spotlight was inside our home. The show, *Full House,* ran for seven years, and even though the TV cameras have long since gone, I can't shake off the feeling I'm being watched.

On the night it all started, I felt unseen eyes tracking us before we'd reached the end of our street. As ever, we'd snuck out of the house under the cover of darkness, avoiding our father's place and the security cams he'd installed. We know people follow us—autograph hunters, paps after a photo, journos after a scoop—so we confound them by splitting up and taking indirect routes to our destination. They want a picture of the twelve of us together, but we won't give them that. They also want to know where we go each night, but we're not giving them that either. Even my sisters occasionally want a break from the attention.

But that's the trouble with fame. You can't have it on your own terms.

"I think someone's on to us," I whispered.

"You're so paranoid," scoffed sister seven, Gina.

"Doesn't mean you don't want to kill me," I replied.

Gina and I don't get on. I wondered if she knew my secret. I shouldn't have done it, I knew I shouldn't. But her boyfriend, Gilchrist, was this beautiful black guy from Putney, tall, built, and bald, with slim, graceful hands. And not so long ago, I'd found him in the cloakroom of Club Sub, sitting on a bench, exhausted, gorgeous, his legs spread wide. His mouth was parted, eyes closed, sweat gleaming on the dome of his head. He was wearing a red military jacket, tasseled epaulets squaring his shoulders, shiny gold buttons glinting in the half-light. The jacket was undone and, oh boy, so was I. His chest, chocolate brown and broad, was scattered with tight black whorls of hair, his pecs perfectly contoured, his stomach taut but not ripped. His flesh folded in a lean band above the buckle of his belt and his crotch bulged.

Slowly, he opened his eyes, giving me a tired, dutiful smile.

The words were out of my mouth before I knew it. "Silly Gilly," I said because that's her cutesy little name for him.

His smile didn't change. "Gina," he said, unable to hide his weariness.

I giggled and swayed toward him, the floor cool through the holes in my worn-out shoes. "I think I've had too much to drink."

Gilchrist looked more interested. "Yeah?" he said, sitting up straighter.

And that's how I came to betray my sister by pretending to be her and sucking off her boyfriend in a nightclub cloakroom. I still get flustered to recall how I'd knelt between his thighs and how he gripped my hair, keeping my mouth low and steady around his hard, fat length. And when he came, his long, tormented groan sounded like a cry wrenched from a creature of the underworld.

"Ah, Gina," he murmured afterward. "You should drink more often."

But Gina doesn't drink.

She dances. We all dance. Every fucking night.

Most people have heard the rumors. Local newspapers report on the Dancing Dozen who keep the area's cobblers in business by sending in their shoes for repair each day, twenty-four soles worn out after who knows what shenanigans. That's not enough of a story for the nationals though. They want the dirt. They want to know where we go, who with, what we're wearing, and whether cocaine or professional footballers are involved. Their desperation is such that one tabloid, let's call them the *Daily Scum*, has offered a substantial reward to anyone who can provide evidence of our late-night activities.

Ordinarily, our father would be down like a ton of bricks on such blatant incitement to press intrusion, particularly when he doesn't stand to profit. However, he also wants to know where we go, and he probably has an eye on a sponsorship deal with Reebok, so with this one, we're on our own. It's a relief, I can tell you.

In our separate groups, we made our way through London's late-night streets, reconvening at Waterloo Bridge, where a fog was gathering to swathe the Thames in a spectral murk. Sisters three, four, and ten were late, so we hung around at the top of the steps, anxious and impatient. The haze was shot through with the city's lights snaking along the banks, reflections on the black water like a sky of fallen stars. To the west, the gleaming palace of Westminster was a golden, gothic ghost casting a stern frown upon our illicit adventures. I swear, that building has my father's eyes.

Across the river, the slow-turning wheel of the London Eye glittered above layers of mist, making it seem as if a phantom fairground were luring us to the other side. Or was it my father again, watching us peep-eyed through the environment?

When our remaining sisters had caught up with us, we hurried over the bridge because, no, it wasn't a charmed fairground that drew us, nor could my father follow our every move, much to his frustration. Our nightly haunt was Club Subconscious, a darkly magical place of music and revelry in a Southwark venue three stories low, a former underground car park now transformed into a night club.

Well, "darkly magical" is their advertising slogan. To be honest, it's a bit of a meat market but at least it's members only and no one cares about our fame. I mainly go because my sisters would kick up such a fuss if I refused. ("We're nothing if we're not twelve!") Plus, it's the only time I get within sniffing distance of any action because we always have our boyfriends, twelve good, strong men, faithfully awaiting us on Waterloo Bridge, ready to dance until dawn.

Trouble was, we'd got the wrong boyfriends. My lover, Leander, hardly ever put out. I wished I had what Gina had. Wished I had Gilchrist. Maybe it was the mist or the odd sensation we weren't alone, but that night, as we crossed the bridge, I felt we were on the brink of change, as if something in the shadows were waiting to upend our lives and sprinkle them with stardust. When that something in the shadows stepped on my toes, I got the jitters.

"Ouch!" I said.

"Didn't touch you," replied sister two, laughing.

"I know you didn't. Something—ouch!"

"What?"

"Well, that felt like an elbow in the tits."

"Lily, have you been drinking?" asked Gina disapprovingly. Man, she is so uptight. "No, Gina. It's the crystal meth kicking in."

I caught a waft of masculine scent, as distinct as the aroma of someone nearby. Confusingly, no one was nearby. I breathed deeply, thinking, since ours was a walk through history and mist, perhaps they surrounded us, the faces of the lost, the drowned, and the long gone, ghosts of boatmen, brawlers, merchants, and dredgers from an era when the city stank and the river banks were sludge.

At the halfway point, when we met our men, I pressed a kiss to the lips of Leander, looking askance at Gina who was drawn close by her Gilchrist, his hand cupping her ass as they embraced. A knot of pain and jealousy pulled below my heart. In his arms, she was as stiff as a board, recoiling from the kiss he sought.

I saw his face tense with a moment's impatience before he regained his composure. He's such a gent—although actually, he isn't. At least, not when it counts, if you know what I mean. He probably would have dumped Gina ages ago if I hadn't given him hope. Oh, idiot, idiot me. If I'd thought more about the consequences, I'm sure I wouldn't have done it.

Well, to be honest, that's probably not true. When I'd stumbled upon Gilchrist in the cloakroom, I was so horny and restless, frustrated by Leander's permanent primness. Leander treats sex like it's a big deal, as if me fucking him means I might want his babies. But I don't care for him that way. He doesn't make my heart sing. I'd simply like a shag every now and then till I'm ready to settle down with someone I love. The problem is, I can't imagine ever wanting to commit to monogamy. I like men too much to limit myself to one. Plus, I'm so accustomed to hanging out with eleven that coupledom is a lonely prospect.

Maybe Gilchrist could make me respectable, but he's my sister's boyfriend and I am evil and wicked for having such unsisterly thoughts.

And Gilchrist, unfortunately, was a man sustained by hope. He still acted as if Gina was The One. I appreciated his spirit but at the same time feared he didn't know when to quit. Determination's an admirable quality, but blind optimism's a bitch. The way he'd caressed Gina's butt when they met on the bridge suggested he hadn't quite got the message. But I'd mixed up the message, hadn't I? I'd made him think his girlfriend might occasionally be up for it, so you couldn't blame the guy for trying. And, although I say it myself, I did give him a spectacular blowjob.

Memories of sucking Gilchrist's cock and an unexpected hand on my own ass got me briefly excited. I thought Leander had turned lustful but when I looked into his eyes, that staid, Thameside Ferris wheel churning slowly behind him, they were as dead as ever. I dismissed the touch as the randy hands of London phantoms but by the time we reached Club Sub, I knew we were being followed.

Our stalker, I soon realized, was wearing one of those new invisibility coats made out of, what was it, negative index meta-materials? I'd read about the technology but hadn't known the coats were on the market. How infuriatingly typical that some sly, skeevy journalist had gotten hold of one. Wouldn't have minded an invisibility coat myself. Damn, he smelled good though, unlike my Leander who smelled of sweet, sanitized nothing.

At Club Sub, we danced under fake stars, over sparkling snowscapes and through sinister forests, each floor of the venue themed like stories from our childhood. When my soles were worn thin, I drifted off from Leander to grab a beer, trying to harden my heart to the sight of Gilchrist whisking Gina around the dance floor.

En route to the bar, Mr. Invisible started harassing me again, a nudge here, another there. Hell, he was annoying. I tried to escape him and wound up on the cold, concrete stairwell of the fire exit. I paused for breath, enjoying the calm of muffled music and my near-dark surroundings, a soft green emergency light the only illumination.

Finding sanctuary turned out to be a smart move, because when Mr. Invisible joined me (jeez, he was persistent), he was manifested as a pale shimmering ghost, outlined in luminous green. I lunged for him, taking him by surprise, and after a few moments' struggle, I had the meta-coat off him and was scampering for the exit. Back in Club Sub, I slipped on my new garment and vanished. Poof!

When Mr. Visible emerged, looking a mite hacked off, I had to stop and stare. While he didn't suit ghostly, he most definitely suited visible. Something about his stature or maybe his short, coppery curls gave him an enchantingly majestic air. We were in the forest zone, and against the backdrop of replica trees with pale, dappled disco lights swooping across the room, he could have been a medieval prince on an heroic quest.

Color me superficial, but I suddenly changed my mind about him. I might have stared till sunrise if I hadn't been distracted by the sight of my Leander and Gina on the far side of the room, deep in troubled conversation. I threaded my way through the crowds, quickly realizing there was an art to being invisible that I hadn't yet mastered. I left a number of people accusing innocent strangers of feeling them up and gained a new insight into Mr. Invisible's difficulties. Perhaps I'd been over-hasty in my earlier dismissal of him as an opportunistic lecher. Funny how much more forgiving you can be of someone when you'd like to get in their pants.

Leander touched Gina on the elbow, stepping closer.

Oh, I thought, *it's like* that, *is it?*

Gina pressed her hand to her heart, shaking her head, but she didn't retreat. I moved nearer.

"But it's you I want," said Leander.

"And I want you," said my sister, "but it's not that simple."

Well, I never! Fancy the two of them sneaking around behind my back! How very dare they? I realized my anger made me a total hypocrite because after all, I'd sucked off Gina's boyfriend. However, that didn't ease my temper. If anything, I got ever crosser because I was cross with myself for not having good reason to be cross. I searched for excuses as to why my betrayal was different to theirs but found nothing that convinced. Nonetheless, their duplicity stung.

I stomped off to get a beer. By the end of the glass I could see the main damage was to my ego and pride. And hey, didn't this leave the way open to Gilchrist? After all, we were sisters. We've been happily swapping stuff since we were born. Okay, so we'd never swapped boyfriends—well, not officially—but there was a first time for everything. The thought rallied me. Now where on earth was my big-thighed, black-skinned, dark-eyed soldier?

I wandered from floor to floor before checking out the cloak-rooms in case he'd taken refuge in there again. Cloakroom attendants at Club Sub smoke a lot of weed, and security's lax. But I was invisible so I didn't have to cajole anyone into letting me pass. Instead, I clambered over the counter, and when I accidentally kicked the book of tickets to the floor, the guy in attendance simply giggled.

The cloakroom was large and L-shaped, an extravagant room tiled in Egyptian green, with honey-colored benches and golden lockers, coats on rails waiting to be reanimated by their owners. Sure enough, tucked away around the corner was Gilchrist. But this time he wasn't resting, not by a long shot.

He was standing, his head tipped back, his eyes closed. As ever, because he has a wonderful theatrical streak, he was wearing a military jacket, this one a deep indigo adorned with silver buttons. Again it was open, his chest bared. He was naked from the waist down. His elegant hands, tipped with shell-pink nails, were resting lightly on the flame-red curls of my newly visible journalist friend who was on his knees, shirt off, lips wrapped around Gilchrist's cock.

I stared like a slack-jawed idiot. My heart and hopes went up-down, up-down, much like Mr. Visible's mouth. My thoughts veered from a fear I'd lost my guys to man-love to a brand new awareness that, wowzers, this scene was horny. My groin thumped with lust, my lips swelling fast. I drew closer, worried that the drumming of my heart might alert them to my presence.

Mr. Vee's hands were clamped to Gilchrist's thighs, his skin pale and stark against the velvety darkness of my darling. Well, my sister's darling, technically speaking. Rich, purplish shadows hollowed out the dip in Gilchrist's buttocks, and he seemed so sturdy and corporeal compared to the kneeling beauty whose shoulder muscles shifted under translucent, blue-tinged skin, his armpit hair a wisp of fire. Gilchrist was a mighty storm and Vee was a forest wraith, strong but otherworldly.

Gilchrist groaned quietly and clasped his lover's head, his dark fingers sliding through Vee's russet curls. He held him close on the downstroke, and Vee, adjusting his position, edged toward Gilchrist's black-haired crotch, slow and steady, until he'd taken him throat-deep. "Oh, mate," croaked Gilchrist, eyes shut, knuckles blanching, "hold it there, oh fuck, that's good."

Vee's neck bulged with the effort. My cunt pulsed as I remembered how Gilchrist had directed me to do similar. I moved closer, prepared to run the risk of discovery in return for the joy of being near them. They looked edible, like ginger snaps, licorice, brown sugar and ice cream, but man-sized and a lot less sweet. They smelled of skin and beer, of being underground for too long. I wanted to taste them, and so I did, leaning in to lick Gilchrist from the base of his spine to his neck, careful to touch him with nothing but my tongue. He was warm and salty, and he made the strangest sound, arousal warped by disbelief. I blew on the back of his neck then stood on tiptoe to stream cool air across his gleaming, stubble-shadowed head.

He moaned again and dusted the back of his head as if an insect were bothering him. I dodged his hand, ducking sideways to see his thick length slide from the grip of Vee's mouth, his shaft cabled with dark violet veins, saliva lending him a silvery sheen. Avoiding Vee, I cupped Gilchrist's balls, fondling their shifting weight, making him moan. He didn't seem to know or care that my touch was surplus to possibility.

Then Vee moved. He withdrew his hand. I was too close, didn't budge fast enough. He knocked me, realized I was there. He snapped back from Gilchrist and flailed in my direction. Hitting and clawing at me, he tried to grab what he couldn't see.

"You!" he said.

"What the fuck?" said Gilchrist, staring at Vee in amazement. "Oh shit, are you having a fit? Do I call an ambulance? Don't swallow your tongue! That's all I know. Don't swallow—"

"Give me my coat," yelled Vee. I wanted to run but Vee had hold of me, arms around my thighs. "She's got my coat!"

I fell to the ground, wriggled and kicked. "Get off, you're hurting me!"

"Oh fuck," said Gilchrist warily. "How do you do that? In that girly voice? Mate, you're scaring me now. Ouch, ah! Who the—" Gilchrist frowned at Vee's wild antics, eyes flitting in search of something.

"She's invisible," said Vee. "Get the coat off her, you'll see."

Gilchrist dropped to his knees, and I then had a seriously hot time as the two men grappled to undress me, their confused, eager hands flying all over my body, ebony and porcelain tugging at this, pressing on that. Before long, the coat was off and I was on the floor between them, visible, disheveled, and breathless, my dress torn, my arousal threatening to melt me.

Gilchrist stared. "Gina?"

"Well, don't just kneel there," I said. "Fuck me!"

"Lily!" he said, clearly relieved.

"Is it obvious?"

Gilchrist grinned. "I never forget a blowjob."

"But I thought you thought I was—"

"Gina? As if," he said. "Anyway, I can see it in your eyes, Lil. Your dirtiness twinkles."

"Doesn't it just," agreed Vee.

"Now get on all fours," said Gilchrist in a bossy tone that made me weak, "and show my new friend your skills."

Gilchrist pumped his length, working himself back to stiffness, while Vee hurried out of his jeans. I swiveled on my hands and knees, ready to take both men, and take them hard. I wasn't going to waste time pretending I wasn't sure this was a good idea because at that moment I was hot and wet, and it seemed like the best idea in the world. Gilchrist flipped up my dress and yanked down my knickers. He circled his hand over one cheek while Vee presented himself for my mouth, his boner jerking up from a thatch of rich, copper curls. I tongued his tip and slurped on his end, squealing around him when Gilchrist landed a glancing blow across my butt.

My cheek juddered, a sting flowering to heat, growing hotter and hotter as Gilchrist continued with his eager, erratic spanking. "Great ass," he said.

I slid my lips to the root of Vee, groaning in frustration as

Gilchrist ran a soothing hand over the pain he'd generated. Vee reached for my breasts, rolling their heaviness in his palms and gently squeezing my nipples. My desire to be fucked consumed me. I pushed back in search of Gilchrist, then had to stop myself because I didn't want to lose contact with Vee. My poor body was torn in two, and they hadn't even started on me yet.

I heard Gilchrist chuckle, amused by my torment. He continued to tease me, stroking my skin with those supple, slender hands. I've often thought how his hands are like those of an artist or pianist, and under his touch, I felt he was making something of me, transforming me from a mortal body into a shimmering Sistine Chapel or a glorious sonata. When he slid his fingers inside me, his other fingers on my clit, my conscious-ness became a mess of music and trippy, pulsating images. I was lost, wanting his cock, wanting to come, pleasure waltzing with sanity until I barely knew who I was.

Then, oh, he pulled away when I was on the brink and his cock nudged at my wetness, so firm and stout. I lifted my head from Vee, wanting space to gasp, but Vee drew me back. "Keep my dick in your mouth," he warned, clutching my head.

As Vee surged past my lips, Gilchrist plunged into my depths, and I was strung between them both, on ecstasy's edge. I reached for my clit, circled and rocked until I was coming over and over, my body buffeted by two guys as they thrust and froze, trying the keep their rhythms in synch as mine scattered into orbit.

With a gasp, Vee snatched himself from my mouth, jerked his fist along his length then offered himself to me. His come was light, swift and fluid. I drank willingly, happy to consume his bliss, and then tenderly he kissed the remnants from my lips. Gilchrist was a stayer. He didn't come for a long old time, by which point I'd peaked again and so had Vee. I'd been turned this way and that; I'd taken one guy in my mouth while another had feasted between my thighs; I'd straddled Vee and sucked Gee; I'd sucked Vee while he'd sucked Gee; I'd bobbed from cock to cock, and on and on we'd gone, relishing all the hot, sticky permutations available to us.

Together, we were like a new creation, working in harmony to take ourselves to dizzying new heights. I went to heaven and back, and so did they. We loved our own peaks, and we loved each other's. In our easy, instinctive choreography of lust, there was a unity, trust, and understanding that transcended fucking. I felt we were a team, and we had a secret to cherish and nurture, far away from the world.

Afterward, we lay in a tangle on the green tiles, lips and fingers maintaining languid contact. When the smug glow of contentment began to fade, I said to Vee, only half-concerned, "You'd better not put this in the papers. I don't want my dad thinking I'm a tramp. Although he probably does anyway. Who do you write for?"

"I don't write for anyone," he said. "I'm just a huge fan of yours, Lily. You're beautiful, you're funny, you seem—"

I sat up, alarmed. "Oh hell, I fucked a fan. Don't stalk me, please. If you do—"

"No, I'm cool, I swear." He reached to tweak a nipple, making me laugh. "I just wanted to...to talk to you. To say hi."

I smiled down at him. "Hi."

He grinned. "Do you come here often?"

Gilchrist guffawed, taking the filthier meaning.

"Every sodding night," I said. "I'm like Persephone, forced to spend half my life in the underworld. It sucks. We're famous for being famous. My sisters love all that crap, and so they've created this big mystery to make it seem like we've got something worth hiding and being famous for. But we haven't. There's nothing to us except people's fascination."

"I'm sorry," Vee said guiltily.

I sank back into their loose embrace. "I'm sick of it," I continued. "I'm going to pack it in soon. I want to go to college and do media studies. I'll make a pair of shoes last a year, no repairs."

"Oh god," said Gilchrist, pressing a hand to his forehead. "What are we going to do about Gina?"

"Gina's cool," I said. "She's hooked up with Leander. I think they're a better match. And so are we. Don't you reckon?"

Gilchrist laughed darkly. "I've always thought that."

I slid my hand across his chest. The thud of his heart beat in my palm like something hatching in a dawn of new possibilities.

Vee sat up and shrugged. "Well, hey, this is all very nice but you know what they say. Two's company and—"

"And three's even better company," I said, pulling him back down. "Twelve, however, is pushing it."

The three of us fell into light, lazy conversation until Vee asked, "So what next?"

"Same again tomorrow?" suggested Gilchrist.

I laughed. "I'll be fucked to pieces. But okay, I'm game. Let's see how it goes, shall we? Tomorrow and tomorrow and tomorrow."

Somewhere in the distance, the stoned cloakroom attendant giggled.

"Save the last dance for me," said Vee.

"And me," said Gilchrist.

I reached out to caress them both. "And me."

NAME

A.D.R. Forte

They called the girl, Elisse, clever. Her fingers were the nimblest on the shuttle for seven villages round, the work of her loom without flaw. She won first prize each year at the fair, and the traders filled her father's pockets for the scarves she painted with scenes of dappled leaves over the mill stream and hollow hills beneath towering oaks.

The miller complained all the same when he bought her a pair of spectacles that she might keep up her work.

"Can't marry you off like this," he lamented. "What man'll have you looking like a hunchbacked crone?"

She said nothing. Only dipped her brush into blue paint and swirled it across the sky on her flaxen canvas.

And so the years passed and might have passed forever, until the trader came. He had heard of her work in a distant port, he said, and come seeking her art. He spoke their tongue strangely, and his clothes were quite fine, but she only nodded and asked what he would buy.

When he had made his selections from the rainbow piles of

scarves, haggled with her father, and finally disappeared into the dust raised by his wagon wheels, she thought no more of it. That is, until the leaves turned from green to flame and gold and overripe apples fell from laden branches. That was when the king's summons came.

"How is it...," demanded the king, "...that I have an artist of such skill in my land, but I must buy her goods from a foreigner's cart?"

Elisse watched her father stutter and stammer and grovel before the throne, tongue-tied with fear. Then she stood straight, pushed her spectacles up, and met the king's cold, green gaze.

"I thought my humble work too poor for Your Majesty's taste," she said. "The error is mine. Let me repay the royal household with what craft I can muster."

The king looked at her for a long moment, and she saw that behind the lines of duty his face was yet young, his body still hard with muscle. His eyes, green as the forest, were bright as they appraised her faded dress, the plain scarf bundled around her straw-basket of hair.

"This is nonsense," he replied at last. "Your work is the finest I have ever seen."

"Yes, yes!" cried the miller. "The finest indeed. She is a true genius, Your Majesty. The best in the land. There is nothing of skill she cannot do."

She watched the king's jaw clench as he turned.

"Yes?" he said, and she prayed her father might hold his tongue, but the miller rattled on, as if once his words had begun to fall he could not stop them.

"And tell me," interrupted the king. "Can she, this genius daughter of yours, better my own alchemists? Can her magical spindle transmute my straw into gold?"

"Aye. Even so," crowed the miller.

In horror she stared at her father, in mute appeal she shook her head, but the king had already beckoned forward the guards.

"Well then. We shall see what she can do, this weaver of dreams," he said softly. He turned to her once more as the guards seized her arms, and his words echoed in her head like thunder before rain.

"If you succeed, clever girl, I shall marry you and make you my queen. Your father shall want for nothing so long as he lives. Fail, and both of you shall die."

Tears served nothing. She would not shed them. For a long time she watched the light cross the dungeon floor. Then she slept a while. If she would never see the waterwheel, the river, and the silent depths of the summer forest, she might at least dream them one last time.

Thus she saw him, for the first time, in the twilight land between slumber and consciousness. And he called her name.

"Wake, Elisse, and tell me why you seek my woods in such distress."

She sat up and wiped her eyes before settling her spectacles on her nose. In the twilight gloom of the straw-packed dungeon, he knelt beside her, but she couldn't see his face.

"Your woods? But I do not know you."

"Yet often I have seen you. Sitting beside the waterwheel alone or picking flowers to braid your hair."

She raised a hand to touch him and shivered at his cool skin, smooth like stone or the glossy underside of a leaf.

"Why are you here now when I wait upon my death?"

"Death?" he said, though his voice held no emotion, only curiosity at her plight.

"The king will kill me if I do not spin his straw into gold."

At that he laughed, and she looked in terror at the iron-barred door, but no guard came to rattle it. He lifted a handful of the straw and blew the pieces from his palm.

"Is gold all he desires? Gold is a simple thing. Ugly and bright and the cause of many sorrows. But if it is what he craves, he may have it."

Elisse scarce dared to breathe. It *must* be a dream, a desperate fantasy to lull her mind's fear, yet she felt the heat of his body and smelled the scent of his skin, warm as summer-baked earth, light as a springtime morn.

"It will save my life," she said at last, and his eyes shone in the half-light like a cat's as he turned to her.

"But I require something in turn, Elisse."

"Anything," she said.

A moment later she thought it had been a very foolish thing to say. Such a promise to one of his ilk she might well regret, but there was only his price or else the executioner's rope.

"What can I give you?" she asked, between lips as dry as straw as he pulled her to her feet. The rapid thud of her heart told her it had already guessed the answer, even if she herself remained ignorant.

"This," he replied, and he touched her lower lip, then the hollow of her neck, and then her breast where his fingers lingered until her flesh responded to the weight and heat of his touch. She hadn't known arousal before. If ever the thought came to her in an unguarded moment, if a breeze washed over her skin while she bathed, she transmuted the craving into pale colors in her mind. Held them away until she could pour them onto cloth or stitch them in fine, dyed thread.

He gave her no such escape. His hand on her breast, he bent and covered her lips with his. She tried to breathe and found only his warm breath and his tongue, and when she thought her legs might fail her from the shock and the lack of air, his hand gripped hard between her thighs, and she broke the kiss with a cry. Now indeed she must fall, but his hand and his arm gave her no room to sink into a maidenly faint.

His fingers dug into her flesh through her clothes, holding her in place, and impossibly, his grip tightened. He massaged her knowingly, roughly, and she felt her skirts grow wet against her flesh, her stomach quiver.

"These you will not need," he said, releasing her abruptly so that she stumbled and gasped. He lifted the spectacles from her face, and behind him the walls and the straw blurred into a palette of blues and greys. But he filled her vision, his face just above hers. So close that with the tiniest stretch her mouth could meet his again.

But before she could fully make sense of the thought, he turned her about and guided her hands to the cold, uneven surface of the wall. He closed the metal of the shackles hanging there around her wrists with no sign of lock or key. Now her heart raced, and in vain she tried to turn. But he stood behind her, one hand warm on the small of her back, and his hair tickled her cheek as he leaned his head beside hers.

"Only bid me leave you, and I shall go and touch you no more."

She shook her head, refusing his words and her own fear.

"I have no choice," she said.

But her body trembled at his breath on her neck, and she wondered, *Had she the choice,* would *she say the words?*

The old fabric of her clothes ripped easily, fell in tatters to the straw. Some remaining thought of the Elisse she knew wondered what would happen when he left and she waited for them to open her cell door.

She couldn't think of it as he untied her scarf and ran his

fingers across her scalp and through all the length of her thick, golden hair. It fell warm against her back, not like the cold of the stone before her bare torso, contrasting to the heat of his touch. She tightened her stomach when she felt his hands slide up over her ribs, and a tiny cry escaped her as his fingers closed on her nipples. The swirling sensation first kindled by his touch became hunger, became madness.

She hadn't known her own flesh could hurt so, or so betray her as the blood beat quick and urgent in her groin, making her twist her hips and thrash in his embrace. His fingers were steel or stone, their bite on her tender flesh unbearable. She flung her head back and he released her with a last vicious tweak, but before she might even breathe, might even realize the respite, he drew his palms lightly down, across her tingling flesh, and she moaned at the torment.

"Ah. What have you done to me?"

Without seeing it, she knew he smiled.

"Wakened you at last."

He shackled her ankles next, wider apart than the spread of her hands, and she balanced precariously now on the tips of her toes, for otherwise she must fall against the unforgiving wall or strain her arms in their sockets. She sobbed as he ran his fingers along the back of her taut legs and followed his touch with his tongue: liquid silk and flame. Fists clenched, she waited, but he had pulled away, and though she turned her head this way and that, he might have melted into the shadows and left her, he was so silent.

But she knew he was there. She heard the whisper of straw, the step of a boot behind her, caught the glimpse of motion in the greyness.

"And now to lay you bare," she heard him say, voice as deep and still as the flagstones under her toes and the ground beneath that. But how much more bare could she become?

Straw whispered across her bare buttocks and thighs, striking her skin gently. A hundred or more tiny fingers that scratched and pricked as he struck her again. Harder this time. He had twisted the straw into a tool, a switch to punish her. Or to please her. The distinction had become blurred, become confused, and with each stroke on her back, her buttocks, the tensed, sensitive muscles of her arms and calves, the confusion deepened.

The tingle turned to stinging, made her eyes water. She flinched as the blows came, but there was no way she might evade them. When he paused to run a finger across her skin, his touch burned like hot iron. Behind eyes closed against the agony, she imagined it branding her flesh with the spirals and knots and lines he traced.

His lips found the places she hurt most: the undersides of her arms, the curve of her buttocks just above her thighs, and she bucked and gasped, rattling the shackles. She screamed as the knotted end of the switch landed hard on the backs of her upraised feet. He trailed the strands up her legs, the stalks like hot needles against her inflamed skin, and she felt her throat constrict with pain. A tight, burning vise that choked her.

He brought the switch around her body, flicked it against her breasts, and she tried to press her body to the cold wall. But he caught a handful of her hair, dragged her back. The stalks caught at her bruised nipples, and she cursed him, railed at him, begged him to stop.

But she did not bid him leave her.

Instead, she looked up, staring into the darkness that hovered at the ceiling. The light was fading fast now. They had left her a candle and tinder box, but she had no way to light it. It didn't matter, for she was herself burning, melting, floating away, incorporeal as a ghost. She was pain that shivered on the verge of oblivion.

Would death, she wondered, *be any different than this?*

Then she felt his fingers between her legs, stroking the center of the madness that consumed her. His kisses fell on her neck, and his other hand stroked her nipples, so gently now she felt the pain in her throat break, releasing the dam. The tears trickled hot down her cheeks and the most exquisite sensation flowed into her from his fingers. Despite the shackles, despite the pain, she arched against his hand, seeking more of the sweet, sweet throbbing. Welcomed pain filled her groin with heat and she cried out, trying to spread her legs wider for him though they were stretched already to their limit. His laugh echoed off the walls, triumphant as he moved between them and filled her. Hard as stone, hot as lusty summer.

She heard her voice, but it sounded nothing like she knew, so breathless and so rich with pleasure it couldn't be hers at all. And yet...and yet, it was.

When they unbolted the door, they found her sitting on the floor with her arms about her knees and her head pillowed upon them.

She'd woken in the hour before dawn and found her clothes, whole and untouched, draped across the wheel, her spectacles atop them. Dressing had been a slow task, agonizing beyond measure, but as the sun rose, she'd finished knotting the scarf around her hair and sat to wait among the glittering skeins that glowed and shimmered across the murky dungeon. Her reward. For which she'd traded body and virtue and breath.

Or perhaps it was her price, and he had paid it gladly.

The buzzing, burbling crowd at the doorway parted for the king, and chin held high, she met his gaze before sinking to her curtsey, though the effort to stifle any cry of pain cost her dearly.

"Here is your gold," she said. "Does it please you well?"

The king came to stand before her, and she felt his hand on her chin. A mortal man's touch, flesh against flesh, and she struggled up to her feet again, blinking with surprise.

"I am pleased," he said and his voice was low and full of wonder. "How you have done it, I cannot tell. And I do not demand the secret. Only know it is the most wondrous thing I have ever seen."

She took a step back, and for a heartbeat his fingers hesitated as if he would touch her still. Then his hand fell to his side.

But she cared nothing for it.

"You are most kind, Majesty," she said, her voice tight with hidden disdain. "But shall I not now weave it to cloth of gold for you? That you may have tapestries the envy of all other princes?"

"Nay. You have humbled me, Elisse." His voice deepened, and a pang shot through her heart as she remembered a voice too much like it saying her name. "You are magical and fair and wise, and all I can offer you is a kingdom when you could buy ten times that if you wished. Still I am bold enough to ask if you will have me."

She wanted no kingdom. No gold. No power. What she desired, she could not put into words. But the light in the king's eyes turned them green as newborn leaves as he knelt at her feet and reached for her hand. She put one hand over her stomach and felt the morning sun warm on her face.

"Yes, I will marry you and be your queen," she said.

They loved their new queen well, even if she worried them a little. Her maids noticed the high, unsettled color in her cheeks and the way she never sat still for long. Often she went walking in the woods alone, sending away even the guards, who fidgeted and fretted and peered unhappily at the trees as if they might somehow be granted a vision of her whereabouts and thereby not fail in their duty. But she never came to any harm.

And never smiled. She laughed, but the laughter fell brittle on the ears of those around her. And often she stared out of windows, as if searching for something. But for what, or who, they could not tell.

In due time after the wedding, a child was born and the kingdom rejoiced over its prince. A bonny lad they said: hair as golden as his mother's and eyes as green and sharp as his father's. But his mother watched his cherubic face and waving fists silently.

She took him with her to visit her father's old mill, crooning softly as she walked beside the waterwheel and sat near the river. She picked flowers and let them fall into the water, watched them float away while the babe chuckled and gurgled on her knee and reached chubby arms after the spinning blossoms. But at last she came home and sat many an hour in her private tower, staring out of the windows into the world as if she might discover some answer there hidden from her gold-rimmed spectacles. She grew thin again, as thin as when she first came to the castle, and some worried that she might think herself into nothing.

Not least among them was the king, but to him she spoke least of all.

On a summer morning when the sun seemed to stand still in the sky, she woke early, earlier than any in the castle, and took her paints and a bolt of fine linen to the topmost room in her tower. She shut her door and bolted it well. Then she rolled out her tools and knelt on the floor and swirled her brush through green and russet and ebony and silver.

She painted a forest of autumn with leaves of silver. With her thinnest brush, she shaped mountains of black against a sky of emerald. From a river of pale blue a flock of white birds took startled flight. She painted until her wrist ached and trembled, and the fierce morning sun stuck her gown to her back with perspiration.

Exhausted at last, she fell asleep on the floor. And there between dream and waking, he came to her again.

"Wake, Elisse. And tell me why you have called me here."

Through paint-smeared lenses and tired eyes she saw him, a silhouette with broad shoulders against the bright window-panes, and her heart raced as it had not in an age. She sat up and vainly tried to see his face, but the sun was too bright and her spectacles too spotted with paint.

"The child is yours," she said at last.

"I know it," he said, quietly. "He is a beautiful boy."

She slammed her fist against the wooden planks of the floor. "Is that all?"

"What would you have of me, Queen?"

"Stay." She sobbed as she saw the lines of his body waver and blur, and she knew it was not just from her tears. "Stay. I beg you."

But his voice echoed, drifting between the worlds.

"Say my name and I will stay. I will love you as your heart and your body desire, Elisse. But only if you call me by name."

"But I don't know your name!" she cried. "How shall I learn it?"

Sunlight flooded the room, and the window was empty.

Now she knew utter despair, for there was no lore in the world she dared try that would give his name to her. She was a scholar and a crafter, neither a sorcerer nor a witch.

Her maids fussed around her when she came down from the

tower with slow steps. They clucked their tongues over the paint under her fingernails and the knots in her hair, and she let them wash her and dress her in a gown of turquoise blue. So flattering, they said. A present from His Majesty.

She barely heard their words.

For a while she played with the babe, but his chuckles failed to bring her even a laugh. When he slept, she left the nursery and walked slowly along the farthest turret rooftop where the sun baked the stone like an oven.

It was there the king found her, standing beneath an archway with her face to the wind, letting it demolish the maids' painstaking work with her hair piece by piece by piece.

He caught an errant strand and she turned, lips parted with surprise. But when she recognized her companion, she composed her expression into careful neutrality.

"My lord," she said.

"Lady."

Staring at the ground, she jumped at his sudden touch on her cheek. His thumb outlined the shape of her cheekbone, a gesture unusually demanding and possessive, and she swallowed hard as she looked at his face.

"For many a day," he said. "I have watched you pine for something all the gold in the world cannot buy. Tell me, fair Elisse, what I must do to unlock this fortress you have built for yourself."

Even in the shade his eyes seemed to catch the turning light of leaves trapped between sun and wind. Pale green. Like her son's eyes.

She shook her head, dislodging his hand. Her throat felt stifled. Her eyes burned.

"Nothing," she whispered, and her voice scraped across the words.

"Nothing?"

She shook her head, desperately looked at him, willing him to understand.

"Can you not see? There is nothing to be done. I am warped like tangled thread."

She dropped her gaze to his boots, twisted her hands together. Beyond their feet, the black, severe shadow of the archway arced, and about them, the wind had nearly stilled, save for a breath now and then as if the sun hung in suspended silence. Listening.

"Then," he said at last, and his voice hummed in the stones around them. "If we cannot untangle you, we must cut you free."

Slowly, so slowly, she raised her gaze again. The king was smiling, stroking his beard while his gaze traveled from her flushed face to her neck to the turquoise gown cut, she realized, lower than any other she owned. So consumed had she been by her melancholy she had not even noticed it when they dressed her.

"I think," said the king, "...we shall start with these laces."

The sun glinted on the blade of the dagger twisting so quickly she could only gasp as the blue ribbons fluttered, severed, to the ground. Pain grazed her chest, belated like the tiny thread of crimson across the white surface of one bared breast.

Half-unclothed and marked, she stood before her lord, and he, smiling, sheathed his blade. It had been no accident.

Her chin came up.

"Ah," he said. "There is the girl who first came to my court. Who dared me to challenge her."

A giddy sensation swept through her chest, heating her naked skin. She recognized it as mischief when it whispered to her that she should run. Run and see if he gave chase. Too late she heeded it, but by then he caught her easily about the waist, spun her around to face him. Deftly he tied her wrists. With what, she could not see but much as she struggled, he managed to hold her fast.

No dreamlike, magical binding this. She heard his grunts as he drew the knots tight, and his arms, bared against the summer heat, pressed muscled and damp against the skin her torn and slipping gown revealed.

This, she thought, was how such things should be.

His savage kiss, when once her hands were tied, took her breath away. His scent was leather and steel and earth and air, his hands roughened from blade and harness. And he made no attempt to soften the force of his touch.

Why had he waited so long to take her this way?

Hands on her naked shoulders, he forced her to her knees, and the hard ground met them without mercy. The sudden impact rattled her teeth, made her unbound breasts sway, and she heard the king's harsh intake of breath. Between sun and shadow, she could not see his face as he stood above her, the smooth, taut fabric of his breeches before her lips.

Heat made the ground shimmer and the metal on his buckles and weapons as he undid his belt. It blurred her vision like a veil between worlds. The sun's scorching fingers raked her back, and the stone burned under her knees. She knelt in flame and his voice rang in her blood, a musical, resonant note. Husky with his need.

"Now to make you mine."

Laces dangled free. His flesh was smoother, softer on her tongue than she had imagined. Like stone, or the glossy under-side of a leaf. She closed her eyes, her body aching from the strain of her position and faint from the heat that enfolded her. Unaccustomed to his width, her jaw hurt, and her lips, and her throat. Hair fell into her eyes and his hands smeared it over her face, smoothed it back, tangled it again. The space between her legs knew the pleasure her mouth gave, and it hungered for pleasure in kind.

But her mind. Oh, her mind was clear. She tumbled with the river's flood between banks of red earth, through the heart of forests thick with trees. She moved with the wind over expanses of purple heather and sang through muddy reeds of the fens.

She was heat and flesh and she was nothing at all.

Until she heard his roar, louder than thunder, and she marveled at the taste of him, a taste like nothing she might name. Greedy, she wanted all of him. She would share him with none.

The sun caught his hair as he shuddered one last time. She lifted her lips and watched light catch in the strands of his beard, on cheeks and chin tilted to the sky as his passion ebbed. Her heart pounded madly, urging her to her feet. Get up, get up, it insisted. She must see his face.

He looked down and saw her trying to rise, caught her bare arms and raised her to his chest. She looked into his eyes, green like spring itself. His face perfect in the light of midsummer sun. Human.

But not.

"You," she breathed. "I know you."

The king smiled. "Yes. You do."

"But how? But why?"

She shivered as he untied the thongs about her wrists with a warrior's capable fingers. And with unearthly ease. Free, her hands reached up to touch his face in wonder. The silk of beard and skin, the beads of perspiration that trickled from his brow.

"I wanted all of you, my love," he said in a voice she knew from dreams. "Your body and your dark passion and your pride and your hand, all willingly given. But I wanted your heart too."

Joy bubbled through her entire body like the flush of passion.

"And I know your name."

He nodded. Her king and her husband and the father of her child. She laughed and laughed again, and then, slowly, she smiled.

She had learned more than need.

"Say it, Elisse. For I love you more than your heart desires."

He stroked her bare breast and she leaned into his touch, craving more. And then she said his name.

SENSITIVE
ARTIST

Donna George Storey

The storm hit just as I pulled into town. Exhausted after a five-hour drive, I crept slowly through the unfamiliar streets, windshield wipers slapping, until I reached my final destination: 777 Prince Lane. I was looking for a charming Victorian, but the jagged slashes of lightning made the place look more like Dracula's castle, a hulking structure with turrets soaring into the night sky. The rain was so violent, even the sprint from the car to the porch left me soaking. Foolishly, I'd packed my umbrella deep in my luggage.

It wasn't the way I would have chosen to meet Alex face to face for the first time—my curls pasted to my cheeks, my blouse clinging to my body as if it had been painted on—but I was so relieved to be inside, I wiped my hand on my jeans and offered him a cold handshake.

His fingers were slightly tingly against my skin, like champagne.

"I wasn't sure you'd make it here tonight," my new landlord

said, giving me a pitying once-over.

"Orientation for the summer session starts tomorrow. I have a thing about keeping commitments."

"Very responsible of you," he replied with an approving smile.

After bringing me some fluffy towels to dry off with, Alex led me up to my apartment on the third floor. "Speaking of being on time, I'm afraid there's been a delay in the delivery of your stove and refrigerator. But you're welcome to use the main kitchen downstairs. Consider breakfast tomorrow on me."

I murmured thanks, but in truth I was busy appreciating his sturdy male form as I followed him up the stairs. My friend Lily had been talking up her old college buddy since she suggested I rent a suite of rooms in his house; he lived in the same college town where I'd be taking an art education course for the summer. Alex was such a great guy—a sensitive artistic type—and handsome, too. He'd just never met the right woman to make him happy. The handsome part was now patently obvious, given the way he filled his jeans and those beguiling sea-green eyes, but the sensible side of me counseled caution. While our increasingly friendly emails over the past weeks were a promising sign, I pictured a long, uncomfortable summer if we took things too fast and foundered.

We reached the top of the stairs, and he opened the door with a flourish. Alex had sent JPEGs of the rooms, so I was expecting the antique four-poster bed, but not the gorgeous damask coverlet or the gauzy canopy.

"What a magical bed!" I cried out without thinking.

He smiled. "I'm glad you like it. It's made up for summer weather though. Here, let me get you some quilts to keep out the damp and cold."

His unerring thoughtfulness charmed me. I decided to keep

an open mind about the summer's possibilities and wished Alex a warm good night.

"Sleep well," he said with a final nod.

"I will," I assured him.

But I didn't.

In fact, it was one of the most tempestuous nights of my life. The rain pelting the tall windows was the least of it. Although it looked new, the mattress had a dreadful lump right in the center, an oddly shaped area of about one-by-two feet. It wasn't exactly painful, but whenever my body rested against any part of it, my skin began to prickle. I tried shoving the extra comforters under my back, but they gave no relief from the unnerving sensation.

The worst was yet to come.

When I finally dozed off, curled up at the edge of the bed, the dream began.

"I know why you're here. Properly dressed for the occasion, too."

He was only a voice at first, yet my whole body blushed at his insinuating tone. Looking down, I realized I was wearing some sort of pale, silky robe that was tied loosely to expose plenty of cleavage.

"Don't just stand there. You want this as much as I do."

I nodded, although I had no idea what he was talking about. Fortunately my body seemed to understand. I found myself walking over to a Victorian fainting couch and perching primly at the edge.

"Well, are you going to open the robe?" The voice was clearly annoyed.

Bashfully I unknotted the belt and parted the silk. My stomach did a somersault. The view before me—suddenly it was as if I were standing outside myself watching—was frankly obscene. My upper half was wrapped in a scarlet corset with generous holes to expose my nipples, which seemed as red and glossy as the fabric. Down below I wore nothing but black stockings attached with ribbon garters to the corset. I felt like a whore.

"A fitting outfit for a trollop like you," the voice agreed, "but you know what I really want to see."

My pulse was racing and my throat dry. I knew I needed to please this regal male presence, but I wasn't quite sure how.

His right hand made an impatient, sideways wave. For the voice had a body now, tall and sturdy, holding a pad of watercolor paper in one hand, a delicate paintbrush in the other. "Come on. Show it to me."

Show you what? Then, as if they understood, my knees began to part, slowly, shyly. I glanced down. My vulva was deep red, moist, swollen with arousal.

He clicked his tongue. "Well done. Now all of your female secrets are revealed to me. All but one."

The man had a face now.

It was Alex.

"Touch yourself until you come," he ordered.

This time, at least, I had some clue as to what he wanted me to do.

"No, please." My protest was faint, unconvincing even to myself.

"If you can't do that much for me, then we're through. Please go now."

"No," I pleaded again. "I'll...I'll do it."

I felt rather than saw his smile.

My whole body was trembling as my hand crept down between my legs. My flesh there was unbelievably tender and smooth, like silk. At first I stroked the lips gently as I might a kitten's belly. Then my middle finger wandered to my clit. I pressed down.

And immediately had an orgasm, a body-wracking wave of pleasure that came crashing down upon me again and again and again.

I woke up bathed in sweat, my hips still jerking from the climax. I'd never had a wet dream before, and it took a few moments to recover from the shock. During the night, I'd rolled back onto the lump in the mattress; it still throbbed faintly beneath my buttocks like a pulse.

I leapt out of bed, rushed to the bathroom, and splashed some cold water on my face. That was one hell of a dream. I stared at my own haunted face, trying and failing to make sense of what had happened. Finally I decided I simply had to get some sleep before class, so I dragged the quilts from the bed and curled up on the floor. No more dreams tormented me in my drugged, post-sex sleep. I awoke to buttery sunlight streaming through the windows.

Before I went down to breakfast, I ran my hands over the center of the bed. It was flat, firm, and cool.

Alex had a lovely spread waiting for me: French press coffee, fresh strawberries, a Greek yogurt-granola parfait. He asked how I'd slept with such genuine concern, I had to admit that I'd been troubled by a rather strange dream.

"Are those rooms haunted by any chance?" I asked playfully. In the light of day it all seemed almost amusing, if you discounted the fact my stomach muscles were still aching from that nuclear orgasm.

"Not that I know of, but it is a house with a history. What did you dream about?"

If only he knew. Now I regretted mentioning it at all, but I could hardly refuse to answer. "There was a man. An artist," I said, choosing my words carefully. "He wanted to paint my portrait, but the interaction between us was strange, as if he thought I were someone else. He was obviously angry with this other woman. I wanted to help him, I just didn't understand how." While sanitized, I realized my summary gave the nightmare a new coherence for me.

Alex lifted his eyebrows thoughtfully. "Only a sensitive artist would have such a dream."

I laughed. "Perhaps. If being an art teacher with a few local exhibits on her résumé counts as an artist. By the way, I'm not usually a complainer, but the mattress has a hard spot right in the middle. It's shaped like a large box. Perhaps there was an irregularity in the manufacturing?"

Alex face took on a strange expression—if I didn't know better, I'd say he looked guilty. "Really? Listen, I've got to do a photo shoot this morning down at the beach, but I'll check out that mattress as soon as I get back. I'm terribly sorry about this."

In his contrition he looked even more appealing than he did the night before. No doubt about it there was powerful chemistry between us.

"Thanks, I really appreciate all your help," I replied with my sweetest smile.

Since the orientation for my program ended at noon, I decided to skip the class tour of the university art museum and head home for a nap. I slipped into my Japanese sleeping kimono and was just about to get into bed when I heard the jiggle of a key in the lock of the apartment's main door. A moment later Alex walked in, briskly, like a man with a mission. He stopped short when he saw me.

"My apologies, I didn't mean to come in without your permission. It won't happen again."

"That's okay. I sort of gave you permission to check the mattress this morning," I said lightly, although this did indeed feel like a violation of my privacy.

"I'd forgotten that I'd stored a few old things under this bed, and I thought I'd remove them for your comfort," he said hurriedly, avoiding my eyes.

"Oh?" Instinctively I knelt down and peered into the shadows under the bed. A single cardboard moving box was stationed dead center under the mattress, but it wasn't even touching the box spring. I laughed. "I don't think one little box is causing the problem."

Alex cleared his throat. "Yes, that would be unlikely. I'll order another mattress right away, a different brand."

"Thank you." As tired and indecently dressed as I was, I was tempted to ask him to stay for a chat.

"We're not getting off to the best start, are we? Freak storms, lumpy mattresses, rude intrusions. I feel like I owe you a home-made dinner tonight at least." With this, he met my eyes and smiled.

I felt a sexy pang between my legs. "You don't owe me anything, but I'd be delighted."

He'd hardly closed the door behind him when I was back down on my knees gazing at that intriguing box. I didn't want to snoop, but then again Alex had showed himself capable of bad manners. Plus, now I had the weirdest hunch this box had something to do with my lascivious dream.

With some difficulty, I reached under the bed and coaxed the box out into the open. It was marked "Laura—Personal." My friend Lily had given me a thumbnail sketch of Alex's past. A family with a history of prominence in the community, pressure to abandon artistic interests for something "real" like law school, a beautiful fiancée who betrayed him but also gave him the excuse to escape from lawyering to live the life he'd always wanted as a photographer and restorer of old houses. Was Laura the fiancée? I decided a quick peep inside wouldn't be too terrible an infraction. If it were full of moth-eaten sweaters, it would at least put any supernatural fears to rest.

Taking a deep breath, I opened the loose flaps of the box. A cold hand closed around my heart. Folded on top of few photo albums was a length of pale peach silk. I picked it up and shook it out. It was the same robe I'd been wearing in the dream.

With a shiver, I tossed it on the bed and pulled out the album on the top of the stack. The first photograph was a professional quality black-and-white headshot of a lovely, dark-haired woman. In the next, she wore a black veil over her face, but her eyes shone through the lace, drawing the viewer deep into her soul. The next series of pictures showed her lounging on a couch in the silk robe. None roamed beyond the bounds of tasteful sensuality: a glimpse of bare thigh, a hint of cleavage, the generous curve of her buttock outlined in silk.

And then, gradually, just as in the dream, the woman loosened the robe. At first the camera merely appreciated her body at a distance, then in close-up, the nude as art. As I turned the pages, my hand trembling faintly, the poses became more willful and dynamic. Eventually she was fully reclining, her legs spread to reveal her most intimate secret, a split, ripe fruit framed by dark curls. In the last photograph, her blurry hand was positioned over her vulva, her mouth gaping in a cry of ecstasy. This woman was obviously coming for the photographer, the man she loved. The twist of lust in my own belly told me that.

I reached for the next album. I shouldn't have been surprised, but I jumped and let out a soft cry at my next discovery—a black satin teddy, crushed into wrinkles by the weight of the books. I lifted it out of the box. The garment was like a soft corset with dangling ribbon garters. The chest area was nothing but a sheer black nylon, which would leave the wearer's breasts fully exposed. It was the kind of thing a woman would put on if she wanted to feel like a prostitute.

I was finding it very difficult to breathe.

But I had to know the rest of the story. I turned the first page to find close-ups of the same beautiful model as before. However, this time her mouth was hard, even triumphant, as if she had taken something important from the photographer but wanted still more. She certainly gave more to the viewer. Quickly adopting sinuous, pornographic poses, she seemed to taunt the camera, fondling her own breasts, bending over the couch and smirking over her shoulder, her exposed cleft glistening, as if to say, "*He* took me this way, like an animal, and I liked it."

Just looking at these images made me feel dirty—and fiercely aroused.

The final photo was the most revealing of all: a close-up of her dark eyes, disdainful yet adulterated with something I could only call regret.

Betrayal. He's captured it well.

In spite of the ache in my heart for him and my own past heartbreak at the hands of a faithless lover, the pulsing knot of lust between my legs required my immediate attention. On impulse, I shoved the box back under the middle of the bed and positioned myself face down above it, naked. Within moments, the sheet began to feel warm and spongy, like flesh.

"In spite of what I've done, you still want me, don't you?"

This time the voice was female, a rich alto. Confident,

teasing, a bit cruel. I began to rock my hips into the bed, as if I were fucking my lover oh-so-slowly.

"Your lips might deny it, but I can see you're hard in your pants, Alex. You're hard for your Laura, aren't you?"

Was it my imagination or did I hear another voice, male, sighing in reply?

"I want to make you suffer like you made me suffer all those months when you abandoned me for work you didn't even love. And what else could I do on those lonely nights? I'd masturbate all night, crying out your name as I came over and over again until I collapsed. If only you'd been there to do it for me, we wouldn't be here now."

I began to pinch my nipple rhythmically. Moisture pooled under my abdomen. The sheets were going to be soaked.

"*He* had time for me when you didn't. *He* told me I was beautiful. Said it was painful to watch me waste myself on a man who didn't appreciate me. He was rougher in bed than you are, but I liked that. Because I felt guilty at first, and it helped me forget. But then I became addicted to it. The way he'd tie me to the bed and feed me his cock, then pull out at the last second and empty himself on my face. Then he'd take me from behind, pumping patiently in and out for a full half-hour until I had no choice but to climax around him. I never could manage to reach orgasm that way with you."

I heard another sound in reply—a groan of anguish—mixed in with the gentle *click, click* of a camera shutter. My hips moved faster, grinding into the mattress, which seemed to push up and back in response.

"But I'll give you one more chance, Alex. He might know how to fuck dirty, but you make it into art. I'll never forget that first time when I came for you on camera. I never felt so beautiful, so loved. Is it possible to find that feeling again?"

Someone was moaning now. Me.

"Take me, Alex."

A pulsing like a hard cock filled my belly. Large hands gripped my ass, possessive and hungry.

Who was rough in bed now?

The throbbing heat rose into my chest, my skull. No one had ever filled me so deeply. My cunt muscles twitched, desperate for release, but I held back my orgasm, hovering on the verge as long as I could bear it. When I finally came, so blindingly hard, it was as if every orgasm in the world—hers, his, mine—were packed into one explosive, bruising finale.

When I returned to my senses, the sun was low in the sky.

Alex served a fine dinner, too: grilled salmon, a salad of baby lettuces, a cabernet from a boutique winery owned by a friend, another ex-lawyer who'd followed his dreams. Slightly tipsy, I joined him on the sofa for dessert. Talk came easily to us. He told me about his growing photography business—mostly weddings and portraits, but a few personal projects that were less profitable but he hoped would find a gallery some day. We inched closer as dusk fell.

Then Alex hit me with the bombshell. "To me you look exactly as an artist should, a unique beauty who creates beauty. I hope you'll let me do a photo session with you while you're here."

I almost choked on my Grand Marnier. To my guilty mind, he'd just asked me to put on skanky lingerie and masturbate for his camera.

"Are you all right? I know you didn't sleep well last night."

He put a hand on my shoulder.

My flesh seemed to melt into his fingers.

I'm not sure why I confessed my transgression so easily. I'd always felt a special connection between us, even by email, and now his touch seemed to draw the truth from me as if I'd been enchanted. Besides, I was an idealist. Lies and secrets pained me physically, like rusty shards of metal pricking my heart.

"Ah, so you know all about Laura now." To my surprise, he didn't seem angry, only sad. "You probably found those pictures disturbing. I suppose any woman would."

"To be perfectly honest, I felt them before I saw them. I mean—and I hope you don't think I'm crazy—I dreamed about those pictures last night before I had any idea there was something under the bed. The first album wasn't disturbing at all. It was beautiful, very erotic. But the second, well, it must have been difficult, but that's what a real artist must do. Capture the Truth, no matter how painful."

Alex turned to me and looked deep into my eyes. "I have something to confess to you, too. I put that box under your bed on purpose. Now you might think *I'm* crazy, but we had so much in common, I was starting to like you even before we met in person. I suppose that box was a kind of test or a way to exorcise my own demons through your innocence. I never thought you'd be affected by it. For that I am sorry."

I laughed wryly. "I understand these things. I'm a sensitive artist, too."

"That you are. I have plenty of proof." He smiled. And leaned toward me.

It was, officially, our first kiss, and yet I know he felt it, too. This was only the next step in our journey together, taking the bitter along with the sweet.

When he finally pulled away, every inch of my body was humming, awake. He took my hand. We rose and walked upstairs together to that magical bed.

* * *

"I think it's finished." Lips pursed, I ran an appraising eye over the latest watercolor in my series *Summertime on Prince Lane.*

"Does that mean you can come to bed now?" Alex was lounging under the canopy, shirtless, his legs lean and endless in faded blue jeans. In fact, I'd been dying to jump him for hours, but I had to finish my homework first.

"Stay there, I'll bring over the easel and show you how handsome you are."

"Ah, I love the way you capture the afternoon shadows. But you made that fellow too good looking."

"That's exactly how you look through the eyes of love."

Alex grinned. "Or maybe your model has that glow about him because I was thinking about making love to you the whole time?"

He pulled me down beside him. The thrum of desire between my legs burst into crackling flame. His brushed my breasts knowingly. I bit my lip and moaned.

"You are such a *sensitive* artist," he murmured, pulling up my shirt and camisole to take one stiffened nipple between his lips.

I pressed my crotch against his thigh and cupped his erection through the jeans. I was always impatient with Alex, as I'd never been with any other lover. My lust was on overdrive, as if he'd fed me a magic potion the moment I arrived. Yet I knew after my first skull-shattering, selfish orgasm, there'd be another on Alex's terms, slow and teasing and boundless. But, well-bred gentleman that he was, he always obliged my urgent needs first.

Without another word, he yanked down my pants and ran a delicate finger along my slit.

"You're so damned wet. It must have turned you on to paint a half-naked man who was dreaming of all the ways he wants to fuck you."

"Yes," I whispered. "Because I saw how much you wanted me."

"My response was obvious, wasn't it? But you are such a fine lady, you only gave a hint of a bulge for viewers who were *sensitive* to such things."

I would have blushed, but Alex was right. Although no one could accuse me of crossing any line of propriety, the work I'd done this summer was the most erotically suggestive of my career.

"I wanted you, too, Alex, and I want you inside me now, please."

He laughed and took me in his arms. "I can't deny a damsel her desire, but one favor deserves another. Next time you'll pose for me. You show me all your secrets, and I'll show you how beautiful you are in my eyes."

Even the mere thought of baring myself to him like that made my cunt turn to honey.

I clutched at his belt desperately. Still laughing, he struggled out of his jeans and briefs, his stiff rod twitching and eager as I was.

After hours of visual foreplay, I was so horny, I swung a leg over Alex's hips and immediately sank down onto his cock. He let out a deep "Ahh," and I tightened my pussy around him, squeezing and massaging the shaft, making the pleasure last as long as I could. I did feel everything more with Alex, my senses heightened to the point that I was almost embarrassed at the speed and intensity of my orgasms.

I nudged my left thigh into his, our signal to roll, a two-backed beast, into the center of the bed. Alex's body enveloped mine, and he began to thrust into me slow and deep. His lips at my breast sent pulses of pleasure all the way down to my pussy. My inner muscles continued to milk him, and I felt my climax begin to bloom, a fluttering tickle deep in my flesh.

How could I capture this feeling and make it last forever?

I remembered, in a sudden flash, how I'd once made love to ghosts in this bed. Now the mattress was smooth and flat beneath me. The boxes were gone, the lingerie discarded, the photo albums stored, at my urging, with his other work as lessons of craft and history. The heat and sweat was ours—and very, very real. The throbbing deep in my pussy began to rise, up and up, a fiery flower of pleasure, banishing all thought of the enchantments of the past that brought us here together.

We had our own magic to make.

YOU

Charlotte Stein

I confess I thought the stories were little more than fairy tales when my sisters first whispered them through the darkness at me. *He has the horns of a beast,* they had said, *and teeth like knives. And if you go to the bridge between the forests at a minute past midnight, he will come to you and grant you a wish.*

How childish it had sounded then!

But it does not sound childish now, as the pale moon above seems to dim, and his footsteps ring out slow and heavy on the cobbles—like the sound of my heart. My heart, that cannot bear his heavy, slumberous approach a moment longer.

His footsteps are like the end of the world. They will ring out inside me until the day I die, I know it—and that day comes soon, soon. My sisters were wrong. He does not grant wishes. No monstrous dark shape such as his could ever grant wishes. He comes to you in the night, instead, and steals away your soul.

Or at least I think so until the clouds part around the moon, and light paints one side of him. And then I'm not quite sure what to believe, because he is neither as monstrous as the stories made out nor as fearsome.

It is true—he does not have the legs of a man. They are the legs of a deer or a goat, I'm certain of it, furred all over and strangely shaped. And these legs end in hooves rather than feet, as though he really is Pan or the Devil or some beast-god, the way everyone claims.

But his horns are not great monstrous things, sprouting from his forehead. They are the smallest nubs, set within the rich tangle of his dark hair. And his eyes are not slits, burning out at you like the deepest fires of hell. Even through the darkness I can see they are blue, a dark, deep blue like stones at the bottom of a lake.

He regards me with them, silently, and I do not fear for my soul. Instead I find myself looking at him, in return—at his mouth like a slash in his face, and his arms so pale and sinewy in the dim light. He looks like a man who spends all of his time running through endless forests, with hounds on his heels and nothing but trees and vales and mossy banks ahead of him.

And then I realize I've thought of him as a man rather than the thing he is, and I don't know what to think of that. I don't know what to think of it, other than, *He makes it easy.*

"Have you come to ask of me, maiden?" he asks, finally, and I know by heart what I am supposed to say in return. I'm supposed to say, *I have come to ask of you, He Who Has No Name.*

And yet I do not speak the words. Instead I think of the word he used—*maiden*—and I wonder if he knows. If he has some power that sees inside the hearts of women and understands that they are pure or tainted, good or wicked. Can he see my wickedness clear, when he looks at me? I have never lain with a man, but there are other ways to do evil. A part of me did not want to come here, after all, and make these wishes for my sisters.

A part of me was afraid and could not be brave for them.

But that part is done with, now. He is not so monstrous that he can frighten me off and force me not to speak. *He is like the forest,* I think instead, like a wild and untamed forest—and I can ask. I put my shoulders back. I steel myself.

"I have come to ask of you, He Who Has No Name."

He inclines his head the moment I speak, like a nod only not. In truth it seems more like a salute, a sealing of the pact we are about to make. He has done this dance before a thousand times and probably knows what I will say before I say it. When he looks at me with those blue-stone eyes, I feel as though he can see right into my being, through all the places I hide within.

But he still asks it of me.

"Speak your wish, then," he says, in a voice as clear and cold as a mountain stream. It strips me down to nothing and makes me shiver, but I find the words inside myself anyway. They have been there a long time—ever since I saw Eladria sobbing for want of a husband.

"My sister cries for her true love. She cries day and night, and will not rest. I would ask that you bring this true love to her, oh He Who Has No Name, and end her torment."

He is silent for a long time after I have spoken, but I cannot tell why. Did the words sound like a lie? Can he see that deeply inside me, to the place where my sister resides? If he can, I am not sure what he might see. Eladria can be fickle, and sometimes I am half-certain her weeping and wailing is not in earnest.

But then, surely he must know. Surely he must understand that as spoiled or false as someone might be, to be without love is still a torment. To have no one to walk beside you, no heart that beats as your own does...

Can he not simply see inside my own heart, and know that this is true?

"Are you sure that this is your wish, maiden?"

Apparently he cannot. He has spent his existence as impassive as stone, a granter of human wishes, an observer of their faults and foibles. But there is no true understanding inside him, I am sure.

"It is," I say.

Strange, that he looks almost disappointed when I do. However, he still finds it in him to name his price.

"A kiss, then," he says, and for a moment I am sure I have misheard. Why would a creature such as him want a kiss from the likes of me? I spend my life sewing buttons on shirts and soaping clothes in water. I read books and marvel over all the things I've never done in my life.

Only fairies and beautiful damsels and women like my sisters get kisses from beast-gods. Though mostly they seem to despise and hate it when things like that happen to them. They all want princes, handsome princes—and I'm quite sure he thinks the same of me.

He thinks I'm going to refuse, I know it, but the thought only makes my hand steadier. My head clearer.

"Agreed," I say, and I do as the book told me to. I put out my hand for him to shake, which had seemed like a very poor sort of mystical agreement sealer to me. But he takes the outstretched offering all the same and laces his fingers with mine, and just like that the deed is done.

No lightning strikes. No mist rises. The coldness of his palm thrills through my entire body, and I am certain for a second that I am about to drown in his eyes, but that is all.

It's quite disappointing, I must confess. I don't know what I had imagined, but this wasn't it. And then afterward his stony touch drops away from me and he just waits, as though I told him a moment earlier that a wagon would be along soon and we should both catch it, if we hoped to be home before morning.

It's a dull, mealy, mundane sort of moment, made more so by my own littleness. A greater woman would know, I'm sure, what should be done here. She would reach up and offer the price he asked for, rather than just standing here in a cloak too big for her, eyes downcast, everything in her saying *Go on, go on.*

Only then I do go on, and it's all wrong. I know it is before he's even said a word, because as I reach up on tiptoe toward his strange but beautiful face, he shies away from me. Not enough to be rude—oh dear me no, a godly creature such as him could never be rude—but certainly enough to make it clear.

He does not *really* want me to kiss him. It's some other kiss he meant, or maybe...yes maybe it's the kiss of another person he's after! These devils are all known for making tricky bargains, and what would be trickier than asking me for a kiss *from someone else?*

I think about my still-lovely mother. My other sister, Luvia. In fact, I'm still thinking of both of them when he finally explains, in a voice that stills my blood.

"The kiss I have asked for is not one you can give with your mouth."

Or maybe it's the words that still my blood. The ones that tell me I have made a grievous error. Of course the book *told* me that he might change one word for another and mix me all around. But it seems that I did not listen—or at least, I did not listen half so well as I thought I had.

I thought I was clever. But I have to admit I cannot think of a kiss I could give without my mouth. I'm not clever enough for that. And even if I were, I'm not sure I'd ever want to know. A kiss without mouths is undoubtedly something so rude, so illicit, that no mortal woman should ever be allowed to think about it.

Though somehow it still comes as a surprise, when he says: "Lift your dress, Ren."

I consider many things, then. How he knows my name, how I'm supposed to do what he has asked, how a mouthless kiss can happen with me bare below the waist. But none of them help me in the task I now have to perform, not even the slightest bit.

My hands are shaking as I stoop down to grasp the hem of my dress, but I do it anyway. Because I have to—I swore. I shook hands with the Devil, and even if the Devil meant something else entirely by *kiss,* you can't go back on it.

He might poison my sisters if I go back on it. He might poison me. He might look on me with his stone-eyes now bright with the light of a thousand years and put his hands on my face as though I am suddenly something precious, and say:

"Do not fear me."

And I wish I didn't, I do. But the funny thing is, I don't think this would be half so thrilling if I were not so afraid. I can smell him now like the forest and like something burning, and when he drops to his knees my mind swirls with all the things he might possibly do.

Because of course he said *kiss.* And he said that I might not do it with *my* mouth. But he didn't say anything about his own, or all the possible places he could press his lips, or how tremulous and on the cusp of something wicked I would feel, the moment I felt him *there.*

I try not to make a sound. The road stretching away on either side of us is silent, but in this moment of bared legs and strange hands on my thighs, it feels as though a million eyes are watching us from the forests.

And it grows steadily stronger when he leans forward quite

suddenly and gives me that kiss he promised.

Of course, I have no idea why I use the word *promise*. He didn't promise me. I promised him. And yet it swims up inside me anyway, unbidden, as he lays his mouth on the warm, wet split of my sex.

Maybe because it's like a gift. It shouldn't feel that way, I know. I should be crying out over my womanly virtue, but instead I cry out in a different way altogether. He's found some secret heart between my legs, some well of pleasure, and the water from said well flows up and up inside me until it comes right out of my mouth.

And then my whole body sways and I simply have to touch him, I have to—if only to hold on. Though of course once I've done it—once I've put my hands in his hair to steady myself—I can't help but marvel over the feel of him.

The tangles are like the roots of a plant, I think. Like grass, so cool and slippery between my fingers. And when he kisses me more deeply—more deeply than he should be doing, oh far more deeply—I dare to do more.

I feel out the little rough humps of his horns, to remind myself of what he is.

And then he kisses me harder, wetter, oh god he uses his *tongue*, and I don't pull away. Lord forgive me, I don't. I know I should, I know I should think of the word *maiden* and not make a slattern of myself, but I can't help it.

He spoke so ill of this, when he called it a kiss. I've seen kisses—they are not like thing he is giving me. I'm swooning—though I keep my footing—and when his narrow devil's tongue slides through my slit I feel every fold and whorl he uncovers. I feel all the things I didn't even know existed, including a sweet little swollen spot right where everything begins or ends.

I've never known this. I didn't understand that people could do things like this—though likely as not *people* don't. It's just him, it's just creatures *like* him, and now I'm going to hell right along with all of them because he's licking that little stiff point and *oh* it feels so good.

How could I not have known that such pleasure existed in the world? It swells and gushes and bursts through me, so all-consuming that it's hard to imagine a time when it *didn't* exist. Every lick sends another wave through my body, until I'm sobbing, I'm sobbing.

I hardly care that anyone could hear me. I don't even care that it's this beast between my legs, making sounds so hungry-seeming and abandoned that I couldn't call it anything but obscene.

He is obscene, and I am damned, I am damned. Because when he leaves one last wet kiss on the swollen bud at the top of my slit, I give in to him. I do. I give in to the kiss he fooled me into having.

I don't mean to go back again, I swear I don't. But Eladria's prince comes and then Luvia cries all day and all night and I have to, I simply have to. It's not fair to do it for one sister and not the other, after all.

And yet he still looks surprised to see me. I'm not sure how his great, still face even manages to show surprise, but it does, and then I am not sure how to ask. Clearly he thinks I should be feeling all the things I know a proper lady must. I should be outraged and horrified, ashamed of the wicked kiss he gave me.

But instead I am here to trade another part of myself for my sister's happiness.

"Come again, have you, maiden?"

I try to think if this is the first or second time he's deviated from the words written down in the book, but I don't know. I'm not sure it matters anymore. I'm not sure I really have to explain—stating my request flatly and without much embellishment seems to be enough.

"I have come for my other sister."

"The same need?"

I nod, even though I know there are two possible interpretations of the word *need*.

"Then you were happy with the gift I gave you?"

Again I think of other interpretations, dual meanings. We could be talking about anything now, but I carry on with it anyway.

"Very happy. More than happy."

"And if I ask a similar price of you this time you will give it to me freely?"

He's offering me the chance to take my leave now, I know. To understand completely what our transaction may be and refuse it before it goes too far.

But I only say:

"Always."

And I continue to mean it when he tells me what he wants.

"A touch is my price," he says, and though he could be suggesting almost anything I clasp his hand. Only this time the cold of his palm goes straight to my core, to that place where all feeling bloomed the night before.

He is not natural, I think. *He is almost unreal.*

But those things have ceased to matter, I know. Instead there is just the expectation of his hands on me, of his fingers brushing over my swollen mound and between those lips he kissed last night.

So it's almost a disappointment when he doesn't do it. I feel it burning at the back of my throat and behind my eyes, and it lasts all the way up until he takes my hands in his and lays them on his broad, hard chest.

And then I don't know what it is I feel. It's something like apprehension, but heavier and yes, sweeter, too. He has tricked me again, though I hardly know how. I understood the way he works, I saw his trickery clearly, and yet here I am with my fear in my throat, waiting to find out exactly what he meant this time.

He is the Father of Lies, I think, but oh I live for every one of them.

"Tell me," I say to him, and he does. He tells me with his hands over mine, pushing me to explore the strange landscape of his body. I've never touched a man like this before, and the very fact of that is enough to set my every nerve on edge.

But then I remember he is not a man at all, and that edge gets sharper, steeper, more impossible to traverse. I feel how marble-like his skin is, and how alive and strange the hair grows beneath my fingertips, and I can hardly bear to carry on.

I can hardly bear not to. He's so firm—why did no one ever tell me how firm a man could be? And when I slide my hands down over his taut belly he makes a sound, so soft and whispering I'm sure I've imagined it.

How can a creature such as him react like that to a woman like me? I am so small and slight in front of him—so small and slight that for a moment I am sure I'm about to blow away. My body sways beneath a different kind of pleasure as I curl my fingers through the fur between his legs, and another touch will send me over, I'm sure.

But he keeps me steady. He clasps my shoulders in his long-fingered hands, and murmurs to me to *go on, go on, do not be afraid.* And I confess that I am not, anymore, not in the slightest, though the anticipation remains.

I search through the fur looking for I know not what until I feel it and then I understand so clearly. I see the men of my village capering naked in the river, something soft and sleeping between their legs. But the thing my beast-god has is not like the thing they have; it is long and thick and stiff, as stiff as the little bud I have between my own legs.

And when I touch it, when I run my fingers over the shaft of it, he shivers the way I do. He shivers and whispers my name in a way I never thought I'd hear it—like the sound of the forest sighing or a maiden swooning.

So I touch him again, and again, stroking over the only place on his body that feels fever hot and thick with life. Following instinct rather than knowledge, of which I have none.

Though if he understands this, he doesn't show it. He bucks into my twisting grip instead, body suddenly strung taut, eyes as bright as they were once dark. He's enjoying it, I think, and the thought spurs me to greater daring. I cover the tip with my palm, just to feel the slickness growing there. And when he moans—so deep and long it's like hearing the world turn beneath my feet—I fall to a rough kind of tug. Back and forth along the length of him, everything getting more slippery by the moment.

Things are reaching some sort of crescendo, I know. I'm not quite sure what I expect—something like the feeling that burst through me, perhaps—but the reality is so much more thrilling. So much earthier, somehow.

His back arches and that forest scent of him grows stronger, and richer. I lean into it—I can't help it—and the moment I do I feel his shaft leap in my hand. A great groan moves through him, more powerful than the one that came before and certainly enough to turn the world this time, and then he clasps me tight.

He holds me to him, as though I am his lover.

I think it's this that moves me more than any other thing. The feel of him in my hands—so hot and pulsing—is good, and it forms an ache in me like no other. And I admit I enjoy the spill of his seed over my fingers, so slippery and illicit.

But his arms around me...that is what I remember, later on. I think of my own girlish thoughts about love and not living without it, and I remember him holding me the way no man ever will, while pleasure made him weak in my arms.

And then I know. I know what I must do.

He does not say, "Come again, have you, maiden?" when I return. He doesn't even use the word *maiden*—though I suppose that is fair enough. I am no longer pure, after all, and even if I was I'm not sure I'd hold to the title any longer.

There is something burning in me, something I did not see on my sisters' faces when their princes came. I see it in my own mirror, though, and I have learned to recognize it inside myself.

It comes most strongly when he says just the one word:

"Ren."

His face is different now, I see. There is something less than impassive about his expressions, and his eyes are no longer stones. They shine out brightly through the darkness, full both of a sort of hope and a sort of despair.

I understand why. I feel the same every day of my life—like I dream of beautiful things to come and yet know they never can. Or at least, they never can if I don't dare everything. If I don't say yes, when he asks me:

"Have you come to ask another wish of me? Any one person may only have three—you know this, don't you, sweet Ren?"

I do, I do. The book said as much, and so I spent the night thinking and thinking of what I would ask for myself if I had the chance. I know what it is, now, but I also know I must be wily. I must be as tricky as he was, if I want my heart's desire.

"Then strike quickly, if you would. I hear it in you, the whispering desire for that which your sisters now have. Did they seem gay, as they disappeared into the night with their husbands? Did they seem fair and fine?"

"Is this where you tell me that I must be careful what I wish for?" I ask, because I can see the warning in him. I can see what he is thinking—of false-faced princes, who sing of love and then prove themselves dastardly.

"I am not such a beast that I cannot tell you truly, Ren. The world of men is harsh and cold, though it may seem otherwise on the surface."

"And the world you come from? The world of the forest?"

"Is red in tooth and claw."

My heart beats wildly when he says it, but I cannot turn back now. I have decided, and it is time to make him my offer.

"I have a wish, He Who Has No Name. But much as you have kept the price for my requests from me, I ask one thing of you now. I wish to keep my heart's desire from you until it has been paid for."

His eyes glitter, glitter. I can see him considering, but of course things might go either way.

"And if I grant you this consideration—as vast and impossible as it may be—what do you think would be payment enough?"

I think of many things, then. My collection of gleaming beads, my dress of green velvet, my books. Though of course I know that none of them will ever be enough for what I ask.

"My maidenhood," I say, and he takes a step forward as though he cannot help himself, just as I knew he would. Few offer such payment, and yet nothing will mean as much to him as this does.

Nothing is as precious to one such as he, because one such as he dwells in darkness—without love, without the touch of another, without the thing that burns inside me, even now.

"You would give me this gift?"

"I would," I say, and he clasps my hand before I can take it back.

This time, he kisses me. He kisses my mouth, while I think about his warning over and over again—that people aren't always as they appear. That things may seem fine and fair, but really, underneath...

Oh underneath there is this, as sweet as summer rain. His mouth tastes like elderflowers, and when he spreads me out in the grass by the forest's edge I don't resist. I don't have to be bought, or bargained for, or asked of. I only want to feel my beast-god between my legs, as rampant as I always knew he would be.

Of course there's pain. Everyone speaks of the pain, and I knew it would come. And yet when he lays his hands on me— warm now, instead of cold—and cups my bare breasts against his rough palms, and kisses me again, again, the sharp sting melts away.

I think only of the root of him, working slow and steady in that place between my legs. Everything there feels so sensitive and so slick, and though he fills me to the point of bursting I find I like it.

I wrap my legs tight around his great furred body. I kiss him in all the places I've longed to, since the moment I laid eyes on him. And when he says my name I say his back—I say the one I know he secretly has, below all the myths and the legends and everything hidden.

He looks down on me, then, face as open as I've ever seen it. It sends a spike of pleasure through me, though I do not let it show. Not yet. I want him to rut against me, first, I want him to pant and throw back his head. And after a long, long moment he does.

He moans like a wild animal, teeth bared, back arched. And

I feel him swell inside me, so good and so strong. It's as though I'm being split apart and put back together at the same time, and through it all great shivers of pleasure run through me—far sweeter than anything my sisters have ever claimed, when they speak to me of lying with a man.

But then, he is not a man. He is not. He is my beast-god, my Father of Lies, everything about him so different to those sunny-faced princes.... And yet it is better this way, I think. Better to hear it in his name and see it in his face and know all perils that you might face instead of coming to them later.

I know the perils. And yet as the pleasure blooms fresh inside me and he leans down to ask, "What then is your prize?" I tell him clear as a bell ringing and twice as strong:

"You."

KIT IN BOOTS

Sacchi Green

Kit gazed into the miller's open grave and vowed silently that Puss would be forever buried with him. As the gravediggers shoveled earth over the coffin, she thought of tearing off her drab, shapeless gown and shawl and tossing them in as well, revealing the shirt and breeches and, yes, even boots, she wore beneath, but some of the mourners would enjoy that scandal all too much. Just a few more hours and she could shed entirely the life she'd led.

What lay ahead…well, the course of a new life was always unclear, but she knew where to begin the search for all that she wanted and needed, whatever the price. A certain memory drove her on, so vivid yet unreal that by now she could scarcely tell what was truth and what was dream.

There had been high winds hurling cold spray from the waves on that moonlit night as she tramped along the shingle beach. In her rare hours of respite from tending the old man, she often walked two miles from the inland village to feel that wind and space and illusion of freedom. Sometimes she yearned toward faraway places she had heard of beyond the sea. But this time, a great dark figure on the low cliff above had been watching, clutching his hooded cloak about him so that even his eyes could not be seen, though she felt their gaze like a searing touch.

Kit's hedge-witch mother had given her little power and less instruction, but enough that she could feel the aura of fierce desire emanating from the brooding watcher. It inspired a tremor of fear, yes, but a wild, wanton impulse as well that made her spread her arms and let the wind blow her threadbare cloak out behind her and mold her damp, shapeless dress tightly against her very shapely body. Long hair whipped about her face at one moment and streamed free like a banner at the next. She flashed a look of challenge, a laughing invitation, upward to the cliff-top; he raised an arm in salute, letting his cloak rise in the wind like a mighty wing—and then he turned and was gone. Kit had waited on the shingle as long as she dared, shivering in the cold wind yet burning with anticipation, but he had not come.

Even now, by the graveside, she yearned to feel again that aching intensity, that fierce power and irresistible force of nature that might yet be bent to her own desires. She would begin her new life by searching out the mysteries surrounding the man on the cliff. In the harbor town of Rockbay, she knew, they called him The Ogre, but had little more to tell, though he had taken residence in the old castle on the coast more than six months past.

The diggers signaled Kit that they had finished. She tossed a handful of daisies onto the new-turned earth. The old man had been kind, in his way, taking her from the workhouse at fifteen to keep house and cook for him and his three sons. Five years later, as he'd grown ill and blind, she had nursed him through his last days. If calling her "Puss" and stroking her tangle of hair the color of a ginger cat soothed him, so be it.

But no one else should claim that liberty. Rolfe, the middle son, had tried and still bore the scars of her claws. He had tried a good deal more than that, in fact, and Kit had chosen to give in to him a few times, on her own terms; satisfying a man she despised might be a useful skill some day, and learning to satisfy herself, since he could not, was a valuable lesson as well. Having soon wrung from him what little he offered, she fended him off once by force and afterward when necessary by twitching her fingers to make his old scars burn anew. Her mother, who had come and gone unpredictably throughout her childhood, had at least taught her a few tricks, bare essentials for survival, just as her poacher father had taught her the survival skills of trapping and snaring wild game before he'd been hanged for shooting deer.

Now Rolfe would be off before the funeral dinner had entirely cooled. He would ride the horse that was his only inheritance in search of a fortune to be made by any means possible, a rich widow or tradesman's heiress being his preference. The local rich widow had already been appropriated by his oldest brother, Willem, who inherited the mill and had grand plans to expand and update it with his wife-to-be's wealth.

*Just a few more hours...*Kit drew a deep breath and turned from the grave. She had already prepared the dishes for the customary dinner, more bountiful than the family could have afforded without her skill at snaring rabbits and pheasants. Now she must serve the guests, clean up afterward, and then she'd be free to go. More than free. The rich widow had no intention of sharing the house with Kit, being shrewd enough to recognize her allure for men in spite of Kit's own attempts to conceal it. The wedding had been delayed only until there was no more need for her to stay and nurse the old man.

Free, except for one detail.

"Kit?" The youngest boy, Jotham, turned back from following his brothers. "Are you feeling all right?" His blue eyes filled with honest concern. He had a kind nature, a hand-some—some would say pretty—face, flaxen hair, and very little sense. Kit merely surveyed him without answering. "I mean..." Jotham hesitated. "Well, Father said that I must...must stick by you. Help you, I suppose, although I don't know what I'll do myself."

Yes, that one detail. "Take care of the boy," the miller had pleaded on his deathbed, and what could she do but promise? There would be no place for him, either, in his brother's house. The widow had a certain partiality for pretty boys, and Willem had no intention of sharing.

"I will work out a plan," Kit told Jotham, "but you must do everything exactly as I tell you, or I'll leave you to your own devices. Do you understand?"

"Oh...yes, of course." Jotham's face eased in relief. He was in the habit of being led by Kit.

"And tell no one, no one at all, about anything I do or say." She steered him along the path back toward the mill and the house.

"No one." He nodded vigorously, then nearly stumbled, and stared down at her feet. "But Kit, you're wearing boots!" He looked harder. "My boots!"

It was too late to arrange her skirts to conceal them, so she pretended her carelessness had been planned. "Yes, the boots you outgrew before you were fourteen." She raised the skirt higher. "And your old breeches as well. But that is just the sort of thing you must not reveal to anyone, or I will wash my hands of you, and use them to good purpose first!" She raised one fist, and Jotham, whose ears she had boxed more than once, flinched.

"See that you remember," Kit said in a milder tone. "Now go to the house, eat your dinner, make proper responses to those offering their condolences, and then pack up all the belongings you can easily carry in a pack on your back."

She strode off ahead of him, feeling as though the boots were carrying her into a different life, as a whole new person.

Without Jotham to consider she would not have paused at the mill longer than it took to retrieve her own meager bundle of belongings, already packed. As it was, she finished her work with unobtrusive efficiency, feeling the tug of the boots and her own deepest yearnings, tinged with darkness, all the while.

"Meet me in an hour in the copse past the mill," she whispered to Jotham at last, and was off and away before anyone else noticed she had gone.

Before the hour had passed, Kit heard Jotham approaching and stepped out from the trees to meet him.

"Who...what..." he stammered in astonishment, in spite of the hint he'd been given. Kit was every inch—every visible inch, at any rate—a young man, or a boy on the cusp of manhood. Her hair had been cut short to about the length a page might wear and brushed to a smooth, gleaming russet. The clothes that had once been his were of good quality, if somewhat out of date; the breeches, shirt, and jacket fit her slender figure perfectly, with only the aid of some inner binding about her breasts. Jotham's mother had favored and indulged him while she lived, dressing him above his station; now even his Sunday-best suit worn for the funeral was a hand-me-down from his brother Rolfe.

"We must find positions, you and I," Kit told him, "and I refuse to consider any that I might be offered as a woman."

Jotham nodded. "Yes, I had thought about seeking a position

at a wealthy man's estate, but I worried as to what you would do."

Kit's surprise was nearly as great as his had been. There was hope for the youngster yet. "Good! Have you chosen a first place to apply?"

"Well," he said, "the few manor houses nearby are too small. That huge dark castle on the north coast might need staff. They say he has none but a housekeeper and a deaf-mute gardener. But they also say he is an ogre who can transform from hideous beast to man. Nothing could make me approach him! So...," here a blush rose on his cheeks, "...my only choice is to try those foreigners renting the fancy villa to the south."

Kit knew at once what he was about. "Ah yes, the royal something-or-other from the minor princedom with an unpronounceable name. And his very beautiful daughter." Not a bad idea, even if Jotham was so obviously smitten with the girl. He would make a fine and tempting figure as a footman. "Let us both try our luck, and meet again in three days at dusk where that old fisherman's shack was half blown down in the gale last summer."

"You aren't going with me? What will you do?" Jotham's concern was touching.

"Oh, I'm all for the dark castle. And the ogre. Those are more to my taste," Kit said, and strode off without a backward look.

Even the boots and the freedom of breeches did not quite give her the courage to brave the castle that night. In any case, it would be impolite. She could see a light in the castle, high in a tower. If the man had been alone, she might yet have risked all, but with a housekeeper present it would be a different matter.

Kit paced on the shingle beach near the castle for a while, imagining a watcher's gaze on the slender legs and hips so brazenly displayed by her snug breeches and short jacket. After a while she even seemed to sense such a gaze, but that was impossible. This night the sky was dark and moonless, and only the faint phosphorescence of the now-placid wavelets showed her the boundary between land and sea. Even if there had been moonlight and a watcher, he might have been deceived by her disguise and thus shown no interest. But oh, to feel this freedom and be swept by desire; to be exposed, vulnerable, and yet strong, meeting passion with passion, and returning bruise for bruise, if it came to that!

Eventually Kit trudged up the narrow path to the cliff-top, rather enjoying the mild discomfort of breeches dampened in the crotch and pausing at the top to add to the sensation by stroking her own so-accessible limbs. She followed the path back toward the town and the abandoned fisherman's hut, which had still enough wall and roof in one corner to provide some shelter, and there she spent the night.

At a civilized hour of the morning Kit stood at the castle entrance, bearing a brace of newly snared pheasants as a gift. There was no knocker or bell-pull to be seen; perhaps she should seek out a tradesmen's entrance at the rear. But the forbidding iron gates swung open at her approach, with much creaking and grating. After one glance back at the brightness of the day, she plunged on through the stone arch into a dim walled courtyard.

A massive wooden door in the inner building swung slowly open, though there was still no one to be seen. Kit hesitated a moment, thinking of old tales meant to frighten children, then shrugged and stepped on through into a corridor with reassuring light at its end.

The room she entered was indeed well lit and comfortably furnished. The woman seated by the hearth seemed at first glance old, fiercely ugly, and forbidding, but Kit could see beneath the illusion; her mother had often used a disguise very similar, though not as skillfully.

"Well," said the pleasant woman of middle years—though Kit could not be certain whether that too might be an even more skillful illusion—"So he was right. You do have a touch of magic about you. I had thought his judgment was swayed by his desires."

Kit struggled to maintain a cool exterior and proceeded with her planned speech. "Indeed, ma'am? I've merely come to apply for employment, since my old master has recently died. Have you need here of a page, or footman, or even gamekeeper?" She lay the pheasants on the hearth. At the housekeeper's raised eyebrow, she added, "These are from the common heath, not any nobleman's estate."

"Have you other skills?" The woman's amusement was clear, as was the fact that Kit's disguise had not deceived her. "Did you not nurse your old master through his final illness?"

"I did," said Kit, since it was clear that her past was no secret here, "and kept him alive and comfortable far past any expectation of the doctors or his family. Past any desire of his family, indeed, though they would not dare to admit that openly."

The housekeeper surveyed her long and thoughtfully. Kit did not try to conceal anything about herself, but finally she blurted out, "Is it an invalid's nurse that you need here?" It was far from what she had wished for; then again, one never knew.

"Not precisely. Or, rather, not in the common way, but you might yet be of use. Sometimes pleasure can heal flesh and mind better than any medicine, or even magic." She rose. "Come along. You must meet the master, something he both wishes and dreads. We shall see how much you can endure. They do call him an ogre, after all." Kit, though she could seldom read minds, caught a further thought from the housekeeper's mind, no doubt intentionally unguarded: *Once they called him General, the savior of his country! And she, his wife, with her mincing, dainty ways, called him her hero, then turned away in revulsion after that last battle. Gold enough they gave him, as though that could ever heal such wounds!*

Kit felt chilled and heated at the same time. She followed along a corridor and up winding stairs, only asking, "What shall I call *you*, ma'am?"

"Mrs. Thorne," the housekeeper said over her shoulder; then, turning for a moment to face Kit, added with a hint of menace, "and do not try the sharpness of my barbs!"

"Yes, Mrs. Thorne," Kit answered meekly, understanding her perfectly. "My name is Kit, but I can sheath my claws when I wish."

"As to that," Mrs. Thorne said, "best keep them sharpened nonetheless."

By that time they had come to a landing giving onto several doors, one of which the housekeeper unlocked with a key from the bunch hanging at her waist. Before opening it, she murmured into Kit's ear, "Do not injure him more than the world has already done." Then she motioned Kit through, backed away herself, and went down the stairs.

This was clearly a test. Kit braced herself for whatever might come and entered a great room richly furnished but somewhat dimmed by heavy curtains at the windows.

"Sir," she said to the dark figure seated at a desk, "Mrs. Thorne thinks that I may be of some use. My name is Kit." She ducked her head just enough to show respect.

He rose slowly and came toward her, tall and powerful but with the gait of a man who refuses to limp though his body demands it. His features could not be made out clearly, with such light as the windows provided still behind him, but she could see that a patch covered his left eye.

He circled her, and she stood still to let him assess her as he would. Desire was still apparent in his aura, and she felt it grow as his gaze swept along her legs so exposed by the breeches, but a profound loneliness was there as well, and sadness, and echoes of old anger. Even, possibly, a trace of fear.

"So you've come to see The Ogre," he said, a note of bitterness in his deep voice as he stopped at last in front of her. "Does he disappoint you?"

Kit took that as permission to look more closely. She *was*, at first, disappointed. His silver-streaked mane of black hair was striking, but his face was unremarkable, even bland, like a... yes, like a mask, as indeed it was, she realized; an illusion Mrs. Thorne must have provided, for Kit detected no personal magic in the man himself.

"Yes, I *am* disappointed," she said. "I came to see the true man, beast and all. The man who watched me from the cliff. If I am to help you, and if...," she took a great daring leap into the truth, "...if I am to achieve my own deepest desires, there must be no deception between us."

His mask wavered just slightly; out of sympathy Kit looked away and pretended not to have already seen what he tried to hide. Not until he was ready to bear it. The cruel scars descending from his left temple along his cheek and neck and down under his collar evoked compassion in her, not revulsion.

"I will begin the revelations myself," she said, knowing that he had never been deceived by her disguise. "First this." She unbuttoned her jacket and shed it, along with her muslin shirt. "And this." The inner cotton bindings came off, freeing her breasts, their rose-tinted nipples tightening into thrusting points as he watched. "Not yet enough?" She bent and wriggled free of breeches and boots, and the stockings beneath, feeling her naked buttocks flush in the heat of his gaze. Then she straightened and turned to expose her full womanhood, slick dampening folds beneath a light furring of russet curls. "Enough now?" she asked, with all the challenge she had projected that moonlit night by the sea, and even more.

"Enough!" he said sharply, stepping back, though now she felt from him a surge of need pent up so long that it towered like a giant wave suspended above them.

"Not quite enough," Kit said. "Your turn now for revelations," and before he could prevent it, she reached up to his cheek below the eye patch and brushed the long scar with a touch so light, so tender, she doubted he could feel it, though he grasped her hand and pulled it away.

"Do not bait the lion in his cage," he grated, his grip tightening until it was painful.

"It is the lion I came for, both man and beast." Kit expertly extricated her hand. "I am strong enough to bear your anger and sorrow, as well as lust—but I must begin with the lust, or go mad!"

Before he could resist, she dropped to her knees and reached out to the mighty bulge in his trousers. His growl of warning turned to a growl of quite another kind as she swiftly unbuttoned his garments and freed his demanding flesh. By the time her mouth was on his cock, sliding over all that could fit of its great length and thickness as her hands worked at the rest, he had given in to deep groans and rasping breaths. His hands wove deeply through her hair and pressed her face ever harder into his raging need.

The giant wave crashed over them. Kit's ears rang with sounds like thunder and the screeching of sea birds combined. Her own need was still great, but elation at her new master's release buoyed her up, and indeed it was mere moments before his desire began to revive. He pulled her to her feet, then crushed his mouth against hers and ran his hands roughly over her body, arousing her to the edge of pain. She scrabbled at his clothing until it was all in a heap along with hers, and skin could press against hungry skin. When he lifted her so high that he could tantalize her breasts with nips and bites, she wrapped her legs tightly about him, his cock hardening once more beneath her buttocks; he forced his mouth roughly onto her aching nipples, one after the other. She could hear herself growing shrill with the desperate need for more.

He carried her through another door into a second room. Soon a bed was beneath her, lurching under her thrashing body as she opened to him, begging to be filled. He responded with more than she had thought she could hold, thrusting hard, sending bolts of pleasure into her deep, ravenous core until her own wave hit, overwhelmed her, and receded in ripples of such joy that she scarcely felt his second eruption.

In the aftermath Kit noted drowsily and with gratitude that her ogre's long scar, and several others she had not seen while he was clothed, ended well short of what had given her such piercing fulfillment. With one hand she stroked tenderly all down his body, noting the effort he made not to wince away.

"Does it still give you pain?" she asked gently.

"No. Or, at least, not enough to signify. But...how can you stand to touch me? To even look at me?"

She wriggled onto his belly and chest. "It is you yourself I see and touch. Not merely certain parts, except when they are in a particularly interesting state." She touched his cock, hardening yet again. Good. Let him not regret his moment of vulnerability. Better to distract him.

Kit reached up to the posts at the head of the bed. "What are these contraptions? Playthings?"

He tensed in quite the wrong way. "Cuffs and fetters. Restraints. There are times...dreams of battles...when I must..."

She could feel him retreating from her. "Well, all the better to have someone attend you who knows how to deal with them. Especially if you should wish to travel abroad, as I have always longed to do. Besides, I have also heard of such things used for pleasure. Perhaps you should show me...restrain me, punish me, have your will with me, test my strength. I might surprise you."

She saw his arousal revive, and knew, with a prickle of anticipation, that she had succeeded. If there had indeed been a test, she was sure that by now Mrs. Thorne would know that she had passed it beyond any possible doubt.

Two nights later Kit met Jotham at the abandoned shack. She was moving a bit stiffly, still savoring the soreness. "I have a most secure position," she assured him. "How did you fare?"

"Oh, Kit, she is the most beautiful creature!" he gushed. "Sweet and delicate...she thought all our countrymen were rough louts until she met me! They are leaving very soon for their own land, but I have hopes...."

"Hopes? Of going with them as a footman?" But Kit could tell already that there was more to the story than that.

"Well, at first it was like that, but when I told her I was the impoverished younger son of a nobleman, and my horse and fine clothing had been stolen as I swam in the sea so that I was reduced to common rags, and I had only applied as a footman because I had seen and loved her and wished to be near her...and when she told her father she would have no other husband..."

There was definitely more to Jotham than Kit had ever suspected. And possibly a good deal less. "Can this all be truly settled?" she asked dubiously.

"Oh yes. At least...I told him that my distant cousin owns the castle by the sea, and now he wishes to see it. I was sure you

would succeed there, so if you could arrange to let them come
at least into the gardens and have a cup of tea, saying that your
master is not at home, my entire life will become a heaven on
earth!"

Fools and their luck, Kit thought. *And their wild, if senti-
mental, imaginations!*

Two days later, while Mrs. Thorne served the guests tea in the
castle gardens, the master of the castle was unfortunately indis-
posed. In fact, he was fettered to his bed, after Kit had pointed
out that it was all very well to let loose the lion or ogre within,
but it took even more strength of will to submit like a lamb, or
perhaps even something as outwardly weak as a mouse. By then
there was enough trust between them for him to acquiesce, and
while tea and conversation were consumed below, Kit was in the
tower making submission very much worth her master's time.
Among other delights, she had but to twitch her fingers toward
a part of his body to make him writhe with remembered pleasure. If she had a few tricks, why not use them?

Six months later, in a great city on the continent, a wealthy
and imposing figure strolled amid the demimondaine with an
assured bearing that made one overlook his scars and eye patch.
The sleek and charming page so often beside him inspired
sighs from both men and women, but their highest awe was
reserved for the lady who sometimes hung on the gentleman's
arm, dressed in the finest and most severely tailored of women's
clothing in greens and bronzes that set off her shining russet
hair. Either of those companions wore especially elegant boots
suited to their respective costumes. No one was truly deceived,
of course, but that made it all the more entertaining.

The chambermaids were well paid to refrain from gossiping
about their household, though of course they did, especially

about the rather specialized accoutrements of their bedchamber. After all, such fur-lined restraints were not unheard of in certain circles. No one bothered to relate how the lady, when the man occasionally tousled her hair and call her "My pretty puss," would stiffen for a mere second as at an old memory. Her lord would beg her pardon, earning a fond kiss and forgiveness. "You may call me anything you like, my love," she would say, "as long as I have such fine boots to wear."

THE LONG NIGHT OF TANYA MCCRAY

Michael M. Jones

I was lost. My guidebook's maps were either out of date or outright fabrications, my smartphone's GPS had claimed I was somewhere in the Atlantic before running out of power, and every set of directions I'd begged from passersby had led me further into the labyrinthine neighborhood of Puxhill known as the Gaslight District. Now, with night falling, the antique lamps that gave the area its name flickered to life, casting mocking shadows against uncaring brick walls and dark windows. I stood on the corner of two nameless streets—one little more than an alley—and threw up my hands in frustration.

My excursion had started well enough earlier. The Gaslight District had evolved out of Puxhill's original settlement some centuries past, a chaotic tangle of narrow streets, scenic court-yards, and old buildings. It was a cultural melting pot, a unique blend of backgrounds and beliefs. During the day, you could find treasures and wonders in its tiny groceries, bookstores, and curio shops. Where it bordered the normal parts of the city, like

Caravan Street or Tuesday University, you could find popular hangouts and hotspots. My mistake had been in venturing too far off the beaten path. Camera in hand, I went searching for new and interesting shots, not heeding those who said it would be a bad idea.

"Tanya," I told myself, "this is all well and good, but standing here isn't helping. *Puxhill through the Lens* won't get finished if you vanish, never to be seen again." I squared my shoulders, pretended I'd given myself a really good pep talk, and picked a direction. I hoped I'd find somewhere still open, where I could get proper directions or use the phone. For all of its many tiny nameless streets, the Gaslight District was still a finite area in a much larger city.

Several blocks later, I wasn't so sure. Twilight had fallen, and I hadn't seen a single other person in ages. I pulled my denim jacket close as a chill ran through the air. All I saw were closed doors, dark windows, and capriciously dancing shadows.

The silence broke. Raised voices. Harsh laughter. A pained cry punctuated by a soft thud. Jingling chains and scuffed movements. Common sense told me to head away from what sounded like certain trouble; other instincts urged me around the corner, where certain trouble was already in progress.

Given the time and place, what I found was no surprise: five thugs, ganging up on a victim. They were uniformly dressed in steel-toed boots, dirty jeans, black T-shirts, leather jackets proclaiming them all as "Corbie Boys." Crows of ill fortune, mobbing the crumpled figure at their feet. Without any thought for my safety, I raced forward, instinctively letting out a war cry. I pointed my camera in their direction and pressed the shutter button as rapidly as possible, the flash disconcertingly bright against the twilight. The gang members froze before scattering, unwilling to face my unanticipated threat.

I knew I'd only bought us a little time. Once the Corbie Boys realized they'd been taken in by nothing more than a woman with a camera and an ear-splitting scream, they'd be back. I offered a hand to their erstwhile target. His grip was firm and warm, and he stifled a pained groan as he stood.

While he dusted himself off, checking for injuries, I examined him, hoping I'd chosen the right side to help. He was a smidgen taller than me, and I come close to six feet in flat shoes—God forbid I wear heels. Weathered skin several shades darker than my own Irish pale, with intense dark eyes, short brown hair, and strong features. In the right light, he'd be a perfect model; I ached to shoot him in some of Puxhill's more interesting locations. Possibly naked. While battered and bruised, he didn't seem to have suffered overly much from the attack. He was dressed far nicer than the area called for, in a dark suit set off against expensive black loafers, a light blue shirt, and a tasteful red tie. He smiled, making my knees wobble. I blamed it on the adrenaline still racing through me. "While I appreciate the help," he said, "I fear you've made some inconvenient enemies. The Corbie Boys don't take well to challenges, and they react poorly to loss of face."

His voice was low, cool, and utterly in control. It was liquid sex and velvet, sending shivers along my spine. I shrugged. "Then I guess we'd better not stick around. Any ideas which way we should go?"

He looked around before nodding in one direction. "That's our best bet."

I fell in beside him as he headed down the sidewalk briskly, easily keeping up with my own long stride. "I'm Tanya," I said. "Tanya McCray."

"Devin Hunt."

"Nice to meet you. Please say you know where you're going."

He chuckled. "Good news and bad news, then. Yes, I know where we're going. No, I can't get us out of here right now."

I stumbled to a halt, then backed up a step. "How'd you know what I was going to ask?" Well-spoken eye candy that he was, I hadn't forgotten that he was a relative unknown, and we were alone at night in an extremely strange part of the city.

He stopped, holding up his hands to show empty palms and an earnest expression. "I'm sorry, I misspoke. It's just—look, I know this area like the back of my hand, but the Gaslight District, it gets weird at night. We're trapped until sunrise, when the paths straighten out again." His expression turned rueful. "My business here ran late, and the Corbie Boys were set on keeping me here until sunset. We don't get along. I don't accept their delusions of territorial superiority."

No stranger to weird corners of the world, I frowned. I'd explored abandoned mental hospitals, decommissioned cold war bunkers, and burned out schools; this somehow beat them all for unsettling.

"So we wander the streets until morning?" I asked. There was no life to be found around us, only gaslights casting inhuman shadows with their inadequate light.

Devin shook his head. "We find safe haven and hole up for a while. Trust me, the Corbie Boys aren't the worst things hiding in the night."

Of course not. I rejoined him. As he led the way, I kept close. Our footsteps were disturbingly loud in the otherwise silent night. I couldn't hear the city anymore. "So you spend a lot of time here?" I asked.

"In the daytime, yes. Work brings me down here frequently, and I know the area pretty well."

"How big is the Gaslight District?"

"As big as it wants to be. The outskirts and main streets

are pretty stable, anchored by landmarks like Club Euterpe or the Theatre of Dreams, but as you've seen, things...change the further you venture."

This wasn't reassuring, but I accepted it for the time being. At least I was in pleasant company. Devin had the cool, self-assured manner I looked for in a guy, confidence without arrogance. I could always rely on a guy like that. Especially in bed, where he turned that confidence into performance and took satisfying a partner as a worthwhile challenge. I glanced sideways, wondering how his lips would taste, how his hands would feel on me, how—I derailed that train of thought. I liked him, and he looked damned good in a suit, and it had been months since my last fling, but this was not the right time.

He caught me looking and quirked an eyebrow; I hoped it was too dark for my blush to show. There was something in his expression that suggested he liked what he saw. That he appreciated lanky blue-eyed redheads with fair skin, too many freckles, and slight curves. A partner once claimed I was built for speed, not comfort, like a greyhound, but Devin seemed fine with that. I reached back to adjust the red braid that fell past my shoulders, then shoved my hands into my jacket pockets instead.

As we passed dark alleys and crossed deserted streets, we fell into a comfortable silence. Soon, we came to a building lit against the darkness. It had no sign, no name identifying it as we approached, just a tall candle in the front window. Devin pushed the door open with a smile, waving me inside. His chivalry warred with my practicality; I almost insisted he go first, just in case. My aching feet and empty stomach cast their votes. Outvoted, I entered.

It was a cross between a bar and a pool hall, the sort of place where people come to feel at home and be themselves. While dim and dingy, it was also warm and welcoming. It smelled of alcohol and tobacco, fried foods and cheap pastries, sawdust and chalk. It smelled like heaven. Oddly, we were the only ones here. I looked at Devin, both eyebrows raised. He shrugged. "There are safe places, and there are places that can be safe," he said. "Unfortunately, this was the best I could do under the circumstances."

"In other words, I might not like the clientele, but it's better than the alternatives?"

"Exactly." We chose one of the booths along the side. Back to the wall, I stretched out, groaning with relief. Clearly amused by my actions, Devin shrugged out of his suit coat, carefully draping it next to him. He removed his tie and tucked it into a pocket. I could feel his gaze on me, almost erotic in its sudden intensity, his eyes lingering like a starving man in front of a feast. I swallowed hard, trying to ignore the way my nipples tightened and a sudden warmth between my legs. Did he have any idea what that look was doing to me?

"Casual Friday?" I teased.

"Trust me, you don't want to see me in Bermuda shorts and a Hawaiian shirt. I strike people blind," he shot back.

I tried to picture Devin like that, but my brain refused to cooperate. Instead, it conjured tempting images of unbuttoning his shirt, undoing his belt, finding out if his body was as lean and lithe as I expected. If he had any lingering bruises, I could kiss them all better....

I turned the fantasy into a cough, distracting myself by looking toward the bar. "So. What are the chances of getting some food and drink as long as we're here?"

"Not bad," Devin said. "It's strictly self-serve here, on the honor system. Trust me when I say you don't want to know how it's enforced. The owner has a long reach and a short temper, for all that he doesn't drop by often." He left the booth for a moment, returning with a pair of bottles, still ice cold. They were dark and brown, sporting stylized labels from some local microbrew. "Cheers," he said. And we drank. To a weird night. To chance meetings. To the mutual attraction simmering below the surface of our words. Potent stuff, it tingled on my tongue, charged down my throat, and warmed me inside.

We drank in companionable silence for a while, well into a second round. As my body relaxed, my imagination took the opportunity to run wild. I barely knew Devin, yet he and I had clicked right from the start. I felt right at home in his presence, and I knew right then and there, I'd be a fool to let him get away come the morning. Startled by the way my thoughts were going, I swung out of my seat, steadying myself with a hand on the table. "We need snacks," I said. "No drinking on an empty stomach."

His hand wrapped around my wrist, pausing me. Our gazes met. I figured he was going to tell me where the pickled eggs and peanuts were kept. His lips twitched. He moistened his lips with a lightning-quick flick of the tongue. "I—" he said. "I wanted to thank you again. For saving me." My skin crackled with unspoken desire where he held me.

"I'm sure you'll find a way to reward me," I said, trying to make light of the wanton desires running rampant within me. I tried to tug free, instead somehow losing my balance. The next thing I knew, I'd tumbled right into his lap, sprawled awkwardly like an overgrown kid visiting Santa at the mall. Devin was warm and solid, and far too close for comfort. He was—oh. He liked having me in his lap, the proof hard and insistent against my bottom. Oh my.

He leaned in, I arched up, and our lips met in the middle. I melted against his chest, draping my arms around his shoulders. We fit together perfectly, just enough space in the seat for me to happily nestle in his lap. Our mouths teased as a series of light, tentative kisses grew longer, more involved. Devin's tongue stroked my lips, and I parted them, letting the kiss deepen. His fingers roamed my back, and I arched as he traced the length of my spine. I ran my hands through his hair, lightly massaging his scalp, thrilling at the low sounds of appreciation he made. I wriggled my rear against his crotch, a frisson of delight sweeping through me as I felt his arousal. It had to be painful, trapped like that, but he made no signs of discomfort.

Devin's hand slid along my waist, teasing apart jeans and shirt, fingers brushing along the rapidly widening strip of bare skin. Goosebumps rose in reaction to the simple yet maddeningly erotic sensation. I didn't know if I wanted him to go up or down. Yes. And I'd help. A whimper escaped my mouth, swallowed by his. He nipped at my lower lip, and the shock ran all the way to my taut nipples. My shirt was shoved almost to my breasts, cool air on hot flesh. I wanted him. I needed—

There was a clatter from outside, an ominous mixture of loud voices and stomping feet and drunken singing. Like a scalded cat, I jumped out of Devin's embrace, stumbling as I got to my feet. I tried to smooth my hair and pat my clothing back into place. He'd gone dead white. "Damn it." I was about to ask him what was wrong when the front door opened amid a terrible racket.

In spilled the Corbie Boys. Not just the five we'd seen earlier but several dozen, a feral assemblage of black-clad villains. They talked and argued among themselves, exchanging obscenities and boasts, and they brought with them a feast: still-steaming roasts and rotisserie chickens, all manner of side dishes and desserts. I didn't know where they'd found such bounty, but I doubted it was come by politely. My stomach rumbled, threatening to carry over the ruckus. The Corbie Boys were here, and it was nigh impossible to miss us. Any second now, and—

The first one to spot us choked on his beer in surprise. "Holy shit!" he exclaimed.

One by one, the Corbie Boys stopped in mid-activity, turning to stare in disbelief. Dozens of hostile glares threatened to kill us on the spot. Devin and I exchanged quick looks, wordlessly strategizing in the second we had before we were mobbed and slaughtered. We couldn't afford to be cornered here. We had to take the initiative. Devin stood to join me, his stance brazenly casual. "Evening, boys," Devin called. "Nice party you have going on. Room for two more?"

It wasn't often their prey came to them, and our bold behavior threw them all for a loop. We strolled toward the bar, pushing past one Boy after another, until Devin was able to grab us fresh drinks. Capriciously, I snagged a drumstick as I passed a bucket of chicken.

"Devin Hunt," growled one man, a burly bald bruiser with cold eyes and an oft-broken nose. "You really got some balls to crash our territory."

"You know as well as I do that this is common ground, Billy, and your only claim lies in strength of numbers—and potency of body odor," said Devin, smile wide and cocky. "We were just waiting out the night, and in you came. Go figure."

Corbies closed in around us, blocking off all escape. Growls chorused from a dozen throats, jackets rustled as hands crept toward weapons. "You got a death wish, Hunt?" Billy shot back.

"Not at all. I just know you don't understand subtlety." Devin popped the cap to take a swig. "I figure whatever happens, happens. You have us at your mercy, what harm is there in letting us eat, drink, and be merry for a while?"

The leader's eyes narrowed into thoughtful slits. Finally, he bellowed a laugh, slapping Devin on the shoulder. "Fine. You dumb bastards can have your last meal, while we figure out what sort of horrible things we'll do to you." He gave me a long, hard look; I shuddered at the hunger in his eyes.

True to their word, the Corbie Boys let us eat and drink our fill for some time, all the while discussing their favorite methods of rape, torture, murder, and mutilation; I'd never even heard of some of what they fancied. They themselves tore into the food with great abandon and appalling manners.

All too soon, they grew restless, our reprieve reaching its end. Devin and I held another silent conversation, his expression telling me all I needed to know: he was out of clever ideas. This one was all on me. I stood. Using two fingers to whistle shrilly, I got their attention. "Gentlemen!" I called. "You've all been such wonderful hosts, it'll be an honor to be brutally killed and molested by you! But before we get to that, I'd like to get a group photograph. Something to commemorate the occasion." I removed my camera from its case, holding it up. I injected a throaty purr into my voice. "What do you say? A group shot of you fine fellows?"

There was some muttering and shuffling, before Billy nodded. "Yeah, sure. Come on, boys, let's let the crazy bitch take our picture. Ain't like it'll save her." Clumping up at the bar, they jockeyed for position, making obscene gestures, grabbing their crotches and scowling for the camera.

"Here's to your health, here's to ours. May you hold that pose for twenty-four hours," I said. Click! A blinding light filled the room; when it died away, the Corbie Boys, one and all, were frozen like statues: unblinking, unmoving, unknowing.

Devin, who'd watched me with morbid fascination, stepped over to peer over my shoulder at the picture captured on the camera, then at the unlikely tableau I'd created. "Tanya McCray, you are full of surprises," he said with awe. "This beats my idea to steal one of their guns and take Billy hostage." His breath tickled the back of my neck, a shiver of need dancing down my spine. That close to me, he was all male, and my body responded.

I blushed. "What can I say, I've learned some interesting things in my travels. It's a variation on an old family trick, passed down through the generations. Legend has it one of my distant ancestors was a German soldier, who won the secret of freezing people from a beggar woman or angry dwarf or the Devil."

To his credit, Devin didn't even bat an eyelash. "How long will they stay that way?"

"For a day and a night, unless I choose to release them first." I eyed the grotesque bunch. "I'm not inclined to break it early."

Devin chuckled, still close, and I wanted to lean back into his arms. "You're something else, Tanya. You charge into trouble with a banshee's wail, face down hostile gangs, and shrug it off as nothing special. What will you do for an encore, slay a dragon?"

I turned to face him, throwing caution to the wind. As the potential danger faded, my body's urges left me charged and restless. "I'll claim my reward for saving your ass not once, but twice," I said, before kissing him, eager to pick up where we'd left off earlier.

Eventually, we broke apart to catch our breath. My skin was hot, a furious flush contrasting its normal paleness, and my lips tingled with excitement. Devin's eyes blazed with hunger; he looked rumpled for the first time all night. We knew what we both wanted. Unfortunately, there was no way we could do it here, not with the Corbie Boys present if oblivious.

We considered covering them with a tablecloth, but that solution didn't thrill us. So we went exploring into the depths of the building. Kitchen, too cramped and messy. Stockroom, too dark and dubious. Then we found what had to be a guest room, a sparsely appointed affair containing little more than a bed and nightstand. "Wish we'd known about this earlier," I said, wistfully thinking of the time we'd already wasted.

Devin kicked the door shut behind us, already stepping out of his shoes. "Just as well we didn't. Imagine one of them coming back here looking for a place to crash and catching us with our guard down."

I shivered, first with horror at the thought, then with anticipatory glee when Devin pulled me back into his arms. The kisses turned fierce, as he tried to devour me, while I gave myself to him eagerly. Our hands roamed freely now, fumbling at clothes in a heated frenzy. I unbuttoned his shirt, letting it hang open so my fingers could run over the firmness of his chest, nails raking over his nipples. He growled, tugging at my shirt, yanking it up over my breasts to reveal my white cotton bra. Had I known what was in store, I'd have opted for something a little more decorative, but he didn't seem to care. Instead, he tugged it up as well, freeing my small breasts, which he cupped in his hands. As he deftly teased my need-stiffened nipples, I moaned, breaking the kiss. It was all I could do to keep a semblance of focus as he caressed me; my own hands resting on his chest, kneading like a cat.

Increasingly tangled in half-removed clothing, we paused to finish the job. His shirt, pants, and socks went flying, leaving him clad in black silk boxers, which did little to hide his erection. Dear lord. Long and lean and well-built, he was a man who kept in shape without going overboard. I think I licked my lips as I eyed him. Meanwhile he busied himself in tugging my shirt and bra off, sending them flying across the room. I helped by shimmying out of my jeans. His desirous look set me ablaze, made my nerves tingle, made me wet with need. He pounced on me, unable to hold back.

We tumbled onto the bed, which creaked in protest under the sudden weight but thankfully held. We ended up in a frenzied tangle of limbs, exploring each other with an initial burst of passion that didn't seem likely to fade anytime soon. His lips found my neck, my throat, my breasts, leaving a sizzling trail of kisses and nibbles that made me squirm and whimper. His fingers stroked and glided over sensitive skin; I arched and twisted greedily, demanding more. Passion driving me, I tugged at his boxers, sliding them down until his cock sprang free, erect and magnificent. "Please," I demanded. I was wet, and hot, and empty. I wanted Devin in me. I emphasized my point by stroking him, fingers gliding along the shaft, nails ever so lightly scraping his length.

"Tanya!" he exclaimed raggedly. My panties ripped as he tugged them down. He paused, responsibility conflicting with need, then rolled off the bed with a muttered curse, diving for his pants. I almost cried, waiting for him to get back to me. He returned, foil packet in hand, and I snatched it eagerly, tearing it open. A moment later, I'd rolled the condom down over his cock, rubbing him all the while, marveling at his feel.

He wasted little time in entering, kissing me fiercely even as he guided his length into my heat, fingers spreading the moisture of my arousal, making me ready. As Devin slowly buried himself in me, I lost the power of speech, moaning as my muscles clenched to hold him in place. Then he started a slow, steady rhythm, thrusting with gradually increasing force, filling me each time. As he took me, he met my eyes. Our gazes locked, a flood of emotions poured between us. The spark was undeniable; I knew this was no one-night-stand for either of us to quickly forget afterward.

I dug my nails into his back, pulling him to me, hips thrusting upward to meet his movements. He quickly abandoned his controlled rhythm for something far more primal; I responded in kind, bodies bucking as we took each other. I came well before he did, an intense orgasm ripping through my core and setting every nerve on fire, a series of ecstatic cries exploding from my lips until he silenced me with a kiss. He continued to pump and thrust, keeping me there on the edge until a second wave of pleasure crashed down, this one encompassing us both. I moaned, he growled; as he came, he held himself deep within me, so I could feel the pulsing release of his own orgasm. Slick with sweat, breath coming hard, we clung together as our motions slowed and stopped. Satiated, I curled up against him, resting a hand on his chest. "Reward acceptable," I murmured.

It turned out to be a reward in several parts, one that kept us busy until morning crept up on us. We hurriedly—and reluctantly—dressed, gathered up our belongings, and left. I threw the frozen Corbie Boys a one-finger salute of my own on the way out. It was easy to navigate our way out of the Gaslight District in the light of day; only a block separated us from the edge of Caravan Street. We stood on the sidewalk as early morning people passed us by and shared a few more kisses. "You never did tell me what you do," I said.

"Real estate agent, specializing in properties in the Gaslight District," Devin admitted. "It's an...interesting job."

I nodded. "Tell me about it."

"I'd love to," he said. "At length. For a long time to come." He grinned, slipping an arm around my waist, and I snuggled in. "Just promise me you'll ask permission before taking my picture."

I snorted with laughter, extorted a promise to meet him in a few hours after I'd gotten some sleep and a shower, and began the trip back to my hotel. I had the feeling my stay in Puxhill would be a lot longer than originally planned.

SHORN

Lisabet Sarai

D o not believe what you hear of me. It was not to preserve
my chastity that I was imprisoned here, in this amusingly
phallic tower with its sealed entrance and single window. I have
not been a virgin for years; even my father knows that. In the
cesspit of hypocrisy that is his court, no one cares what goes on
behind closed doors. Only appearances matter.

And appearances are what landed me here in this unorth-
odox prison. I'm confined to this aerie because despite all blan-
dishments and threats, I refused to cut my hair.

In a society like ours, valuing external neatness and order
above else, my wild auburn locks are an offense to public
decency, or so my royal parents would like me to believe. My
father's crown rests upon a bald pate, shaved daily. My mother
and sisters wear pale helmets of curls that are clipped back whenever they grow beyond the earlobes. Every proper citizen plucks,
trims, waxes, and shaves to eliminate any hint of the hirsute.

Not I. I love my hair, not just the luxurious tresses that flow over my shoulders and down to the floor, but the rest, too: my unfashionably bushy eyebrows, the soft tufts gracing my armpits, the wiry tangle that hides my sex. My hair is a source of my power. My father suspects as much. An ancient prophecy says the kingdom shall one day be lost to a red-haired sorceress, and he fears I am the fulfillment of that promise.

He need not worry. I care not for the sort of power he wields. All I want is freedom—to travel the world, to think for myself, to love whom I please. To my father, I am nothing but a bargaining chip in the game of alliances. For that role, my hair diminishes my worth—as do my forthright tongue and legendary temper. I'm pleased to note that I've successfully discouraged every suitor the king has attempted to lure into taking me off his hands.

His ambitious Majesty sent his minions to my room while I slept, to shear me by force. When one returned with a broken arm, the other soaked with blood from the scissors embedded in his chest, the king decided prison was the only way to deal with the threat posed by my independence. He spread the tale that the servants had been injured fighting off rapists. Under pretext of guarding his beloved daughter from ravishment, he locked me in this lofty turret and sealed the door from the outside.

To discourage rescuers, his magicians established a tall hedge of rose bushes round the perimeter. My father's roses are thornless, as his subjects are hairless, but they exude the seductive perfume of forgetfulness. Anyone who ventures within a hundred yards of the tower forgets not only his intention to rescue me but his very name. He wanders, dazed and content, among the scarlet blooms, marveling at the tower looming above him and trying to recall his mission, until my father's men come to lead him away.

I do not rail against my fate. What would be the point? No, I bide my time in my tower. I gaze out the window, down at my father's people who scurry along the roads of the city like ants, mindless and driven. I brush my hair until it shines like a river of copper, spreading in a lustrous flood across the carpet. My tresses reached to my ankles on that day two years ago when I was locked away. Now they are far longer, piled up in burnished coils around me as I sit on my bed, rustling behind me when I pace my cell.

The days pass. My hair grows. I read, or write, or sing to myself the ancient songs my grandmother taught me. I practice her little spells. And I wait for my prince.

He comes to me on the nights of the full moon, nights like tonight. A potent mage, he rides the moon's pale beams into my room. He sinks to his knees before me and buries his face in the aromatic thicket between my thighs. His tongue is quicksilver and lightning, dancing in my cleft, gathering the nectar that flows just for him. He devours me like a starving man. I lie back upon the bed, pillowed by mounds of hair, spreading myself wide so he can feast upon my flesh.

As he nibbles, strokes, prods, and probes, he kindles two kinds of pleasure. Sharp, electric delight crackles across my moist skin, so intense it is almost pain. My every nerve sparks in response to his knowing mouth. At the same time, a sweet ache swirls deep in my belly, swelling and tightening as he draws me toward release. He bathes the swollen button at my apex in hot saliva until I am ready to boil.

I lace my fingers into his jet curls and pull his face deeper into my cunt. He burrows into my hungry depths, eager to give me what I crave. I struggle against the bonds holding me back from release. I feel them weaken. Arching up, I grind my soaked, hairy pussy against his nose, his chin, his protruding tongue, any hardness he can offer.

His teeth close on my clit, cutting me free to fly. Bliss shudders through me. I drift weightless, buoyed by joy, among glittering copper clouds. My lover's strong arms cradle me as I sink back to earth.

My prince smells of horses, leather, sweat, and new-mown hay. His scent makes me want him naked. I tear madly at his jerkin and leggings, seeking his bare, burnt-oak skin. He looses a soundless laugh and rises to strip away his clothing. Saliva pools in my mouth as I watch. He is dark night to my midday brightness, with ink-black hair that tumbles to his shoulders and eyes like chips of obsidian. His leanness counters my ripe curves. My softness balances the taut power in his muscled limbs.

We are two halves of a whole, my prince and I. We both know this. He's the youngest son of a neighboring king, and mute from birth. That scarcely matters—everyone tells me I talk enough for two. In any case, when we are together, we have little need for words. Like me, he's a disappointment to his parents—an outcast. He chose to be a wise man rather than a warrior, and his father will never forgive him.

Nude, gleaming like a statue in the moonlight, he stretches out beside me and gathers me into his arms. He claims my mouth in a kiss dark and rich as chocolate. I taste my ocean flavor on his deft tongue. I close my eyes, sinking into his presence, and let him carry me away. His heart beats against mine. Our breathing synchronizes.

He trails one finger along the outside swell of my breast. My nipples snap into tight, hungry points, rasping against his black-furred chest. Of course he does not miss the change. Sliding his hand between our bodies, he pinches one aching nub until I gasp. Then, before I have a chance to recover, his lively fingers are in my sex, delving into the wetness and spreading it along the hard shaft that presses so deliciously against my belly.

Some nights he'll tease me for hours before he enters me.

He'll flip me onto my stomach and lick his way down my spine, circling each vertebra, in a kind of delicious torture. At long last, he'll reach my buttocks, which he'll kiss and fondle until I'm jerking my ass in his face, pleading for his cock. Even then he might continue to inflame me, pulling my cheeks apart, laving my rear hole, silent laughter vibrating against my sensitized skin.

Tonight is not one of those nights. I sense his need, matching my own. He rolls me onto my back, onto the sleek, soft curtain of my hair, and slides into me in one smooth motion.

It's always ecstatic, regardless of how often we couple. When his flesh pierces mine—when he fills me, stretching me to the edge of pain but not beyond—I'm ready to drown in pleasure. We move together, arms and legs entwined, like a single being. I don't know if it's his power, or mine, but I swear we hear each other's thoughts. He knows what I want almost before I do.

Some nights he's rough. Some nights he's tender. It is always perfect. Tonight there are no games, nothing but pure hunger. He holds himself above me, muscles knotting in his shoulders, and drives his cock into my clinging sex. His strong, even rhythm sends me spiraling toward climax. Each thrust pushes me further up the sweet slope.

I clamp my thighs around his waist, tilting my pelvis to take him deeper. He slows, especially on the upstroke, so that I feel every inch of his hardness moving over my tissues. His earthy scent fills my nostrils. I laugh, drunk with joy, no longer a prisoner. There is no reality but our conjoined flesh and the communion of our spirits.

We rock together, slithering back and forth upon the silky waves of my hair. It surrounds us, caressing our naked skin, as though we coupled among a crowd of lovers. Red-gold strands stick to his sweat-beaded forehead. Vagrant locks tickle my buttocks. I want to bathe him in the river of my hair—my pride, my power, the pure expression of my womanhood.

I flip our locked bodies over, so that he's on his back, cradled in the copper tangles, and I'm straddling him, his cock buried deep as it can go. There's a tug at my scalp, which I ignore. I gather handfuls of shimmering curls, brushing them over his nipples and belly, while I clench my muscles around his bulk. He pulses and swells in response. Pleasure ripples out from my center in strengthening waves.

"I love you." The words are superfluous, but I want to tell him anyway, to give voice to the truth we both know. We hover on the edge, together in a new way. A single breath will send us tumbling into orgasm.

A new sensation stops me—a new sort of stirring, deep in my belly, an odd feeling as though my organs were rearranging themselves. My prince searches my face with those glittering, ebony eyes, and I understand that he feels it too. It's foreign, outside our charmed circle. At first I'm frightened, thinking that my father's magicians have found a way to undo our magical connection.

Then simultaneously, we understand. A third. A child. My womb bears the fruit of our love. The realization looms up, enormous, terrifying, and unbearably sweet. Like a tsunami it sweeps us into a wild, shuddering climax. We cling to each other, pleasure wracking our bodies, as he pours his seed into my depths. Meanwhile, the child—our daughter, I'm quite certain—moves with us.

We lie together, exhausted by the intensity of the orgasm and the unbelievable new shape of our relationship. The child is quiet, as though she had fulfilled her goal by announcing her presence.

The moon is setting. My prince helps me to sit up, more gentle than ever. He retrieves my silver-backed hair brush and starts to work the knots out of my tresses. I close my eyes, to concentrate on the warmth of his hands, the soft tug of the brush, the light scrape of the bristles against my scalp. It takes a long time for me to relax. I don't want him to leave, especially not now, given what we have learned this night. Still, I can't help but give in to the peace that comes with his presence.

He stops. I drift, lost in dreams of a time when we can be together always. A sound of metal on metal drags me back to the present.

My prince stands at my side, clothed once more, brandishing a pair of scissors.

"No!" I scream, backing away, the weight of my hair making me slow.

He raises his hand, palm facing me. I stop, obedient despite my fear. He gestures at the tresses flowing from my skull, stretching across the floor, ordered and smooth now from his attentions. Then he points at the window. All at once I grasp his plan.

He's right. Now that I know I'm with child, my prison will be unbearable—even dangerous. If my father were to find out, he might kill us both, or worse, steal the child and bring her up amid the corruption of the court. I need to escape.

I can't ride on moonbeams the way my prince can. I will need another route out of my lofty prison.

I sink back onto the bed. My lover strokes my silky hair back from my brow, then sets to work.

The first snip of the shears makes me shudder. He ceases his efforts long enough to kiss my lips and fondle my breasts. After-shocks of our previous passion rumble through me. I nod for him to continue. My gleaming locks fall to the floor, one by one.

Morning will be here soon. I'll be alone. I wonder how long

it will take to braid my tresses into the rope I'll use to lower myself to the ground. I'll need clothing. With my shorn hair, maybe I can pass as a boy. My prince will meet me outside the perimeter of my prison, I know, with horses and supplies. We'll leave our respective kingdoms behind and travel as I've always dreamed, seeking a better place to raise our child.

The amnesia-inducing roses are a problem. Perhaps I can hold my breath long enough to get clear of their influence. If I can't, I'll end up witless and confused like the unfortunates who thought to set me free.

The last rays of the moon are fading. My prince has finished his work. He gives me a pained smile and kisses me one last time before he disappears.

My glorious hair carpets the floor around me. I peer out the window. Peach-colored clouds streak the eastern horizon. I feel incredibly light, as though I might float away.

I don't mind that my hair is gone. It is, after all, for a good cause. If I forget I'm Princess Rapunzel, that won't matter either. We might become penniless wanderers. I'll still be grateful for my freedom and his love.

All I care about is being with my prince. And I'm quite certain there's no magic on earth that could make me forget him.

REAL BOY

Evan Mora

In a small apartment above a storefront in lower Manhattan, not very far from where Mulberry meets Canal, lived an aging toymaker named Geppetto and his daughter Giuseppina.

Geppetto had come to America from his village near Naples some eighteen years earlier, intent on a new beginning in the New World following the death of his beloved wife.

"A fool's journey!" His friend Mastro Cherry had said. "You are already an old man, and New York is no place for the old."

But Geppetto had gone anyway, driven away by the grief that had lived in every room in his house and in every shop in the village, filled as they were with memories of his wife.

He'd set up his toy shop and apartment both, and business, while not great, kept him busy. But loneliness was a heavy mantle upon his shoulders, and Geppetto had wished for something to alleviate it.

"If only we'd had a child." He'd said, alone at his near-empty table. "Someone to teach and to love, and whose laughter would fill me with joy."

Imagine his surprise and delight then, when one morning not long thereafter he had discovered a bassinet in the toy shop doorway, and inside, a cherubic baby girl.

"*Toymaker,*" read the note tucked in alongside the baby, "*I have no warm bed or food for this child; with me she will know only hardship. Many times I've passed by your window and admired your beautiful toys. Please give her the same care and attention you've given to them, and love her as if she were your own.*"

Geppetto had thought about contacting the authorities, but he'd known that they would take her away from him. So he'd scooped up the bassinet and taken her inside, and no one was ever the wiser.

"I will call you Giuseppina, after my wife." He'd said, holding her in his arms. Her tiny hand had reached up to grab hold of his snowy white moustache, and he'd chuckled, enchanted already.

"Heh, Pina? What do you think?" He'd whispered to the infant, who'd cooed up at him in response. Taking that for assent, he'd lain her carefully back in her bassinet, and gone to work on fashioning her a cradle.

Eighteen years later, a much older Geppetto called out to his now-grown child.

"Pina!" He shouted, banging his fist on her bedroom door, struggling to be heard over the ear-splitting music coming from within. Abruptly, the door swung open.

"It's *Pino*, Dad—jeez, how many times do I have to tell you? It's been *Pino* for the almost three years. It's never gonna change, okay?"

"Pino—I'm sorry...son." The word did not come easily off Geppetto's tongue, though in truth, there was nothing girlish about the angry teenager. For as long as he could remember,

Pina—no—*Pino*, he reminded himself, had chosen trucks over dolls, pants over dresses, and short boyish hair over the long wavy locks Geppetto had hoped she would let grow. With a child's belief in the magical, Pina had whispered to shooting stars and scrunched her eyes shut before blowing out birthday candles, wishing, always wishing, for the same thing: to be a boy. As a teenager with access to the Internet and resources that could scarce have been dreamed of a generation earlier, she found a new vocabulary, one that included words like *gender dysphoria* and *transgendered*. It was hard for Geppetto to understand these things, but he loved his child with all his heart, and though theirs had seldom been an easy relationship, he tried to keep the peace.

"What do you want?" Pino's tone was aggressive; Geppetto sighed. Pino was ready for a fight. He was, it seemed, always ready for a fight. In the past few years, since he had announced his desire to live as a boy among his schoolmates, he'd come home with more than his fair share of split lips and black eyes. Even in a place as diverse as New York City, children are still cruel and single out those who are different, and Pino had learned that the way to protect himself from this cruelty was never to back down from a fight. He had gained a reputation as a vicious scrapper and had earned the grudging respect of those who had singled him out. His place as one of the boys had been hard earned, but these boys he now called friends were a rough lot, frequently cutting school, drinking alcohol obtained from older brothers and friends, and acting disrespectfully to others.

"You said that you would watch the store for me this afternoon, so that I could visit with my friend Sergio," Geppetto reminded him.

"Well, I can't anymore. Me and Rocco and the guys are going to shoot some pool."

"But Sergio is ill, and I promised that I would stop by the pharmacy on my way over."

"So just close the damned store already! Nobody ever goes there anyway." Pino said these words as he shouldered past his father, shrugging into his jacket and pulling open the apartment door. Then he disappeared into the stairwell, and the door slammed shut behind him.

Now there comes a time in every father's life when he has to say things to his child that they will not want to hear. Geppetto thought long and hard about what he wanted to say to Pino and determined he would speak to him when he returned home. If his child—his son—truly wished to become a man, then he needed to learn how to be a good man, one who was caring and unselfish and who knew right from wrong. He needed to get a job, and he needed to treat others with respect.

The conversation did not go well. Pino erupted into a rage, shouting obscenities at his father, and Geppetto, pushed to his limits, shouted back. Things were said that should not be said between parents and their children, and in the end, Pino had stuffed his duffel bag full of clothes and stormed out of the apartment. That was the last that Geppetto saw of him.

"Pino! Let's go, man!"

"Yeah—just give me a minute!" Pino shouted, stepping in front of the mirror to check his appearance one last time. He ran a hand over his freshly shaved jaw and down over his Adam's apple, making sure no traces of shaving cream remained. He smoothed back the short hair at his temples and tweaked his faux hawk so that it was perfect. He turned a little to the left, then the right, flexing his pecs and his biceps, then cupped the bulge in the front of his jeans, adjusting it so that it was a little to the left and didn't quite look like he had a raging hard-on in his pants. During the day he usually just wore a soft packer, but at night, in the hot Miami clubs that were filled with even hotter women, he needed to be ready to get down to business.

When he'd left New York five years earlier, he hadn't really known where he was going. All he'd known for certain was that he'd had to get away—from his father, from school, from that whole suffocating life. He'd needed to find someplace where he could be his own man—do what he wanted, when he wanted, and not have to listen to all that bullshit about getting a job and being responsible.

Ironically, when he'd landed in Miami, he actually *had* gotten a job bagging groceries at Publix to pay for the room he'd rented—his old man probably would've been happy about that. He'd found a doctor who was cool with the whole f2m thing and had started getting T-shots almost right away. Then he'd found out how much top surgery cost and had given up the room and spent the next eighteen months couch surfing until he had enough money for the whole boobs-be-gone thing.

He'd started working out as soon as the scars on his chest had healed a little, and it was like finding religion. As the months had passed and he'd seen the growing definition in his muscles; seen the transformation of his weak body into the one he'd always dreamed of, he'd thought of little else. He'd lost his job, which hadn't really been a big deal since he hadn't had rent to pay or anything, and had taken to spending almost all his time at the gym.

He'd made some good friends—guys he'd met at the gym who'd never taken him for anything other than another guy— and they'd introduced him to the Miami nightlife. Pino had always steered clear of the club scene because he'd been afraid of picking up some hot chick and then having her freak out when she found out he wasn't a real guy. He couldn't very well explain that to his new friends, so he'd sucked up his courage and gone, hanging out nervously on the sidelines until he'd realized that most of the people there would have been too drunk to spot a gorilla on the dance floor, let alone a guy with a silicone dick. He looked right and felt right to the women who pressed up against him, and that was all that seemed to matter. The first time he'd bent a girl over the bathroom sink and pushed her short skirt up over her ass he'd been in awe, and when he'd pushed his cock into her he'd felt like Superman, never mind a real guy. He'd had an epiphany too, somewhere between tucking his cock back in his pants and watching the sway of the girl's hips as she walked away with a whispered, *"Thanks, stud...,"* these girls weren't looking for Mr. Right—they were looking for Mr. Right Now, and Pino was happy to oblige.

Back in his buddy's bathroom, Pino winked at his good-looking self, splashed on some cologne, and opened the door, ready for another night on the town.

"Dude—you spend more time in the bathroom than my girl-friend!"

Pino punched Marcus in the arm with more force than was necessary and grinned at the other man's grimace.

"Is Katie meeting us there?" Pino asked as the two left Marcus's apartment and started walking the three blocks to the club.

"Yeah, and she's bringing a friend of hers too."

"Sweet," Pino said, happy to have the night's diversion fall so neatly in his lap. Marcus stopped Pino with a hand on his arm.

"Listen man, hands off this one, okay?" Marcus was serious.

"What are you talking about?"

"Look, she's really good friends with Katie, and I just...don't want you messing around with her."

"*What?*" Pino was incredulous.

"You know I love you man, but you know how you are, and I just don't want Katie to get upset if you hurt her friend."

Pino felt a pang of guilt and fired back. "Why do you care so much about what Katie thinks anyway? What, you love her or something?"

"Yeah, actually, I do." Marcus grinned. "I mean, I know I haven't known her for that long, but..." He paused, looking for words. "It's like I'm home when I'm around her. I'm dreaming about a house and babies and growing old with her, you know?"

Pino didn't know. He'd never felt that, and he didn't imagine that he'd ever find someone who felt that way about him. Sure, he thought about it late at night when he was alone in his bed; wished that he could find someone who would love him. But how could he, when every hookup he'd ever had had been based on a lie? He'd fucked a lot of women in the past few years, mostly drunk women in the bathrooms of bars, and he knew what Marcus was getting at—he'd become an ass. He'd steer nice girls away from himself too.

"Look man, just hang out with her and be nice to her, okay? For me. Just this once."

"Sure, no problem," Pino said. He could be a gentleman tonight. Smile. Make conversation. Hell, he thought a little bitterly, maybe he'd fall in love too.

And that's exactly what happened.

Katie was waiting to the side of the line-up at the club entrance as Pino and Marcus approached, and Marcus gave her a sweet kiss on the lips when he reached her.

Pino, for his part, had stopped moving when Katie had gestured to her friend that the boys had arrived and the girl had turned around to get a look at them. He felt like he'd been sucker punched. Like all the air in his lungs had suddenly vanished. She was beautiful. No, she was more than beautiful. She was magical, almost otherworldly. Tiny and fine boned, she couldn't have been more than two or three inches over five feet tall; the top of her head would reach just below his chin, Pino thought. Her skin was like porcelain, so white that it fairly glowed against the backdrop of the night, and her hair, which fell nearly to her waist in silky-looking waves, was the most extraordinary shade of blue.

He forced his feet to move and approached the group with what he hoped could pass for nonchalance. He kissed Katie on the cheek, and she introduced him to her friend, whose name, as it turned out, was also Blue.

"Hi, Pino," she said.

"Hi," he replied, feeling himself blush for no apparent reason.

Her eyes were the same extraordinary azure as her hair, and he felt as though she could see past his surface, through sinews and bones, into to the very heart of him.

"You guys ready to go inside?" Marcus asked.

"We're ready," said Blue, slipping her hand inside Pino's, sending currents of electricity racing up his arm.

That night Pino was more of a gentleman than even Marcus could have hoped for, listening to Blue with rapt interest and doing his very best to make her laugh, just so he could listen to the sound. He held her close when they danced, breathing in the fragrance that was uniquely hers, and he would have sworn—as only the lovestruck do—that when she was in his arms, time itself stood still.

He walked her home after the club, scarce believing his good fortune when she pressed her soft lips to his cheek and asked in a whisper if he'd like to come inside. He opened his mouth to say yes, but caught himself at the last moment. He couldn't go with her, couldn't explain.

"Are you worried about this?" She said gently, her hand cupping the bulge in the front of his jeans. Pino stepped back, his eyes wide.

"How did you—"

"Shhhh...." Blue stepped forward, pressing a finger to Pino's lips. "How did I know it wasn't real? Why it's as plain as the nose on your face."

"But you still—"

"Yes, still." She feathered kisses against his lips until he took her in his arms and kissed her as he'd wanted to from the moment he'd first laid eyes on her.

Pino was a changed man. With Blue at his side, he became the kind of man his father would have been proud of. He became a certified personal trainer and got a full-time job working at his gym. He vacated his semi-permanent spot on Marcus's sofa, and he and Blue moved into an apartment of their own. He was responsible and caring and all the things that Geppetto had wanted his son to be.

Pino thought a lot about his father. He thought about the way he had stormed out of their small apartment all those years ago. He wondered about his father's health; the old man was in his eighties now and had no one to care for him. He realized with horror that his father could be dead, and he'd be none the wiser.

"I've got to go back to New York," he told Blue, and she kissed him and told him to go.

November in New York can be cold, and Pino shivered as he got off the plane. He grabbed his luggage and hailed a cab, and gave the address of his childhood home. When the taxi pulled up, Pino cried out in dismay. The toy shop looked long abandoned. Wooden boards crisscrossed over broken window-panes, and ripped plastic did nothing to keep out the elements. He bounded up the side steps to the apartment, but the door was bolted shut with a huge padlock. A weather-beaten notice of eviction was stapled to the old wooden door, its date too faded to make out.

Pino descended to the street and sat in the empty doorway, head bowed low with grief. He should have been there for his father. He was gone. If he was alive, Pino didn't know where to begin looking for him, and if he was truly dead...he stopped himself. He couldn't bear to think of that now.

Just then, a hunched old beggar in a ratty woolen blanket rounded the corner, pushing all his worldly possessions before him in a shopping cart. He was humming a tune, though he had to pause now and then as he was gripped by wracking coughs. Pino recognized the tune; it was the song his father used to sing to him as a small child!

"Father!" Pino shouted, running to the old man and grabbing hold of his arms. "It's me—it's Pino!"

"Pino!" Geppetto cried. "Is it really you?"

"Yes Father, it's really me!" Pino laughed and the two embraced, father and son reunited, overcome by laughter and tears both.

"I knew Pino, I knew you would come to me," Geppetto said, overcome by a fit of coughing once more.

"But Father—" Pino held him at arm's length, taking in every detail of the old man's ragged appearance. "What's happened to you? Why is there a padlock on the apartment door? What's happened to the toy shop?"

"Sharks!" Geppetto cried. "The sharks have taken everything—swallowed me whole!"

"What sharks Father? What do you mean?"

"Loan sharks! When you left that night, I was sure you

would come home. Even when days became weeks, I was certain you would come back to me. But then weeks became months and I despaired that I would never see you again. I tried to find you. I searched everywhere, and when I found nothing I hired a private investigator to look for you—the very best! But he was expensive, and I needed money to pay him, so I asked the Commisso brothers for a loan."

Pino groaned; even as a child his father had warned him against such people.

"Business at the toy shop was not very good, and when the time came to pay..." He shrugged.

"They took everything," Pino finished.

"Swallowed me whole." Geppetto nodded. "But I knew that I must stay close. I knew that eventually, you would come. And so—" He pointed a gnarled finger at the broken toy shop window.

"You're living in there?" Pino was horrified. "No more, Father! I'm taking you home to Miami to live with me."

And he did.

When Pino and Geppetto arrived home, Blue welcomed them both with open arms. She gave the old man a warm hug and kissed his weathered cheek, and Geppetto declared that she was the loveliest creature that lived. Together they arranged his few possessions in the extra bedroom down the hall, and as evening progressed, Geppetto announced with a yawn that he was tired, and he bade the young couple a good night.

Alone in their room at last, Blue lit some candles and turned off the overhead light. Standing at the foot of the bed, the two embraced, sharing tender kisses in the glow of the candle-light. When Pino would have laid her down on their bed, Blue stopped him.

"Wait." She said, placing her small hand in the center of his chest. "There's something I want to tell you."

"What is it?" Pino asked.

"I just want you to know how proud I am of you, Pino." Blue said. "You're a good man, caring and unselfish, and I think what you've done with your father is a wonderful thing."

When Pino would have spoken, Blue pressed a finger to his lips. She took a step away from him and then another, and Pino thought back to the night they first met, and how he'd thought her skin seemed almost to glow in the moonlight. It looked like that now, only she really *was* glowing, as if the light was inside her.

"And because of these things," she continued, "I can, at long last, grant you your heart's desire."

"What do you—" Pino began, and then stopped. There was a tingling in his chest; a warmth that began in the vicinity of his heart and spread outward, racing through his limbs until he could feel it everywhere; his fingertips, his toes, his—

"Oh my God." Pino's hands flew to his button fly, but they trembled so badly that he couldn't get the buttons undone.

"Here, let me." Blue closed the distance between them, brushing his hands aside and unfastening the buttons. She slid one hand in the opening, cupping his warm, soft flesh tenderly in her palm.

"I can *feel* that." Pino's voice was a rasp of emotion and tears glittered in his eyes.

Blue stroked him gently, and Pino's intake of breath was swift as blood rushed to his cock and he stiffened in her hand.

"Who *are* you?" He whispered.

"I'm the woman who loves you." She kissed him softly. "And a fairy."

"A fairy."

"Mmm-hmm..." Blue trailed a line of kisses along his jaw and down his neck, stroking his erection until he groaned. With her free hand, she tugged at his jeans, and Pino quickly shrugged them down and off, his T-shirt and Blue's dress following closely behind.

Blue knelt in front of him, and when she took him into her mouth, Pino thought it was entirely possible that he had died and had somehow wound up in a heaven where all his dreams had been made real. He could *feel* the heat of her surrounding him, the erotic scrape of her teeth against his shaft, the swirl of her tongue against the sensitive skin on the underside of his cock. He could feel her fingers circling the base of his cock and slowly stroking in time with the workings of her mouth, and her other hand cupping his balls and caressing them gently. He could feel his pulse pounding in his cock and the tightening in his balls. He was rushing toward the precipice with all the speed of a teenage boy, and he stopped her with a hand on her shoulder.

"Pino?"

He drew her up against him and wrapped his arms around her, his cock nestled against her belly.

"Thank you," he whispered against her hair. "I love you so much, Blue—and not because of this; I just want you to know that I am who I am because of you."

He kissed her then, a kiss both tender and passionate. When it ended, Blue smiled at him and took his hand, leading him wordlessly to the bed where she lay on her back and drew him between her thighs.

He knelt there, looking at the vision before him with wonder. Her body, so open and ready for him, and his cock thick and proud between them. He drew her thighs over his and wrapped a hand around his shaft, tracing her opening with the head of his cock, slicking himself with her moisture and spreading it along his length. He shuddered with the pleasure of it and rocked his hips forward so that the head of his cock disappeared into her welcoming heat.

"That's it, baby," Blue murmured, her hips pushing forward in turn so that he was even deeper inside her.

Pino groaned and shifted his grip, his hands beneath Blue's thighs, bringing her even closer to him, opening her even wider as he thrust into her, as aroused by the sight of his cock sinking into her as he was by the sublime feel of *being* inside her. She felt so hot and tight around him, the friction sending currents of electricity tap-dancing from his nerve endings to the pleasure center of his brain.

Pino could feel the tension rising in Blue's body; see the telltale flush on her skin. Without changing his rhythm, he slipped one hand out from beneath her and stroked the pad of his thumb across her swollen clit.

"Don't stop," she whispered, eyes shut, body arching into his touch.

"Never." He loved watching her like this—lips parted, hands fisted into the bed sheets—he swore he'd never get tired of this as long as he lived.

He felt it then, even before her breath caught. He felt the contractions begin deep inside her, rolling through her and over him, her orgasm pulsing around him, squeezing him with vise-like strength.

"Blue!" he cried out, pulled into the vortex, his own pleasure cresting in an explosion of sensation as he shuddered and emptied himself into her.

In the aftermath, Pino moved carefully, loathe to separate his body from hers. He braced his weight on his elbows and her legs wrapped around his waist, his hips still cradled between her thighs. He kissed her slowly, thoroughly, then paused for a moment.

"A fairy?"

"Mmm-hmm." She smiled.

"And this is really real?"

"Mmm-hmm." Blue clenched her muscles around his cock, giggling as he sucked in a sharp breath. Already he was hardening inside her again.

"Forever?"

"And ever," she said, before adding, "that is, unless you do something to really piss me off."

"Never." He said, rolling his hips slowly, and it was his turn to smile at Blue's tiny moan of pleasure.

"Well, what should we do now?" Blue looked up at Pino with feigned innocence, and he kissed her, a deep heated kiss that left them both breathless.

"I can think of a few things," Pino growled.

"Mmm...and then?"

"We live happily ever after," Pino whispered, kissing her tenderly.

And they did.

GARDEN VARIETY

Lynn Townsend

The carafe of wine slipped, unnoticed, from Jackie's hand and smashed onto the patio. Shards of glass and splatters of Chianti barely registered as she stared, gape-mouthed, at the wreckage of her garden.

Before work, Jackie had checked the seedling beans, twining tomato plants, and a few decorative flats of strawberries, and everything had been pristine. She'd plucked a few weeds from the warm soil, bound up a falling tomato vine, relocated a few bugs, and discussed the latest celebrity news with the attentive bean sprouts. After a day of manning the phones at East Agency Collections, being called multiple names—as if she were the one who'd run up thousands of dollars of credit card debt and then tried to default on it—and being bitched out thoroughly by her manager, Jackie had been looking forward to a glass of wine, a book of poetry, and the company of her pleasant, non-meddlesome, non-annoying, *quiet* plants. As far as Jackie was concerned, plants were much better company than most humans.

Especially now.

All four vertical trellises that Jackie had painstakingly put together herself lay in shattered ruins. There was potting soil all over the patio. Her budding garden, lovingly tended, was torn asunder; the plants yanked rudely from their clay pots and shredded. There was seemingly nothing that could be salvaged. This was no act of a careless child, not the destruction of someone's dog that had slipped their leash for a few short moments. This was wanton, cruel desecration.

"Who the hell would do such a thing?" Jackie was barely aware that she spoke aloud, tears of rage and grief spilling over her lower lids. She turned her head from side to side, as if seeking answers, but there was nothing. With all the potting soil scattered all over the patio, she would have thought at least that there would have been some tracks, but the earth gave up no trace of the murderer of her garden.

All she saw was one flicker of life, one tiny, tenacious plant that clung to life.

She dropped gingerly to one knee, avoiding the shards of pottery and glass, scooping up the runner bean sprout. She'd bought them just last week from Garden Variety nursery.

"I'll make it right," she promised. Jackie pulled together a handful of soil and pressed it into her empty wine glass. It wasn't the best solution, but perhaps it would be enough to keep the one plant alive until she was able to get to the nursery. "I'll make everything all right again. I promise."

Just not today, she thought as she closed the porch door on her savaged plants. *Maybe things will look better in the morning.*

Under the full moon, touched by love and grief and hope, the beans swelled. Green vines lifted leaves to the sky, twining and twisting, stretching and growing, hard and fast and turgid.

Jackie slept on, unaware and unmoving. She didn't stir as the stalk groaned and strained, cracking the foundation of her home, ripping free of the porch railings and at last, sighing to a halt.

Jackie woke. The first thing she noticed was that the light was all wrong. Her alarm was usually screaming at her as the early grey strains of sunrise barely registered through her blue lace curtains. She normally stumbled into the shower before 6:00 A.M. and left the house with the inevitably vain hopes that she would be able to avoid the morning gridlock.

Not this day. She woke up to warm sunlight streaming in through an open window. She smelled rich, green vegetation. Slowly, she opened her eyes. Her entire window was filled with plant life. The rigid stalk was thicker than her arms could reach around, spreading joyously toward the sky. The sweet tang of pickwick flowers scented the breeze. Hummingbirds already swarmed around the red blossoms. Her window was broken; the remains of her draperies were tangled in tendrils of the stalk.

"There's nothing to do," she murmured, pulling on a simple sundress, "but to climb up." Dreamlike, she sat on the window sill and then flipped her legs out the window, her naked feet finding easy purchase. The vegetation was warm under her bare skin, firm and soft, smooth. She rested her cheek against the stalk, arms around it as far as she could reach.

"I know I promised to make things right," Jackie said, "You're prompt and enthusiastic in your response, don't you think?"

Ladder-like thick vines dotted the stalk and acted as hand-holds and foot rests. It wasn't long before the ground was lost in the clouds. Blue, clear sky canopied her journey. She spared only a moment to think of the earth, far below. By the time it occurred to Jackie to worry about how far in the sky she was, falling seemed like such a remote possibility that she couldn't spare it much concern.

"You won't let me fall, will you?" she said to the stalk. "You'll take care of me, I just know it."

Jackie had never felt silly talking to plants, and now she felt even more like she was having a real conversation. That her words were heard and understood. Her heart raced, her skin rippled with goose bumps, not from fear, but from desperate excitement. The vines rustled, one twining briefly around her ankle like a caress. She grinned, continuing upward.

She reached the summit; a thick bank of clouds like hills surrounded the top of the beanstalk. In the distance, a castle in the sky, impossibly glittering, towers made of glass and pearl. The very tip of the stalk was crowned by a thick seed pod, secured by dozens of flowering vines.

There, miles above the earth, enclosed in the safe cradle of leaves and vines, Jackie became aware of a thick musk in the air. The warm scent of clean sweat, the odor of a male high in his heat, enclosed her. Blanketed by the sky, secure and secret, Jackie smirked, putting one hand on her hip to regard the beanstalk with a playful attitude.

"If that's the case," she said, "you're the world's largest erection. I'm flattered." She lightly caressed the stalk, noting again its soft, rigid texture, the veins underneath throbbing with a giant heartbeat. She rested her cheek against it, then, feeling a strange attraction, a quivering between her thighs, she opened her mouth and flickered her tongue against the stalk.

The entire stalk shuddered, forcing her to wrap her arms around it, holding her balance. "Liked that, did you?"

The vines around her shifted, moving, enclosing her. Thick coils wrapped around her thighs, forming a swing, spreading her legs. Her feet left the tentative safety of the stalk, and Jackie was cradled in the air, supported only by the vines and leaves. More vines looped over her arms, encircling her wrists like manacles.

Gentle tendrils, like fingers, explored her body. She groaned, arching against the containment of the vines. A vine twined in her thick blonde hair, tugging, prickling against her scalp. More vines formed, touching her, caressing. Jackie writhed, helpless against the overwhelming sensations. Vines wrapped themselves around her breasts, tugging at the sundress until it was shredded, baring her skin. The tendrils, like fingers, rolled her nipples, teasing them firm and taut.

The vine in her hair pulled, arching her spine, drawing her head back to bare her throat. A tendril snaked up her leg, nuzzling at her soft, sensitive inner thigh. Jackie shrieked with sudden wanting, her hips bucking against the maddening, seductive caress. The tendril teased, achingly gentle, rubbing against her suddenly molten clit, drawing moans and whimpers from her mouth. It tickled around her feminine folds, exploring, teasing, withdrawing each time she felt the tension building across her shoulders and chest.

Jackie cried out, thrashing against the vines that held her mostly immobile. Her breasts ached, nipples hard, as the vines twined around the round globes, squeezing and teasing the tips to rosy peaks. She could barely move as the vines tightened, pulling her thighs apart and her arms up, stretching her to every sensation, beyond her capacity for thought, leaving only molten desire, tinged with frustration.

"Please, please," she begged, cresting up toward relief, then pushed back again as the vine between her legs slowed its relentless torment. Slow and easy, the vine stroked her clit, plump and wet. It flicked and squeezed, rubbing, caressing. Jackie grew hot, her muscles shaking and contracting desperately. Sweat beaded across her forehead, along the column of her throat. She panted for breath, air burning in her lungs. A final spasm and she shattered into a million pieces. Cries of rapture and relief forced from her throat as she came, shuddering intensely.

Beside her, the seed pod split with an audible snap.

Jackie, limp and spent, hung in the cradle of vines, barely turned her head. Like a swimmer breaching the water's surface, a man emerged from the seed pod. He was tall, with dark hair the very color of rich earth. His shoulders were broad; his arms well muscled, with a long, lean body. He opened a pair of wide, leaf-green eyes, astonishingly brilliant, with dark, sinfully long lashes. His mouth was lush, berry red, with full, sensual lips.

Wordless, he was drawn to her, like a bee to an open flower. Jackie twisted her arms futilely against the capturing vines, aching to touch him, feel the warmth of his skin, bring him to the same pleasures that she had just experienced. He leaned in, slow and sensual, keeping his body away from hers as he gently touched his lips to hers. Without any expectations of action from her—there was no way she could clasp her arms around his neck or mold her body to his—she was forced to absorb every nuance of the kiss, make the most of tongues and lips.

His kiss shivered along her spine. Despite the lightness of his touch, there was nothing gentle about it as he devoured her mouth. His tongue flickered along her lower lip and then lingered on the sensitive corner. She gasped, panting for breath as he teased her upper lip, planting tiny kisses. At last he relented and Jackie tasted his mouth, like raw peas fresh from the garden, warm with sunlight, full, plump and moist.

His tongue was a welcome invasion, exploring the silk heat of her mouth, her lips quivering with excitement. Jackie moaned deep in her throat as his teeth nipped at her lip. She pulled her head back, allowing him access to her throat, the vine still tangled in her hair aiding her, her scalp tingled with sensation as he laved a trail down her neck, stopping to nuzzle urgently at the dip just above her breastbone.

His large hands traced a line up her ribs, corseting her breasts. He lowered his head to the nipple, breathing warm air over the sensitive nub before finally taking it into his mouth. He lingered over one breast, then the other, before pushing them firmly together, allowing his tongue to wander from one taut bud to the other, sending twin bolts of pleasure down her chest, all the way down to her toes. Jackie uttered a screaming moan, writhing.

His mouth left a warm, wet trail between her breasts and down across her flat belly as he knelt in front of her. Strong hands gripped her hips as he gently licked and tugged on her navel ring with his teeth. Jackie clutched at the warm air, her fingers curling tight against her palms and then relaxing. The hot caress of his tongue both tickled and titillated, leaving her gasping for breath.

Jackie was frantic with need by the time his wicked mouth reached her clit. He licked and sucked at the delicate peak, driving her into delirious spirals of longing. His tongue slid along her moist folds, tasting and exploring. He flicked his tongue back and forth, lightly brushing against the quivering node.

"Oh," Jackie gasped, her thighs straining as she tried to close her legs around his neck, "I can't, I can't...." And yet, she did, a moment later, screaming as she came. He continued to suck and lick as each last, trembling shock swept through her.

Jackie hung, limp and sated, in the cradle of vines, too spent to even move her littlest finger. She concentrated, instead, on just breathing. The light sheen of sweat cooled her and she just let herself relax, splayed out in her bonds. She listened to the sound of her heartbeats thudding in her temples, swift and reckless at first, but gradually slowing. The wind shushed merrily through the leaves of the beanstalk. There was no other sound.

Gradually, Jackie came back to herself and opened her eyes. Her lover was there; somehow she'd come to be cradled in his arms—the vines couched her legs and lower back, but her arms were around his strong shoulders, her cheek laying against his warm chest. She pushed herself back and looked up at his face. He soothed her hair back from her face, the corners of his mouth turned up in a loving, playful smile.

Jackie traced a line up his jaw, exploring the contours of his ruggedly attractive features. A strong jaw gave way to a lushly sensual mouth. He had high cheekbones, a sharp blade of a nose, wide, moss-green eyes, a high, straight forehead that was slightly obscured by a tousle of rich, dark hair.

"You can't be real," Jackie said. "I must be dreaming."

"I suppose that's possible," he responded. She hadn't expected him to speak and she startled in his arms, surprised by both his words and the clear, musical sound of his voice. "I like to think I was just waiting for you to wake up."

If Jackie had a response to that, she was certain she didn't know what it was. Any coherent thought was driven right out of her head by the abrupt, trembling boom that rattled the cloud-bank beneath her and the dark shadow that blocked out the sun.

A thunderous voice, unmistakably female, echoed over the cumulous hills:

Fee Fie Foe Fum
On the air, the stench of come
Be lovers paired or just cheap sex
I'll drain their blood and break their necks!

* * *

The enveloping net of vines gave a final shudder and unceremoniously dumped Jackie onto the clouds. If she hadn't been clutching her lover's shoulders in sudden fear, she would have sprawled at his feet.

"What? Who?" Jackie craned her neck looking around frantically.

"The giantess," her lover said. "You must go! She is hungry, and her favorite food is beautiful women."

"You're coming with me, right?" Jackie clutched his hand. She couldn't help but stare over her shoulder as the creeping shadow covered her, blocking out the sun and nearly the sky itself. She peered toward the heart of the darkness, straining her eyes to see the face of her predator.

"I'll keep her from following," he promised, not quite meeting Jackie's earnest, terrified gaze.

"No, no," she tugged at his arm, trying to pull him toward the beanstalk. "I can't leave you behind."

"Look, Jackie," he pulled her close, prying her hand from his arm and clutching her fingers in a bruising grasp. "If we both go, she'll only shake us from the stalk. I can delay her. Who knows, with you earthside, she may go back to the castle."

"Go!" He kissed her then, his warm sun mouth hard and urgent on hers. Jackie harbored no hope of escape for her lover. He would not kiss her so desperately, so much like saying goodbye, if he thought to ever see her again. "I'll come for you."

He thrust her away from him and ran into the depth of the giantess's shadow.

I'll wait for you, she thought, unable to speak. Tears prickled her eyes and she blinked them frantically away. *Promise.*

Jackie threw herself onto the vine, climbing down with much less grace and more speed than she'd ascended. She wouldn't let his sacrifice be in vain. Tears streamed down her cheeks as she scrambled over the smooth vines, twisting and turning her body lower and lower.

Above her, the sounds of the giantess's thundering footsteps faded. The booming, terrible voice stilled.

Jackie reached the ground.

With a groaning cry, the beanstalk shuddered all over and toppled slowly and gracelessly to the ground. Jackie stared horrified at the coils of vines, the leaves already curling up, the dying seed pods.

"No, oh no."

Exhaustion, horror, grief, overwhelmed her. Jackie fell to her knees, lost all sense of the world among the green smell of withering plants.

"Miss?" A strong hand shook her shoulder a few times. "Miss, are you all right?"

"Of *course* I'm not," Jackie pushed away from the unknown, keeping her eyes firmly closed. "Why would…"

"Did you hit your head?"

"Huh?"

Jackie opened her eyes. She peered around. Her hands were filthy, covered with smears of green and dirt. Most of her patio garden had been cleared and cleaned. Broken pots were neatly in boxes, the potting soil had been picked clean of debris and was heaped on the lawn, awaiting new flower beds.

"I think you fainted," a musical voice scolded her. "It's awfully warm out here for you to be working so hard."

"Who are you?" Jackie turned, squinting up at the figure before her. He was standing directly in the warm summer sun and she could see nothing but shadow.

"I'm with Garden Variety. You called this morning, for some new plants? Mr. Andrews sent me to deliver them?"

"I did?" Jackie blinked.

"Yes, miss," he got one hand under her elbow. "Here, let's get you up."

He pulled her to her feet and Jackie barely saw the crisp nursery uniform he wore, the breast pocket stitched neatly with green letters, *"Thorn G."* She was more concerned with a pair of intensely familiar leaf-green eyes and a sensual, smiling mouth.

"They were very special runner beans," Jackie murmured.

"I've always thought the magic lay with the gardener," Thorn replied.

STEADFAST

Andrea Dale

Want. Want want want.

It wasn't fair, she told herself, to want for anything more. For one thing, she already had what she wanted. Her soldier had come home alive from Afghanistan, and he wasn't going back. They had enough money, a decent house, and although she couldn't dance professionally anymore, she loved being a choreographer.

Wanting...

For another thing, what she wanted was selfish. This wasn't about her.

Her soldier had changed.

Always he had been steadfast, stern, and—once he'd gotten past the idea that women were to be handled like spun-glass ballerina figurines—a devoted but firm lover in the bedroom.

He had been the man she needed, to give her balance when she teetered, near to falling, to show her joy and ecstasy and fulfillment again.

In other words, her dream man.

But since her soldier had returned to her, her dreams had been uneasy, and he had been distant. She knew he loved her deeply still, but his emotions were secured away in a foot locker left behind and buried in the desert sands.

As if something deep had been injured when his leg had been, but as his leg healed, the deeper wound festered.

She didn't know how to treat the wound, find the foot locker, bring her soldier truly, wholly home.

Since he would not initiate, she tried to set the stage. Like a choreographed ballet it would be, she thought, if only she could position the set pieces in the right places, the necessary props where they needed to be.

Silvery clamps that shone and glittered (she shivered, needing to have them adorn her small teacup breasts), pale pink ribbons (their bonds of choice), a pair of worn toe shoes (to effectively hobble her).

A wooden paddle, worn smooth to the touch. A pinwheel with nasty, witch-sharp teeth. Her favorite, the whip, coiled snakelike and wicked.

She knelt before him, a tutu around her waist and a blue spangled sash between her breasts, her hair wound up in an elaborate bun. She raised her wrists to him, where she'd wrapped the pink ribbons; they needed only to be tied together.

He shook his head.

"Please," she said in a voice that shook with need.

He lifted her, unlooped the ribbons, slipped off the sash and tutu. His hands were gentle as he guided her to the bed, his leg not strong enough to support him if he picked her up. His tenderness brought tears to her eyes, but they were also tears of frustration.

He stripped then, except for the bandages he still wore

around his leg. She knew he didn't need them anymore, had seen the puckered scars when he showered and didn't know she watched. She also knew he needed to feel whole, needed to be whole for her, no matter how she insisted that no, he was just as strong and brave as he'd always been.

Come back to me, she wanted to say, but the words always died on her selfish lips.

She rolled on her front, rose up, presenting herself for a spanking, but instead he planted a line of kisses along her spine, over her curves. His tongue flicked against her, into her, tasting her. Where once, though, he had devoured her, now he seemed more intent on her pleasure.

Another woman might have been grateful.

But when she wanted hard, he gave her soft; where she wanted rough, he gave her affection. She wanted passion, he gave her restraint. Although not the restraints she asked for...

Her limbs trembled. Want, need, desire. Please. Arousal built, but needed pain to peak, to give her the release she craved.

When he guided her down atop him, she pinched her own nipples as viciously as she could, and it helped, but not enough.

His hands pinning her wrists, an order from his lips (whether to come or to hold off), the touch of a needle or candle wax or wicked wheel: any of things would have broken through, broken the spell. Woken her half-slumbering desire into crisis and climax.

Instead, she curled around him, silent in the night, stifling tears. She felt as thin as paper, as if a strong gust of wind would snatch her heart up and blow it away, tumbling forever out of reach.

As tightly bound as his emotions were—locked away in that desert as untouchable as if they were in the Ice Queen's palace or the Troll King's crypt—he was not unkind and not unaware that she was in distress. So she tried again to tell him what she desired most: that he punish her, and through punishment, reward her.

His jaw clenched tight, as tight as the iron grip of control he maintained on himself. That was what he feared losing, she knew.

She trusted, as she always had and ever would, that he wouldn't.

Now her desire, fragrant and moist, pooled between her legs, legs that felt weak with lust. After so long, after so much arousal and denial, she would finally get what she needed.

She stood before him, eyes downcast even though this time he hadn't ordered it, wrists crossed behind her back. Nipples hard, breath short, stomach fluttering. Clit aching.

He ran the length of the whip through his hands, and she didn't dare raise her gaze to his face even for an instant. Not allowed, for one thing. For another, she wanted to see the lust in his eyes and feared she wouldn't.

She turned away, gripped the post of the bed, waited.

The crack of the whip, like the crackshot of a gun. For an instant out of time, they both froze. Then the strike reached her, and she shrieked and shuddered in equal measure, pain and pleasure.

But still silence from him. She chanced a glance over her shoulder. He stood straight and unbending like a tin soldier, his expression as faraway and blank.

She whispered his name. And again, a tiny bit louder.

His eyes flickered.

It was okay, she told him. It was what she wanted. And we both, she assured him, have the control we need.

But he couldn't. He shook his head, put down the whip.

She bit her lip to force the tears back, to stave off the disappointment.

Still, one thing prevailed, and that was her love for him. And in that instant, she thought, instead of herself, of him and the perilous journey he had taken.

She remembered what it had been like when the tendons in her knee snapped, and she questioned herself and who she was now that she no longer could dance. That was when they had met, and he had brought her back to herself with the snick of cuffs, the smack of a paddle, the denial and the sweet, sweet release.

Perhaps his voyage had been no different, once the goblin bullet came. The sensation of falling, of being swept away on a current in a paper boat disintegrating beneath you, of falling into cold black water and being eaten alive by something you couldn't even see or feel.

And then, the prison walls splitting open, and sharp sudden bright light spilling through the crack. Into the wound. Healing.

She didn't know how to be in control from the top; didn't know how to take charge except from the bottom. The tables were turned, topsy-turvy, like tumbling out of a window.

But she would be steadfast. For him.

Not the whip, though. It took more mastery than she had, and she feared truly hurting him. Instead she reached for the paddle. He shook his head again, and she guessed that he expected her to hand it to him, a plea in her eyes. A request he again could not, would not grant.

His eyes widened, startled, when she snapped his name, putting every bit of strength she had into the command that he prepare himself.

He froze at attention. Had he not acquiesced, she would never have continued. So she calmed her shaking hands and raised the paddle, and crashed it down on his firm ass once, twice, thrice. Three was a number that held power; surely it would break the spell?

But still he stood, ramrod stiff (even if his cock was also ramrod stiff, she saw; at least that was a good sign), unable to bow or bend, as if he were afraid that if he did, he'd break.

Or, as if he feared that if he opened himself to the heat of her, the heat of them, he would melt away to nothing.

The bloom of red on his cheeks and the purpling of his prick were the first colors she'd seen in him since he'd returned. Could this cut through the grey grief and sallow sorrow?

Seven was a number that held even more potency. She raised the magic as she raised the paddle, cast the spell as she struck him.

Now she was trembling, not from fear or insecurity, but from desire and dreams. She was wet, hungry, desperate for him and terrified he would turn away from her again.

But she had resolved to be steadfast, and so she showed not a tremor, betrayed herself with nary a quiver.

"At ease, soldier," she told him. "At ease with me."

For the first time since coming home, he looked at her, truly looked at her, his eyes (once shadowed, now the blue of her spangled sash) searching her face.

"Always," he said.

She herself almost broke then, but she held fast to her resolve. The walls may have split, the light might be spilling through, but healing...healing took more effort.

He needed more.

The clamps they owned were better suited for a woman, but she managed to affix them to his nipples anyway. When he gasped and shuddered, she squirmed at the slippery throb between her thighs.

A pink ribbon as an improvised cock ring, wrapped around three times and tied with a bow. A butt plug, and although she suspected he wanted to protest, his body revealed his true desires. An order to lick her until she writhed in ecstasy over him, even if the sensation wasn't the full release she needed.

She straddled him once again, sank down onto him, drenching the ribbons tied at the base of him with her juices. They kept him from his own release, and his face showed a mixture of anguish and pleasure.

His face showed emotion. Her heart leapt and her clit shivered. Could she bring her soldier all the way home?

She pinned his wrists with her small hands, whispered to him about how he felt inside her and how she was in control. She plucked the clamps from his nipples, and he closed his eyes against the pain.

When he opened them again, she saw the light spilling, seeping through the prison walls. Breaking free of her grasp, he found one of the clamps she'd discarded and, his gaze never leaving hers, affixed it to her own breast.

A lightning flash of delicious pain as he tugged on her clamp, the hint of a wicked grin on his face. One she hadn't seen since it had been lost in the desert sands. She fluttered. So close...

With trembling fingers she untied the bow, unwound the ribbon. She barked his name—and he cried out hers, half-impassioned, half-commanding.

That, then, was when the fire rose up and consumed them, but because it was a conflagration of their own making, together they could survive it. From the flames they emerged unscathed, and yet changed.

The foot locker, unburied, lay a smoking lump of metal in the shape of a heart, melding with the spangle-bright of her own heart, their emotions entwined as did their bodies.

For the first time since he'd come home, she didn't want anything.

For the first time since he'd come home, they both felt whole.

A SEA CHANGE

Kristina Wright

M ara tipped the champagne bottle to her mouth and felt the cold liquid turn to fire in her throat. She nestled the bottle into the damp sand and looked out toward the ocean. There wasn't much to see. Clouds hung low in the sky, dark ominous things that reached down to the water, obscuring the crescent moon. The only clue that there was an ocean in the inky blackness before her was the steady sound of the waves washing against the beach.

The wind whipped her hair across her face and peppered her face with damp sand. She shivered and pulled her knees up to her chest, pressing her hands to her hot, tear-stained cheeks.

It should have been a happy night. A big promotion for Jack, a beautiful new beach house, friends and family gathering to celebrate their twentieth wedding anniversary. Everyone adored the happy Bennetts. What no one knew, what she wouldn't let anyone know, was that it was all a sham.

Jack had been a ladies' man long before she'd met him. But

she had been so head over heels in love, so flattered that he'd even noticed her—her, the mousy, quiet girl who spent her lunch hour in the library—that she'd ignored his proclivities and pretended not to notice. For twenty years Jack had collected pretty, young executive assistants with the same gusto he used to collect fine wine and expensive electronics.

Mara rocked herself in the sand, releasing two decades of pent-up emotion. Never had she felt more alone than she did at this moment. She should have seen it coming, of course. It was only a matter of time before Jack's running around caught up with him and she—not Jack—paid the price. His twenty-two-year-old girlfriend was pregnant with his child and he fancied himself in love with her. And tonight, while fifty of their closest friends were on their way to celebrate Jack and Mara's anniversary, Jack had asked for a divorce. Tonight, of all nights.

Flinging herself back on the sand, she stared at the storm-clouded sky and imagined how different her life might have been. Her entire existence had been about pleasing others. First her family, then Jack; always compromising, giving in, never feeling like she belonged anywhere and desperately needing to belong. To someone, *something*. She felt like the biggest fool on the planet.

A voice in the darkness asked, "Are you all right?"

She bolted upright, startled that her solitude had been disturbed. The darkness masked the man's features, but she was sure he wasn't someone she knew. Even from her vantage point on the ground, she could tell he was tall. He was also half-naked, wearing nothing more than a pair of faded trousers with ragged hems.

Her pulse accelerated. Jack was constantly nagging the local police about drifters sleeping on their private beach. She should give in to her flight urge, but some small measure of rebellion made her stay. It would be ironic if the one time she stood up for herself, it got her killed.

"No, I'm fine. I live here," she said, mustering an authority she didn't feel. She didn't belong in the house up on the hill any more than this man did.

Rather than walk away, he sat next to her. He smelled of the ocean, a rich, sea-salt smell...and something else. Something decidedly masculine and raw. His hair was as light as his pants—white or blond, she couldn't be sure in the darkness. He had a handsome face with a strong, aquiline nose, though it was impossible to judge his age as shadows played across his angular features.

The stranger smiled, white teeth flashing in the darkness. "I'm Dylan."

"If you don't mind—" She stopped mid-sentence as his gaze met hers. She couldn't tell what color his eyes were, but he stared at her—through her—with such intensity, she couldn't finish her thought.

"I heard you crying."

The sympathy and concern in his voice angered rather than comforted her. "This is a private beach, you know," she said, fueled by too much champagne.

He smiled again. "Do you want me to go?" he asked softly. "I'll go if you want me to."

She wanted to be alone, but suddenly it didn't seem to matter whether the stranger stayed or left. She'd always felt alone even in a crowded room, even with Jack. Her shoulders slumped as she rested her chin in her hands and looked out toward the sea.

"It doesn't matter," she said flatly.

"Doesn't it?"

She refused to acknowledge that he'd spoken. Soon enough, he'd get tired of this game—if that's what it was—and move on. But he didn't. Minutes passed as she counted the waves that rolled softly toward her. Occasionally, she could make out the white foamy caps, but mostly she saw only blackness and was reminded of the black hole that was her heart.

"It hurts," he said a long time later. "And yet, it doesn't."

Mara looked over and saw that he had mimicked her posture. Legs crossed, chin resting on his laced fingers. She felt curiosity tugging at her but dismissed it. Whoever he was, whatever he was doing on this isolated stretch of beach, it didn't matter. And yet, his words echoed inside her. It did hurt, losing everything she'd always had, facing the god-awful truth that had gnawed at her for twenty years. And yet there was an acceptance, a quiet understanding that somehow, someway, she was starting anew. If she could find the courage. If she could stop being what everyone else wanted her to be and figure out who she was.

"It takes time."

Mara couldn't decide if his one-sided dialogue came before or after her own thoughts. She glanced at him. He was studying her face as if he were memorizing every detail. Finally, he paused at her lips, his gaze lingering over her mouth for so long her lips felt warm.

She knew, although she couldn't say how she knew, he was going to kiss her. She knew it just as she knew she was going to let him. She waited, holding her breath, almost afraid of what was to come. When he didn't move, she felt ridiculously disappointed.

She closed her eyes to absorb her disappointment and then it happened, his mouth was on hers. His lips were damp and cool, firm and strong. He kissed her with the same quiet intensity he had in his stare. Tentative at first, but gradually turning bolder, learning every inch of her mouth in slow, deep kisses.

After the first touch, she kissed him back, giving as good as she was getting. For long, precious minutes they made love with only their mouths, their bodies close but not quite touching, their hands buried in the sand.

Finally, Mara pulled away, gasping for much-needed air. She wanted to speak, but no words would come. What she had just done wasn't like her, but it was impossible to ignore the tiny thrill of excitement that slid up her spine.

"Kiss me again," he said, leaning closer so that their shoulders brushed. "Kiss me and stop thinking."

She didn't hesitate. She leaned toward him and pressed her open mouth to his. There was nothing tentative about the way they kissed this time. His hands came up to hold her face as he tasted her mouth. When she finally pulled away so she could catch her breath, he didn't need to ask again. She came back for more, kissing him, devouring his taste and absorbing his touch.

His skin felt damp. Not clammy exactly, but moist. As if he'd just gotten out of the shower and hadn't had a chance to towel himself off yet. She ran her fingertips over his muscular shoulders and a soft, guttural moan slipped from his lips at her gentle caress. He mirrored her actions, using his hands to smooth the thin silk straps of her dress over her shoulders. She shivered, wanting to both pull him closer and push him away at the same time.

"I—I shouldn't do this," she murmured even while her fingers discovered the soft mat of hair on his chest.

"Don't tell me what you should do," he said, his voice as ethereal as the sound of the ocean. "Tell me what you *want* to do."

I want to throw you back on the sand and fuck you senseless, she thought and was startled to see him smile.

"Then do it," he answered, though the words had never passed her lips.

"How—" she gasped, but then he was pulling her onto his lap and smothering her mouth with his.

She felt like she was drowning, but it wasn't an unpleasant sensation. His erection pressed insistently against her bottom and she wiggled, wanting him. She'd never been with another man besides Jack, but suddenly, impossibly, she wanted this man. Now.

"Sit still, sweet Mara," he gasped as she rotated her ass on him. "There is time."

Arousal surged within her at his words. They had time. *Time.* She melted against him, feeling as if every breath she took came from him. She kissed her way across his strong jaw line, his skin as cool and smooth as a bit of sea glass. She continued her exploration down his neck, pausing to nibble the strong, steady pulse that thrummed there.

He spread his legs and she snuggled against him, running her tongue across his collar bone, down to a pebbled nipple. He groaned when she sucked the tender flesh into her mouth. Her own arousal built as she alternated between his nipples, licking and sucking them. He tangled his hands in her long hair and moaned her name.

A sense of urgency was growing between them as she slid down a bit further and swirled her tongue against his muscular belly. He released her hair and lay back in the sand, his magnificent form stretched out before her like the finest of banquets. She stared at the shaft straining against his thin cotton pants. Even clothed he looked enormous. Her breath caught in her throat as she thought about what she wanted.

"Whatever you want, take it," he murmured. Unlike before, she wasn't startled that he could read her mind now. It felt right.

She reached for his zipper with a trembling hand. Only, there were buttons instead of a zipper. She fumbled with them until he helped her. Together, they made quick work of the obstacles in her way. The gap in his pants widened as each button was released until she felt hard flesh brush against her skin. She freed his cock, gently, reverently, mesmerized by the column of flesh that rose from a tangle of blond hair at his groin.

"You're so beautiful," she murmured, not even aware she'd spoken until the words echoed in her ears.

He moaned softly in response. A wave of tenderness so pure it brought tears to her eyes washed over her. She caressed him gently, feeling his flesh pulse and twitch against her. His penis was beautiful, long and thick, the head large and dark like a ripe plum. Unable to wait a moment longer, she ran her tongue over the spongy tip. It was the softest, smoothest thing she'd ever felt in her life. And she wanted more. So much more.

"Oh, Mara," he gasped. When she looked up at him, she saw his head thrown back, the muscles of his neck flexed. "Please, love, take me in your mouth. I need you."

His pleas inflamed her. Mara lowered her head once more and sucked him between her lips. He fit so perfectly, cradled on the hollow of her tongue. Some primal, basic part of her soul knew she had tasted him this way before. She used her tongue to wet his cock until it glided smoothly in and out of her mouth. Once more she felt his hands in her hair, not pushing, never forcing, simply holding her, stroking her.

Mara concentrated on the feel of him between her lips. She stroked and sucked him, worshiping him, kneeling between his legs and coaxing long, low moans from him. All rational thought vanished, all worries and concerns fled her mind. There was only her and this man and the hard flesh in her mouth.

She could feel the need building in him as if she were the one being pleasured. Every muscle in his body drew taut, and he almost hummed with the intensity of his desire. She knew what was to come, and she felt herself grow hot and moist at the thought.

He gasped as he flooded her mouth, and she welcomed the salty taste of his arousal. She rubbed her pussy against his leg, painting his hair-roughened thigh with her wetness as she gently sucked his softening cock. Finally, when she had taken all he could give, she released him. She had devoured him—not just his semen, but his very essence—and it made her feel strong.

He pulled her into his arms, holding her against his chest as his breathing returned to normal. His hands stroked her body, pausing occasionally to caress the mole on her bare shoulder or stroke her hardened nipples through the silk of her dress until she moaned. With gentle hands he stripped her, sliding her dress over her head, unclasping her bra and releasing her breasts, skimming her moist panties down her legs.

When she was naked, he cupped her breasts in his big hands before trailing his fingers down her ribs and over her stomach. His fingers slipped lower to her mound and squeezed her pussy in the palm of his hand until she gasped and pressed against him.

She nuzzled his neck, nipping at corded muscle. She felt the steady beat of his pulse against her lips and heard the matching rhythm of the waves against the beach. Her hand trailed low over his flat belly to fondle his still-damp cock. Much to her delight, he began to swell beneath her touch.

"Wet," he murmured, his fingers caressing the delicate folds of her pussy so gently she thought she would scream. "I knew you would be, for me. As wet as the sea. Taste yourself, Mara."

Before she could refuse, his finger slid between her parted lips and she tasted her own desire. She moaned low in her throat, reckless with her need as she palmed his heavy erection in her hand. Even here, where he should be hot, he was cool. She stroked the velvety soft tip of him, swirling a teardrop of arousal around the velvety head until he captured her hand and dragged it away.

"I want you inside me," she whispered, so softly she wasn't sure he heard her.

"I know, Mara, I know." He pulled her onto his lap and she wrapped her legs around his waist, his erection nudging the cleft of her pussy.

"I want, I want," she gasped, unable to voice her need, unsure even what it was she needed.

"You will have what you want," he said, laying back on the sand and pulling her with him. "As much as you want. Take it."

Their bodies pressed together, shoulder to hip, and she had only to shift her weight and he was inside her. She looked down into his magnificent face, rugged and strong, as he guided into her so swiftly and smoothly it was as if he'd always been there.

No moment in her life had prepared her for this utter sense of completion. Every sad thought, every bad memory melted away as she rocked her pelvis against the thickness of his erection. She was in control, and the rest was all an illusion.

Mara lay across Dylan's body, pressing her engorged clitoris into his flat, muscular belly. She could see her desire mirrored in his expression, could feel his pulse in the flesh embedded inside her. And suddenly, like a flash of heat lightning that's gone almost as soon as it's seen, she felt his thoughts.

Come with me, Mara. Come with me.

She stared into his face, his breath coming in short, rasping pants that matched her own. She wanted to ask *how, why,* but then her physical need took over, straining toward the orgasm that trembled just beyond her reach. She shifted her weight, grinding against him, and that was all it took. She screamed her release even as he pulled her head down to him and kissed her.

She whimpered into his mouth, tasting him, tasting herself.

Wetness, so much wetness. Her climax seemed never ending, spiraling higher and higher as he tensed beneath her. His gasps turned to moans in her open mouth. She swallowed his breath and clenched her body around his as he came.

They lay together in a warm, damp tangle of limbs, hearts beating in sync. She felt no shame or regret, only a strong sense of satisfaction and belonging. She closed her eyes and felt the gentle swell of his chest beneath her head keeping time with the waves.

"I have to go," he said, his voice heavy with regret. He gently released her and rolled away to button his pants.

She reached out, but before she touched him she let her hand fall to the sand. It was better this way. Better or safer? Her mind taunted her, but she ignored the crazy, impetuousness that had led her to make love to a stranger.

Dylan stood, looking down at her. "I must go."

She made no move to cover herself, basking in his approving gaze. "Thank you." The murmured words could hardly do her emotions justice, but it was all she could offer him. "Thank you."

He hesitated, raking his hand through his sandy, tousled hair. "If only..." His words trailed off and were carried away on the wind. "Trust your heart, Mara," he said softly, insistently. "Trust your heart."

Before she could speak, he turned and walked away. He followed the line of the shore for several yards, then veered off, toward the ocean. The tide was going out, leaving a dark, wet stain of sand behind each time the waves rolled back out. Dylan never paused as his feet splashed in the surf. He walked into the ocean, ankle deep, knee deep, chest deep.

Suddenly frightened, Mara stood and ran toward him. "Dylan! What are you doing?"

He never looked back.

Mara watched as he disappeared into the sea, his blond hair disappearing from view. She clutched her hands to her pounding heart. "Dylan," she whispered hoarsely.

She searched the dark void for some sign of him, but Dylan was gone. She turned, blindly looking for her clothes before realizing she'd run some distance away from where they'd been. She had to get dressed and back to the house, call 911, call the Coast Guard. Her mind raced but her body was frozen in place, staring at her footprints in the damp sand. Her footsteps. *Only her footsteps.*

Her mind tried to make sense of what had happened as she stared at the marks in the sand. Dylan had walked this same path, yet the only sign the sand had been disturbed was the footprints she had left. Even while she told herself the tide had washed his footprints away, she heard him call her.

Mara, trust your heart.

She looked frantically out to sea even though she knew it wasn't possible to have heard him. Even if he hadn't drowned, he was too far away for her to hear his voice.

Mara.

The thunderclouds finally kept their promise and opened up, releasing a torrent of rain. The ocean churned violently while rain coursed down her naked body. She crumpled to her knees and bowed her head, feeling as if she were losing her sanity. Sobs racked her body, but her tears were washed away in the rain. She hadn't told him her name. She'd never told him her name, and yet he knew.

Mara, come with me.

Suddenly, his words took on a different meaning. She raised her head, wet hair streaming down her back. "What do you want from me?" she screamed. "Who are you?"

No answer came, nothing but silence and the rain. She curled up on her side in the sand, her body aching, her soul dying. The rain felt hot and prickly on her skin, and she sobbed her fear and confusion into her chest, holding herself the way Dylan had held her only minutes earlier.

Mara, love. Please. I've waited so long for you.

She ignored the voice that penetrated into her conscious. She was losing her mind. There was no other possible answer.

Mara?

She opened her eyes, feeling the sting of tears and rain.

"What," she whispered hoarsely. "What do you want?"

What do you want, Mara? She could hear his voice inside her, soothing her. *What do you want?*

"Love," she answered, feeling small and pathetic and alone. "Peace. Belonging. Everything I've never known."

Come with me, Mara. Let me show you how it can be.

It made no sense, but some small flicker of hope, a need to believe in something bigger and greater than herself, forced her to unfold from the sand and walk toward the ocean. The rain had slowed to a drizzle, fat drops splashing against her hot skin. She took one hesitant step toward the water. Then another.

Come with me.

"I'm afraid," she whispered, knowing no one could possibly hear her. "So afraid."

Don't be, love. I'm here. Always.

She *wanted* to believe. Truly she did. But rational thought told her it was the strain of the day and the champagne and exhaustion that was guiding her. She took a fumbling step backward, reason returning. This was crazy. Insane.

And then she saw him. He stood naked in the surf not ten feet in front of her, the foam of the ocean clinging to his chest, his hair slicked back, his skin glowing with a strange luminescence. Incredibly, impossibly, he was there. He hadn't left her.

"Dylan," she pleaded, not even sure what it was she asked of him.

Come with me, Mara.

She wanted to. Oh, God, how she wanted to. She walked toward him, feeling the first chilly brush of water against her feet. Her skin felt fevered and the ocean felt so good, so right. A few more steps and the water was up to her knees. Her nipples tightened almost painfully, whether from arousal or cold she couldn't be sure. Excitement tinged with fear coursed through her. A few more steps and she was in front of him. Close enough to touch him, but holding back.

Go ahead, touch me.

This time, she knew he hadn't spoken aloud. She had known it all along, she realized, but here now was proof. "How?" she asked softly.

Don't speak. I know your thoughts just as you know mine.

She didn't know how it was possible, but it was true. *I'm afraid*, she thought. *What's happening to me?*

Don't you know? His thoughts teased her senses. *Everything you always wanted. Love. Peace. Belonging. Take it, Mara. You deserve it all and so much more.*

She didn't know what to believe, she only knew she felt a lightness in her soul she'd never felt before. When he put his arms around her, she melted against him. Buoyed by the water, the tide gently pulled them out to sea.

"Where are we going?" she asked aloud, a sense of peace settling over her even as the water rose to her chin.

"Home," Dylan answered, his voice sounding strange, almost foreign, after hearing him inside her head. His fingers, cool and strong, wrapped around her shoulders and pulled her closer.

She clung to him as they kissed, feeling his cock, his thick, exquisite cock, swell against her belly. "Dylan," she murmured against his mouth, ready for him. Needing him. He slid quickly and smoothly into her warm wetness as a wave rolled them higher.

She moaned.

Let go, Mara.

He undulated against her, their bodies wrapped around each other.

She looked past his shoulder toward the shore and was frightened by how far away it seemed. She could see the lights from her house twinkling against the horizon. As Dylan moved into her, she idly wondered how long it would be before they would miss her. Would they think she'd drowned herself? Would they find her clothes and think she'd been attacked? It didn't really matter. None of it seemed to matter anymore.

Cradled in Dylan's arms, she slipped beneath the water. The remnants of fear and uncertainty ebbing away as Dylan's body molded to hers and slipped deeper inside her. Her lungs swelled with her desire to moan, yet there was no overpowering need to breathe. A gentle, fluid feeling coursed through her veins as her skin was soothed by the cool touch of the sea. She felt her body changing, adapting to the new environment of the sea, could feel the same changes transpiring in Dylan's body as he embraced her.

You are so beautiful, Mara. You belong here. You know that you do. With me. Always.

Her hair made a cloud around her head as she arched her back and pressed her body against him. His words floated through her mind and laughter bubbled low in her belly. *I hear you,* she thought. *I hear you!*

At last, she'd found her home. She looked up through the

water far above her and saw moonlight glimmering on the surface of the ocean. She looked at the man-creature she clung to, whose body felt as right and natural as her own, and smiled.

I'm home, Dylan. You've brought me home.

Where you belong.

As they drifted on the ocean's current, Mara let go of everything she thought she was, everything she had ever believed in. She let go of everything she knew and embraced the unknown.

She was home.

ABOUT THE AUTHORS

MICHELLE AUGELLO-PAGE (michelleaugellopage.wordpress. com) writes erotica, poetry, and gothic fiction. Like Little Red, she is haunted by stars and afflicted by the moon. She is also a teacher and a mother and lives in New York. Recent erotica was published in the anthology *Fairy Tale Lust*.

ANDREA DALE (cyvarwydd.com) lives in a fantasy world in her head, weaving tales of erotic romance and magic. Her alter egos write speculative fiction, appear in the front row of Styx concerts, and dance under the full moon sprinkled with faerie dust. Sometimes all in the same day.

EMERALD's erotic fiction has been published in numerous print and e-book anthologies as well as on various erotic websites. She is an advocate for sexual freedom, reproductive choice, and sex worker rights and blogs about these and other topics at her website, thegreenlightdistrict.org.

A.D.R FORTE (adrforte.com) is the author of erotic short
fiction that appears in numerous anthologies, including *Fairy
Tale Lust* and *Dream Lover*, also edited by Kristina Wright.
Her tales of erotic fantasy can be found in collections from Cleis
Press and Circlet Press.

SHANNA GERMAIN (shannagermain.com) grew up with
flowering clover fields, handsome fence-fixers and wild, wild
horses. She still dreams of riding a bucking bronco. Her work
has appeared in *Best American Erotica, Best Bondage Erotica,
Best Gay Romance, Best Lesbian Erotica, Dream Lover, Fairy
Tale Lust*, and more.

SACCHI GREEN's stories have appeared in a hip-high stack
of publications with erotically inspirational covers, and she's
edited or co-edited seven volumes of erotica, including *Girl
Crazy, Lesbian Cowboys* (winner of the 2010 Lambda Literary
Award for lesbian erotica), *Lesbian Lust*, and *Lesbian Cops*, all
from Cleis Press.

After brief, unsatisfying careers in advertising, teaching,
computers, and homemaking, **JEANETTE GREY** has returned
to her two first loves: romance and writing. When she isn't
writing, Jeanette enjoys making pottery, playing board games,
and spending time with her husband and her pet frog (who,
thankfully, has yet to turn into a prince).

MICHAEL M. JONES (michaelmjones.com/wordpress) is a
writer, editor, and book reviewer. He lives in southwest Virginia
with way too many books, a pride of cats, and a delightfully
tolerant wife. His stories have appeared in *Like a God's Kiss,
Like a Queen*, and *Rumpled Silk Sheets*, among others. He is

the editor of the forthcoming *Like a Cunning Plan.*

KRISTINA LLOYD (kristinalloyd.wordpress.com) is the author of three erotic novels, including the controversial Black Lace bestseller, *Asking for Trouble.* Her short stories have appeared in numerous anthologies, and her novels have been translated into German, Dutch, and Japanese. She has a master's degree in twentieth-century literature and has been described as "a fresh literary talent" who "writes sex with a formidable force."

ANNA MEADOWS is a current Lambda Literary Foundation fellow in fiction. Her work appears in five Cleis Press anthologies, including *Steamlust: Steampunk Erotic Romance.* She lives and writes in northern California.

EVAN MORA's stories of love, lust, and other demons have appeared in *Best Lesbian Erotica, Best Lesbian Romance, Best Bondage Erotica, The Sweetest Kiss: Ravishing Vampire Erotica, Bound by Lust,* and *Red Velvet and Absinthe: Paranormal Erotic Romance.* She lives in Toronto.

After living a checkered past, and despite an avowed disinterest in domesticity, multi-published author **ANYA RICHARDS** (anyarichards.com) settled in Ontario, Canada, with her husband, kids, and two cats who plot world domination, one food bowl at a time.

LISABET SARAI has published six erotic novels, three short story collections, and dozens of individual tales. She also edits the single-author charity series "Coming Together Presents" and reviews erotica for Erotica Readers and Writers Association and Erotica Revealed. Visit Lisabet online at Lisabet's Fantasy

Factory (lisabetsarai.com) and Beyond Romance (lisabetsarai. blogspot.com).

CHARLOTTE STEIN (themightycharlottestein.blogspot.com) has published a number of stories in various erotic anthologies, including *Sexy Little Numbers*. She is also the author of the short story collection, *The Things That Make Me Give In*, and a novella, *Waiting In Vain*.

DONNA GEORGE STOREY (DonnaGeorgeStorey.com) is the author of *Amorous Woman*, a steamy novel about an American woman's love affair with Japan. Her short stories have been published in more than a hundred journals and anthologies, including *Obsessed, Passion: Erotic Romance for Women, Best Women's Erotica, Penthouse*, and *Nice Girls, Naughty Sex*.

LYNN TOWNSEND is a displaced Yankee, a mother, a writer, a dreamer, and quite possibly the proud owner of a small black hole residing under her desk that tends to eat kittens, odd socks, staplers, car keys, and that book she was reading and had almost finished.

ABOUT
THE EDITOR

Described by *The Romance Reader* as "a budding force to be reckoned with," **KRISTINA WRIGHT** (kristinawright.com) is an author, editor, and college instructor. She has edited the Cleis Press anthologies *Fairy Tale Lust: Erotic Fantasies for Women*; *Dream Lover: Paranormal Tales of Erotic Romance*; *Steamlust: Steampunk Erotic Romance,* and *Best Erotic Romance.* Her forthcoming anthologies include *Duty and Desire: Military Erotic Romance* and *Best Erotic Romance 2013.* Her first anthology, *Fairy Tale Lust: Erotic Fantasies for Women,* was nominated for a Reviewers' Choice Award by *RT Book Reviews* and was a featured alternate of the Doubleday Book Club. Kristina's erotica and erotic romance fiction has appeared in more than eighty-five print anthologies, and she received the Golden Heart Award for Romantic Suspense from Romance Writers of America for her first novel *Dangerous Curves.* Her work has also been featured in the nonfiction guide *The Many Joys of Sex Toys* and magazines and ezines such as *Clean Sheets, Good Vibes Maga-*

zine, *Libida*, *The Fiction Writer*, *The Literary Times*, *Scarlet Letters*, *The Sun*, and *The Quill*. Her nonfiction essay "The Last Letter" is included in the epistolary anthology *P.S. What I Didn't Say: Unsent Letters to Our Female Friends*, and her articles, interviews, and book reviews have appeared in numerous publications, both print and online. She is a member of Romance Writers of America (RWA) as well as the RWA special interest chapters, Passionate Ink and Fantasy, Futuristic and Paranormal. She is a book reviewer for the Erotica Readers and Writers Association (erotica-readers.com) and the book club moderator for *SexIs* magazine's Naked Reader Book Club (nakedreaderbookclub.com). She holds degrees in English and humanities and has taught English composition and world mythology at the community college level. Originally from South Florida, Kristina has lived up and down the East Coast with her husband, Jay, a lieutenant commander in the Navy. They live in Virginia with their two young sons.

More from Kristina Wright

Best Erotic Romance
Edited by Kristina Wright
This year's collection is the debut of a new series!
"Kristina is a phenomenal writer...she has the enviable
ability to tell a story and simultaneously excite her
readers." —Erotica Readers and Writers Association
ISBN 978-1-57344-751-5 $14.95

Steamlust
Steampunk Erotic Romance
Edited by Kristina Wright

"Turn the page with me and step into the new worlds...where airships rule the skies,
where romance and intellect are valued over money and social status, where lovers boldly discover each other's bodies, minds and hearts." —from the foreword by
Meljean Brook
ISBN 978-1-57344-721-8 $14.95

Dream Lover
Paranormal Tales of Erotic Romance
Edited by Kristina Wright

Supernaturally sensual and captivating, the stories in *Dream Lover* will fill you with a
craving that defies the rules of life, death and gravity. "...A choice of paranormal seduc-
tion for every reader. All are original and entertaining." —*Romantic Times*
ISBN 978-1-57344-655-6 $14.95

Fairy Tale Lust
Erotic Fantasies for Women
Edited by Kristina Wright

Award-winning novelist and erotica writer Kristina Wright goes over the river and
through the woods to find the sexiest fairy tales ever written. "Deliciously sexy action to make your heart beat faster." —Angela Knight, the *New York Times* bestselling
author of *Guardian*
ISBN 978-1-57344-397-5 $14.95

Fuel Your Fantasies

Carnal Machines
Steampunk Erotica
Edited by D. L. King

In this decadent fusing of technology and romance, out-standing contemporary erotica writers use the enthralling possibilities of the 19th-century steam age to tease and titillate.
ISBN 978-1-57344-654-9 $14.95

The Sweetest Kiss
Ravishing Vampire Erotica
Edited by D. L. King

These sanguine tales give new meaning to the term "dead sexy" and feature beautiful bloodsuckers whose desires go far beyond blood.
ISBN 978-1-57344-371-5 $15.95

The Handsome Prince
Gay Erotic Romance
Edited by Neil Plakcy

A bawdy collection of bedtime stories brimming with classic fairy tale charac-ters, reimagined and recast for any man who has dreamt of the day his prince will come. These sexy stories fuel fantasies and remind us all of the power of true romance.
ISBN 978-1-57344-659-4 $14.95

Daughters of Darkness
Lesbian Vampire Tales
Edited by Pam Keesey

"A tribute to the sexually aggressive woman and her archetypal roles, from nurturing goddess to dangerous preda-tor."—*The Advocate*
ISBN 978-1-57344-233-6 $14.95

Dark Angels
Lesbian Vampire Erotica
Edited by Pam Keesey

Dark Angels collects tales of lesbian vampires, the quintessential bad girls, archetypes of passion and terror. These tales of desire are so sharply erotic you'll swear you've been bitten!
ISBN 978-1-57344-252-7 $13.95

Red Hot Erotic Romance

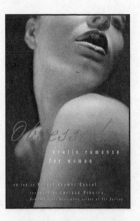

Obsessed
Erotic Romance for Women
Edited by Rachel Kramer Bussel

These stories sizzle with the kind of obsession that is fueled by our deepest desires, the ones that hold couples together, the ones that haunt us and don't let go. Whether just-blooming passions, rekindled sparks or reinvented relationships, these lovers put the object of their obsession first.
ISBN 978-1-57344-718-8 $14.95

Passion
Erotic Romance for Women
Edited by Rachel Kramer Bussel

Love and sex have always been intimately intertwined—and *Passion* shows just how delicious the possibilities are when they mingle in this sensual collection edited by award-winning author Rachel Kramer Bussel.
ISBN 978-1-57344-415-6 $14.95

Girls Who Bite
Lesbian Vampire Erotica
Edited by Delilah Devlin

Bestselling romance writer Delilah Devlin and her contributors add fresh girl-on-girl blood to the pantheon of the paranormal. The stories in *Girls Who Bite* are varied, unexpected, and soul-scorching.
ISBN 978-1-57344-715-7 $14.95

Irresistible
Erotic Romance for Couples
Edited by Rachel Kramer Bussel

This prolific editor has gathered the most popular fantasies and created a sizzling, no-holds-barred collection of explicit encounters in which couples turn their deepest desires into reality.
978-1-57344-762-1 $14.95

Heat Wave
Hot, Hot, Hot Erotica
Edited by Alison Tyler

What could be sexier or more seductive than bare, sun-warmed skin? Bestselling erotica author Alison Tyler gathers explicit stories of summer sex bursting with the sweet eroticism of swimsuits, sprinklers, and ripe strawberries.
ISBN 978-1-57344-710-2 $15.95

Love, Lust and Desire

Red Velvet and Absinthe
Paranormal Erotic Romance
Edited by Mitzi Szereto

Explore love and lust with otherworldly partners who, by their sheer unearthly nature, evoke passion and desire far beyond that which any normal human being can inspire.
ISBN 978-1-57344-716-4 $14.95

In Sleeping Beauty's Bed
Erotic Fairy Tales
By Mitzi Szereto

"Making their way into the spotlight again, Rapunzel, Little Red Riding Hood, Cinderella, and Sleeping Beauty, just to name a few, are brought back to life in Mitzi Szereto's delightful collection of erotic fairy tales."
—Nancy Madore, author of *Enchanted*
ISBN 978-1-57344-367-8 $16.95

Foreign Affairs
Erotic Travel Tales
Edited by Mitzi Szereto

"With vignettes set in such romantic locales as Dubai, St. Lucia and Brussels, this is the perfect book to accompany you on your journeys."
—*Adult Video News*
ISBN 978-1-57344-192-6 $14.95

Pride and Prejudice
Hidden Lusts
By Mitzi Szereto

"If Jane Austen had drunk a great deal of absinthe and slipped out of her petticoat... Mitzi Szereto's erotic parody of *Pride and Prejudice* might well be the result!"
—Susie Bright
978-1-57344-663-1 $15.95

Wicked
Sexy Tales of Legendary Lovers
Edited by Mitzi Szereto

"Funny, sexy, hot, clever, witty, erotic, provocative, poignant and just plain smart—this anthology is an embarrassment of riches. "
—M. J. Rose, author of *The Reincarnationist* and *The Halo Effect*
ISBN 978-1-57344-206-0 $14.95

Bestselling Erotica for Couples

Sweet Life
Erotic Fantasies for Couples
Edited by Violet Blue

Your ticket to a front row seat for first-time spankings, breathtaking role-playing scenes, sex parties, women who strap it on and men who love to take it, not to mention threesomes of every combination.
ISBN 978-1-57344-133-9 $14.95

Sweet Life 2
Erotic Fantasies for Couples
Edited by Violet Blue

"This is a we-did-it-you-can-too anthology of real couples playing out their fantasies." —Lou Paget, author of *365 Days of Sensational Sex*
ISBN 978-1-57344-167-4 $15.95

Sweet Love
Erotic Fantasies for Couples
Edited by Violet Blue

"If you ever get a chance to try out your number-one fantasies in real life—and I assure you, there will be more than one—say yes. It's well worth it. May this book, its adventurous authors, and the daring and satisfied characters be your guiding inspiration."—Violet Blue
ISBN 978-1-57344-381-4 $14.95

Afternoon Delight
Erotica for Couples
Edited by Alison Tyler

"Alison Tyler evokes a world of heady sensuality where fantasies are fearlessly explored and dreams gloriously realized."—Barbara Pizio, Executive Editor, *Penthouse Variations*
ISBN 978-1-57344-341-8 $14.95

Three-Way
Erotic Stories
Edited by Alison Tyler

"Three means more of everything. Maybe I'm greedy, but when it comes to sex, I like more. More fingers. More tongues. More limbs. More tangling and wrestling on the mattress."
ISBN 978-1-57344-193-3 $15.95

Ordering is easy! Call us toll free or fax us to place your MC/VISA order.
You can also mail the order form below with payment to:
Cleis Press, 2246 Sixth St., Berkeley, CA 94710.

ORDER FORM

QTY	TITLE	PRICE
_____	_____	_____
_____	_____	_____
_____	_____	_____
_____	_____	_____
_____	_____	_____
_____	_____	_____
_____	_____	_____

SUBTOTAL _____

SHIPPING _____

SALES TAX _____

TOTAL _____

Add $3.95 postage/handling for the first book ordered and $1.00 for each additional
book. Outside North America, please contact us for shipping rates. California residents
add 8.75% sales tax. Payment in U.S. dollars only.

* Free book of equal or lesser value. Shipping and applicable sales tax extra.

**Cleis Press • Phone: (800) 780-2279 • Fax: (510) 845-8001
orders@cleispress.com • www.cleispress.com
You'll find more great books on our website**

Follow us on Twitter @cleispress • Friend/fan us on Facebook